Lotte R. James traine[...]
director—but spent m[...]
day jobs crunching nu[...]
stories of love and adv[...]. She's turned to be
finally writing those stories, and when she's not
scribbling on tiny pieces of paper can usually be
found wandering the countryside for inspiration
or nestling with coffee and a book.

Also by Lotte R. James

The Viscount's Daring Miss
A Lady on the Edge of Ruin
A Liaison with Her Leading Lady

Gentlemen of Mystery miniseries

The Housekeeper of Thornhallow Hall
The Marquess of Yew Park House
The Gentleman of Holly Street

Discover more at millsandboon.co.uk.

A GOVERNESS
TO REDEEM HIM

Lotte R. James

MILLS & BOON

First published in Great Britain 2025
by Mills & Boon, an imprint of HarperCollins*Publishers* Ltd,
1 London Bridge Street, London, SE1 9GF

www.harpercollins.co.uk

HarperCollins*Publishers*, Macken House, 39/40 Mayor Street Upper, Dublin 1, D01 C9W8, Ireland

ISBN: 978-0-263-34512-4

03/25

To my editor, Hannah, for being an incredible collaborator and reminding me why I love Gothic.

To friends old and new, but especially to Laura N. I hope Juliana's story is all you wished for.

And always to my mother, Brigitte.

Chapter One

Yew Park House,
January 3rd, 1833

Ghosts are not real. Merely fantastical figments of overactive imaginations; ancient superstitions fuelled by howling chimneys and draughts. The dead are dead, and cannot return no matter how we may wish some to.

The dead are dead, Juliana reminded herself ceaselessly, shivering violently as she tore angrily from bed; icy fingers of dread brushing along her spine spurring her into action.

It was baffling that she had to reassure herself of such patently undeniable facts, and infuriating that those reminders did nothing to prevent gooseflesh from popping up on her arms. Thrusting them into her dressing gown, somehow failing to rip it to shreds despite the violence of the gesture, she told herself that the gooseflesh and shivers were merely born from the cold. Only a ruinous voice in her head mocked her, arguing that neither were. They were born from the chill inside her, the one which, like a creeping winter, had been frosting over her heart as it might a lake for days now. *Weeks.*

However, ghosts aren't real, and you must desist with this nonsense now, Juliana.

Sleep certainly would've aided in countering these slips into folly, however it too evaded her of late. Speaking with someone about everything plaguing her might've helped too, however there were some things—*my very greatest secrets*—which Juliana didn't share, and regardless, even if she did, she wasn't about to…to…

Admit I am having to remind myself that ghosts do not exist.

For if there was one thing anyone—including those who knew her only in the slightest—knew *about* Miss Juliana Evelyn Myles, it was that she prioritised reason, and rationality, above all. She was a creature of knowledge, and logic; someone who believed in science, in what could be proven, and what made *sense*. Though she'd been called cold more than once throughout the course of her thirty-five years on this earth, she wasn't *un*emotional, lacking in heart, or immune to sentimentality—in fact she'd once told her best friend, Ginny, to *follow her heart*. Only there were some things Juliana wasn't prone to, chief among which was believing in superstition, magic, omnipotent beings, or anything akin to any of those.

So no, she would not go ask any one of her friends in this house for advice regarding her current *disruption*, for she refused to disabuse anyone of the notion that she was a rational being, by even hinting—let alone admitting—that she was having to work extremely hard to remind herself that ghosts didn't exist; no matter what some might purport.

Bewildering behaviour.

That frustration at her own inability to be as she'd, if not *always* been, then been *most* of her life—*rational*—drove her to move, rather than toss and turn awaiting slumber which would never come, while she succumbed further to the temporary loss of reason. Mindful not to make much noise, though she wasn't close to any occupied rooms, despite what tradition would have considering she was *technically* the governess of this house, Juliana made her way from her room, down the winding and gloomy corridors she now knew by heart, to...

Well, to *where*, she wasn't entirely certain. All that was certain, was that she needed to move, and so, she did, the indeterminate motion soothing her, *somewhat*.

Walking the corridors, descending stairs, Juliana wove her way through the house as eclectic and eccentric as its master, Henry Spencer, Marquess of Clairborne; though it, like its master, had been dulcified these past couple years not only by the presence of its new mistress, but also the revelation of great secrets, and the return of laughter and joy.

If asked, Juliana wouldn't say that she'd always liked Yew Park House. When they'd first moved to Scotland, her, Ginny—Genevieve Spencer, Marchioness of

Clairborne now—and Ginny's young daughter, Elizabeth, renting the cottage across the way, Yew Park had seemed strange. Lonesome, grim, somewhat dishevelled and expertly unkempt; a monument to the fancies of men with too much power and money, and not enough restraint. However, after Ginny had married her marquess, wounds had been healed, new friends met, families had become one, and they'd all begun spending more time here, Juliana had come to love Yew Park. Not only for its treasures—libraries and towers full of books, relics, and art—but also for its simplicity, and warmth, neatly concealed beneath the mismatched wings, and extravagant gardens. It had become a family home such as she'd never known, not only for the Spencers, but for her too.

It was primarily thanks to Ginny, who ensured Juliana remained *part of the family*, and the Spencers— be it the marquess himself, his mother, or sister—who all quickly accepted her as such. They might've very well turned up their noses, and reminded her she was merely, *technically*, a governess. To Elizabeth, but likely someday soon, to young Justine—Ginny's second daughter, who now neared her seventh month. Only neither they, nor any of their friends and growing extended family—the marquess's sister, Mary, having married last year—had ever made her feel unwelcome, or unworthy of inclusion. Even Ginny might've, despite all they'd lived through together, in an effort to *move on*, and Juliana would've understood, though it would've certainly stung.

For once, it had been merely Ginny, Juliana, and Elizabeth, to face the world, then to hide from it, as they had after Ginny's divorce, and their escape from the Hell they'd once dwelled in together. The Hell which had forged their bonds of friendship, and sisterhood; Hadley Hall, the family seat of Ginny's former husband. A house which, much as the one Juliana had been raised in, could never be called *home*; a place which had served as Ginny and Elizabeth's prison until the divorce.

Dark days were those...

Shaking off that portion of her past, Juliana slipped into the orangerie, which, despite the bitterly cold night outside its great glass walls, appeared as warm and bright as ever. Those dark days were long past, and the point was, with all that had changed since Ginny had remarried, and Elizabeth had gained a proper father, she might've left Juliana behind, or asked for their relationship to change. Only she hadn't, and coupled with the fact that Juliana just bloody well liked it very much, it meant that Yew Park had become a true home as Juliana hadn't ever known. A home such as she might've liked to build herself, once upon a time; though that *once upon a time* too—*most of all*—was best left to the past.

Which was all she was desperately trying to do of late—leave *once* in the past, feel the comfort and safety of this home again—yet tonight… Tonight, like every other night since before Christmas, Juliana failed to find here what she had before. There was no longer any comfort, nor safety within Yew Park's walls, for the spirit-like memories of days *long* long past had returned to haunt her with vicious vengeance. Days, a life, a version of herself…all she'd left behind eighteen years ago, and which not even Ginny knew of.

For none of it bears thinking on. It was done. He's gone. The past cannot be changed.

Unfortunately, saying it, thinking it, believing it, didn't make it so.

December, like March…the grim anniversaries she'd seen pass seventeen times now, were always difficult periods of the year. Only she'd faced them so many times now… It wasn't that they'd got easier, however, yes, with every passing one, the demons of her past held a little less bite in their claws, and her biannual visits to the depths of their abyss became slightly shorter, and less tortuous. Perhaps this year, she'd got too comfortable. Exhibited too much hubris, thinking she knew what each anniversary held for her, and those demons had all the while been sharpening their claws, and that was why this time she couldn't leave the past where it belonged.

Or perhaps it was her brother's annual end-of-year letter which was to blame.

Their correspondence had begun thirteen years ago, four years after she'd run away from the family home. She'd told herself those years of silence were to keep him from finding her, and forcing her back to Barrow Heath, and Stag House—where he lived still, to her greatest incomprehension. But the truth was, she'd always known he would never *force* her, whether or not she'd attained her majority. It had been as good an excuse as any to fade away into the world, and try and forget. Time, for her to ignore, then unmuddle her complicated feelings towards Rourke; to make peace with the role he'd played in the grim events that had sent her running. Though even then she'd known, her brother had only ever sought to protect her.

As he always will.

Since she'd found the courage to reconnect with him, their correspondence had become more frequent, and they'd found the closeness they'd had as children again; as much as they could considering the circumstances and distance. A distance—from him, and Barrow Heath—that Rourke had always been understanding of, accepting that some wounds, some memories, were too great to be healed, or faced. He'd understood why she could never go back; that sorely as she wished to embrace him again, to find a way to be in his life, she hadn't the courage to seek out such a path, even for him.

Oh, she'd tried to coax him from Gloucestershire, especially once Ginny and Juliana had joined the Spencer clan, except it was the only point on which they could never reconcile. She could never go back; he couldn't leave. And so they'd tacitly agreed to never push, though each knew the offer, the welcome, remained, always; at least until his latest letter.

I shall be at John and Celia's for the holidays, though I couldn't but decorate Stag House more extravagantly than last year. John joked this is my tradition now, and I wonder if the house shall be full to the brim of greenery, baubles, and candles with nowhere to sit or breathe by the time you return, Jules.

I know why you feel you cannot. None of us will ever be able to forget, but I cannot bear to think that night robbed me of you too. That my attempts to preserve and protect you divided us, and I cursed myself to lose you. I'm sorry to bring up these memories, however the season makes me long to have you here; for us to be a family again, celebrating as we were never allowed to. Your happiness will ever be paramount, and so I let the conversation rest, yet tonight, I wonder if your current course will bring you happiness. If you are certain it will, I will bless you until my dying breath. But are you certain? Or having seen your friends settled, beginning their new lives, is it not perhaps time to move on?

Whatever you decide, I am here, always for you...

And for the first time, Juliana had wondered if perhaps he was right. If it was time to move on, and let Ginny and Elizabeth live their own lives. Between Spencer himself, exemplary father that he was, the Dowager, who doted on her granddaughters as she'd never her children, the Spencers' friend Freddie Walton, who spoiled Elizabeth, sharing his wealth of travel and trade knowledge every moment he could, and their newest addition, Sofia Guaro—Mary Spencer's sister-in-law—who had taken to doting on Justine, Juliana was...*needed but not.* She helped, but was governess and nurse in name only—room and board her only payment since Ginny's divorce—and not solely because Ginny refused to delegate her children's care entirely, but because they were sisters, and Juliana loved the girls as though they were her own.

Except sometimes love means bidding the other Godspeed, and letting them move on.

Still, as much as that thought, her brother's letter, all of it troubled her...none of it was the root of her discombobulation. None of it was what made her feel incapable of finding anything certain enough to cling on to. Made her feel as though she'd learned that no, two plus two, did not equal four; that all the laws of earth were wrong. No. Juliana felt unsteady, as a wave of long-tamed, but never buried emotions—*guilt, heartbreak, disgust, guilt, woe*—engulfed her, because...

I saw a man who looked like him, or rather, as he might've had he...

Lived.

Except he hadn't. He'd died eighteen years ago, and though every day since she'd wished her memories were nightmarish fantabulations, *not* memories, they were, and Sebastian Francis Lloyd was dead. Juliana had seen it done with her own damned eyes.

And though I don't believe in Him, I pray God forgive me for that, and the rest.

Shivering again, Juliana held herself tightly, forcing herself to breathe, rather than be drowned by memories and heartbreak. She walked through the bright vegetation surrounding her, bursting with colour and light despite the darkness; begging the trees and blooms to keep the shadows at bay, as they did the night itself. She tried to see the radiance, feel it, seeping into her, yet she couldn't.

'Tis only lack of sleep. Once...we return to London, all will be better.

Yes. Weather permitting, they would return to town within weeks, and so whatever ghost of flesh now dwelled in these parts, reminding her so of Sebastian, soon she wouldn't see his shadow in the town's alleys, or on the edge of the hills above the loch, or by the roadside or...

In my dreams.

Soon, they would leave, and she could return to herself, and this good, worthy life she'd found and built. A life, a family in which she *did* still have a place, and in which she could, if not be at peace, then be... as at peace as she would ever be permitted to be. For despite a disavowal of God, forsaking of organised religion, and all things superstitious, she admittedly still believed in *repentance for sins*. And regardless of whether she had sinned, failed, and deserved to bear guilt's weight—a constant, internal debate—her past meant that things like true, lasting peace, would for ever be out of her reach.

Whether that is truly repentance for ancient sins, or merely unhealable wounds, I'll never know.

Glancing to her left, Juliana stared at her own shadowed reflection in the glass walls; a ghost herself in her white wool dressing gown, and had she not been so distracted by the rest of the picture, she might've been mirthlessly amused. The lines and form were her own, but unfamiliar, ill-fitting grimness, and hesitation marred them. Desperation bloomed in the shadows around her eyes, born from sleepless nights spent watching memories of lost days, and of this new man who so resembled the one she'd loved, dance before her eyes. Nights of whispers and howling wind carrying his voice, rough and ragged from the *other side*, beckoning her ceaselessly.

Juliana...

Even now, she could hear it on the whistling of the snow and ice-laden whipping wind as it passed and whirled through every crevice, tearing her heart evermore to shreds. Still she stared at her ghostly visage, desperately trying to convince herself there was a rational explanation to it all feeling so *real*, as though Sebastian *were* truly here. That there was merely some stranger roaming these parts who reminded her of Sebastian, which coupled with the dim light of the season, exhaustion, and guilt, made her lose a sense of reality. Such things happened; she was neither the first nor the last. There had even been such an occurrence at Aconite House last All Hallows' Eve; a maid had believed she'd spied a ghost, until she and a guest had uncovered a murderer of flesh and blood. There had been a rational explanation *then*, and so there was *now*.

For you don't believe in ghosts, or voices from the other side, or even another life beyond this one.

Still, tears pooled and fell heavily onto her cheeks, and Juliana swiped them away roughly, hating her body and mind for their weakness, their inability to carry her on, this exhaustion, this—

Juliana froze, a flurry of movement catching her eye. Stepping forth, her eyes readjusted to see beyond the reflections on the orangerie's glass walls, into the obscured gardens, and her breath shallowed as she approached the limits of the space, the cold permeating vividly, inviting her into its embrace.

There.

A figure, cloaked in darkness, and layers of dark clothing, yet unmistakably a man. It was his coat, flapping in the wind that had caught her eye, and somehow, Juliana knew two things.

This man was not a figment of her overtired mind or guilty soul.

This man *was* whoever had been taunting her these past weeks; and he had been *taunting* her—her mind was instinctively correct.

Anger rushed through her. She'd allowed herself to be so silly, imagining spirits when it was merely some ill-intentioned rogue.

How dare he? Why her?

She should go fetch someone, right now, have them chase down this villain, and see to it—

No. Impossible...

Juliana gasped as the wind forced the tumultuous clouds from before the nearly full moon, and she might've fallen to her knees had she not crumpled against the glass instead.

No, no, no...it cannot be...

Her heart threatened to leap from her throat, and she thought she might be ill, right there, even as she remained frozen, staring at the figure before her, brightly illuminated for the briefest moment, which felt like eternity stretched out. For she knew those features well, *by heart*, having committed them there two decades ago, and there was no mistaking them beneath the markings of years passed, a life lived, and time itself.

Sebastian.

Not someone who looks like he might, but him.

Impossible, her mind reminded her, with such force, conviction, and intent, it launched her towards the door just as the moon passed back behind clouds, and the figure turned away.

Enough, her mind screamed, propelling her on, fumbling first with the key, then with the handle. Onwards, out into the worsening storm, which lashed her with pelts of brittle ice, gentle snow, and thick rain. Out into the sloping garden, through the gales threatening to knock her down. She was frozen through within seconds, drenched, numb, and in pain, yet still she moved, onwards, chasing the shadowed figure as it hurried away.

I cannot continue thus, she cried, silently, her tears freezing on her cheeks, or blowing away with the precipitation. She didn't know what cruel joke this was, why someone had sent this man to torture her, but she didn't care. Tripping and sliding and tumbling, she gave chase, her breath a continuous stream of mist for each exhale was so quickly followed by the next.

It didn't matter *why*. What mattered was putting an end to this hellish farce, and had she not been driven so close to the brink these past weeks, perhaps her famed rational mind might've averted her to the dangers of this pursuit, only it had truly abandoned her, and so, on she went.

Until finally, as the figure reached the edge of the loch, he stopped; the water fiercely lapping at the toes of his boots as if beckoning him into its freezing self.

Juliana's frenzy didn't diminish, yet her body suddenly found strength to contain it, so as not to chase him away with her desperation. Her body vibrated, holding itself back, forcing caution so he wouldn't flee as she took those last few steps to within nearly arms' reach of him. Only he wouldn't flee; she saw then, felt, *knew*, he was waiting for her.

He turned to face her, and it stopped her, momentum pulsing through her with as much force as the invisible strike to her heart. For then, there was no denying the truth before her eyes; the reality of impossibility.

And so after one shuddering, stilted breath which

may have carried with it a cry as well as a name, Juliana did something she only ever had once before; she fainted.

Sebastian.

Chapter Two

Sebastian stared out into the tenebrous mire of noth-ingness beyond the fire-tinted glass, a mire he couldn't see, yet which remained infinitely preferable to star-ing at Juliana's unconscious form, now tightly tucked in her bed, beneath thick layers of blankets.

If he hadn't needed her, he would've left her right where she'd crumpled, all pale and dramatic like some pathetic heroine; more a ghost herself amidst the tem-pestuous wintry night than he. If he hadn't needed her, he would've left her there, on the unforgiving, frozen loch's shore, likely to die; or so he was forcing him-self to believe.

Forcing, being the operative word.

For no, despite it feeling better to believe the con-trary, the truth was that he *wouldn't* have left her there. Not because he cared for her in even the smallest pro-portion, but because he valued a life; perhaps even more so than many others. Though the value he placed on a life only meant that had he *not* needed her, he likely would've merely brought her inside, then been on his merry way. He certainly wouldn't be standing vigil as he was now, waiting for her to wake. Unfortunately for them both, he *did* need her, and so, here he was, ensuring she lived through the night, so she could serve his purpose tomorrow.

Nothing more.

Sighing and massaging his brow, Sebastian tried in vain to untangle the mire of thoughts furrowed beneath; an endless mess of Sisyphean proportions. A mess for which he was solely responsible, having not *stuck to the plan.* An already flimsy plan, consisting solely of: *find Juliana, convince her of who you were,* and *force her to help.* Three explicitly simple steps. Yet despite this straightforward simplicity, he'd mucked it all up, because of…

Surprise and sentimentality. Two things I swore off long ago, and which in this endeavour would undoubtedly spell ruin.

And what, precisely, could surprise a man who had died eighteen years ago, been reborn, and built himself into a man of means, with a thirst for revenge? A man who knew the darkest parts of humanity as he knew the back of his hand, and who could decipher people better than scholars could ancient texts?

The answer was simply: a woman. This woman.

Juliana Myles.

She'd recognised him.

Not just tonight, but weeks ago, when he'd finally tracked her down, and watched her from the shadowed alley beside the old cobblers' in Aitil, with as much anger and envy as he'd ever felt in his heart. Oh, he'd been careful—he'd like to say he *always* was, however at the very least his actions since returning to this cursed isle would belie that—but yes, he'd been careful *then*. In fact, his being there that day had been about being careful, *preparing*, getting the lie of the land so he could finalise his plan. Watching his opponent, finding weaknesses and opportunities, ensuring his own safety. Strong man that he was, he'd even had the forbearance to prepare himself for the likely onslaught of emotions he'd face when he saw Juliana again; knowing that seeing her again would be *something*. His intent had been to watch, wait, learn, and prepare, nothing more. Except that day, she'd sensed him, then spotted him skulking.

Fair, he'd thought—prey could sense a predator's watchful eye. So like those great beasts who lurked in shadow before pouncing, he'd not moved, merely watched, until he'd seen recognition dawning in her own eyes, behind doubt and incredulity.

If there was one thing he'd been reassured of—*reassured, ha!*—since returning to these shores, it was that he was in every way the new man he'd crafted himself into. No trace at all was left of *Sebastian Lloyd* for anyone to recognise. Nearly twenty years of toil, torment, success, and ageing, along with fine new clothes, better speech, and a new name, were all it took to wipe Sebastian Lloyd from his own countenance. The man he'd once been was truly dead to all who had known him, just as his name was in most people's minds.

And yet.

That day, Juliana's recognition, had pinned him. Discombobulated him. For to him, that eventuality had been discounted as *impossible*. He'd not counted on her looking at him and seeing Sebastian, *and yet*, she had. So then, in the days and weeks that had followed, he'd followed her, watched her, *not* to prepare—though to his credit he had managed to make *some* useful moves as regarded his plan—but because he simply couldn't *discount* her recognition. He had to be certain, beyond the shadow of a doubt, that it wasn't merely the last shreds of his own imagination and twisted hope that made him believe in it. Therefore as he watched and followed and gathered information, he occasionally gave her a glimpse of himself, as a test. A test, which she passed every time—or failed, depending on how one looked at it—by recognising him, through the layers of years, hardships, woes, and even through his own death. It was troubling.

To say the least.

And it prompted him to make mistakes, which resulted in enormous messes, like tonight, the most shining, glorious example. He wasn't sure *why* he'd come tonight, to stare at the darkened, strange old house; it served no purpose considering he knew it well enough now, knew where she slept, how to reach her, the inhabitants' routines, *and yet*, he'd still come, and she'd spotted him, *pursued* him, and...

A mess. A gigantic, unacceptable mess.

He needed to pull himself together. To get his plan

back into action, forget this bout of surprise and sentimentality, and move on, for it he was only delaying the inevitable, endangering his chance at redemption, and true, everlasting peace. Really, he needed—

Behind him, Juliana stirred, and he clenched his jaw, forcing away *any* trace of sentimentality or nostalgia as he crossed his arms, and finally turned to face her again, though he didn't budge from the window.

It proved a greater struggle than expected—particularly considering the amount of practice he'd had over the years—shoving all the flashes of memories, and emotions back into the depths of nothingness where they belonged. Only, there was something about seeing her thus again, barely unchanged by time, ever as beautiful, slowly waking from what could've been a peaceful slumber, which made his heart ache and twinge most unacceptably.

There was just something about the way her straight, thick, waist-length raven hair lay against the pillows; he could perfectly recall the feel of it through his fingers. The pale skin, dotted with freckles only those closest to her would notice, or be able to describe the locations of like seasoned sailors. The squared yet delicate sharpness to her features and fingers, and the bluntness of those thick eyebrows, and rather long ears. The stubbornness of her straight nose—complete with an imperial bump. The wide, catlike quality to her eyes—how he once could just put his thumb on the eyelids, and brush sleep away for her. The memories, no matter how he attempted to cast them away, clung to him like imps, reminding him of those precious few mornings, when she'd awoken thus, and he'd been beside her, to feel her warmth, and smell…

Jasmine, apple blossoms, the first dew of the morn, and the southern breeze of freedom…

Even had he not been encased in her scent, from carrying her inside, and remaining trapped here in her room so long, where her scent permeated everything, he would remember it perfectly. If he had to choose, he would wager it was that which had taunted him most over the years; every note of Juliana's scent thrusting him remorselessly into the past until he could barely breathe for the pain renewed within him.

It was everywhere here, and he hated that, almost as much he hated her, and how she looked, and—

'You're dead,' Juliana declared, those dark brown eyes of hers which had once hypnotised him, now as cold as he needed them to be, still focusing as she chased away the remnants of unconsciousness.

The placidity, the certainty, the regret contained in that comment, might've injured him, had they not bolstered him, reminding him of *who* he faced now.

Not the girl you loved; if indeed she ever was.

She may be the reason you're here, but she isn't the reason for your return.

With those reminders, the memories shut themselves away into nothingness, and he smiled most wickedly. Juliana studied him questioningly, slowly forcing herself back into the now as she pulled herself to sitting weakly.

He and his heart almost went out to her.

Almost.

'You're dead,' she repeated, her voice a scratchy whisper, laced with less conviction. 'I watched you die.'

'I wasn't the first to survive too short a drop, and I shan't be the last. Though it was mercy which spared me any further attempts.'

'How...?'

'That isn't a story to concern yourself with, nor which has any bearing on the matter at hand.'

'Which is?' Juliana asked flatly, that great, steely strength and mind he recalled in full view. *There you are, my darling.* 'If it is my torturous punishment, rest assured there is nothing you could dream up which would rival what I've done to myself, though I'll admit your recent hauntings were rather effective. Whyever it is you are here, tell me, and be done with it, for the house will be awake in a few hours, and I am tired.'

Sebastian sneered, shaking his head.

He'd never felt Juliana's famed coldness, he'd always seen through it, to the strength, rationality, warmth, and vulnerability beneath it. Not even in those fateful days during his own trial when he'd felt her distance, her betrayal, her silence, had he felt it, but now...

All these years, he'd made excuses, telling himself so many things which now were moot, for he saw plainly how right they'd all been; whatever he'd thought he'd seen in her had either never existed, or was long gone.

She is the unfeeling wretch they said her to be, and that will make this all much easier.

'You cannot think of another reason I might come after you?' he taunted, determined to elicit *some* reaction, because…

Well, there was no *because*; there couldn't be, as all he wanted—*needed*—was her cooperation.

Nothing else, including an emotional reaction, he reminded himself.

'I may not know the man you are, but the man you were would never…'

Juliana trailed off, stopping herself from speaking a lie.

'Hurt you? Kill?' he finished mockingly, grinning. Juliana clenched her jaw, and looked away, staring unseeing at the perfect stripes of the wall-hangings. There was something about the gesture, what he'd glimpsed in her gaze before she turned away… *Do not start imagining things.* 'Eighteen years…it's been long enough. I thought I could live without the truth, *live* my second chance through, only as it happens, I cannot. So here I am, come to take you home, Juliana.'

Now, *that* elicited a reaction; Juliana's wide eyes found him, fear and refusal painted within them.

'No.'

'No?'

'Is that monosyllabic word somehow unclear, Sebastian?'

On a growl, Sebastian stepped forth, his arms uncrossing as his fists clenched, intent on…well, he wasn't entirely sure, which was entirely distressing.

It wasn't as if he *would* ever harm Juliana, yet as she was now, calm, biting, and unmoving, still tucked beneath those covers as though nothing extraordinary or in any way worthy of *some* interest was coming to pass, was unnerving, and infuriating. How dare she, how *could* she be so calm, so placid, when he—

Ah, now *that* was the problem. *He* wasn't in control and for this, for all that would come to pass for he would make it so, he needed to be. Taking a deep breath, he settled, stalking forth until he was at the foot of her bed.

If he wasn't approaching any further, it was because he didn't need to, certainly not because he feared closer proximity with every ounce of his being.

'My sincerest apologies if I in any manner implied you had a choice, Juliana.'

'How precisely do you intend to bend me to your will? Will you kidnap me, shackle me, and drag me with you? Or perhaps will you threaten me with bodily harm or the revelation of secrets? I have no secrets great enough to compel me to do your bidding, and I know you would never hurt me, nor anyone I hold dear enough to place myself in jeopardy for,' Juliana taunted, her temper flaring, taking Sebastian's own with it, for it was naught but the truth.

He couldn't compel her; he'd counted on surprise, and guilt being powerful enough allies, he'd counted on—

Nonsense. Fix it; there are other ways.

'You would go to your grave, meet your maker, with this travesty of justice on your conscience?' he asked, attempting to appeal to her rational mind, since her heart seemed now entirely frozen over. *Ah yes, using theology to underline rationality; very effective on such a person as her.* 'You would live your life, content in having enabled lies to breathe and breed?'

'Justice was served. You were tried, convicted, and sentenced, though you apparently survived that meted out to you, so call it a miracle from that God you always believed in, be grateful, and go live this new life of yours. You can die satisfied that in the next life, His judgement will prevail.'

'I've tried!' Sebastian screamed, rage, and pain taking hold as they hadn't in a very long time. 'Tried to have faith in the God I once believed in, and accept my fate, only I cannot. Eighteen years, Juliana, I've lived as a man not myself, yet with the sins of another on my soul, unable to live truly free! I deserve justice in this life, and I deserve to see the true beast punished for his own crimes! I did not kill them, and I will not die with that stain on my name! I will have the world see the truth at last: *I did not kill them!*'

Silence echoed around them, as they stared at each other, he willing her to see, to understand, to take pity, remember what they'd once shared, and…

That is the hope talking. The hope which cannot be slain, and forces me to want her to believe me.

For this to go any other way than even now I know it must.

* * *

'Please refrain from shouting down the house,' Juliana quipped viciously, startling Sebastian from his stark, seething desperation, old habits burrowing their way back into her tendons, as she'd hoped they never would. *Attack, distract, stall.* 'Neither of us wants the headache of explaining your presence to those who would come to my aid.'

'I would ask why you haven't called for your friends to come save you from the evil phantom, only I see now that it is embarrassment and concern for your position which has kept you quiet,' Sebastian sneered, his mocking tone coloured with hitherto disappeared notes of his original, broader accent.

Juliana bit back another retort, but only because succumbing to further argument would negate the aim of her initial remark, which was to buy herself time, a moment to…

Find some semblance of my reason; something to anchor myself so I do not crumble to pieces…

For the truth was, all she'd truly wanted to say, confess, was that she *knew*.

When Sebastian cried out in denial of his crimes, of those murders, Juliana's heart, soul, mind, *all of her*, had declared silently: *I know*. However, to declare it aloud, to utter those words, reveal that secret she'd never uttered to another living soul, and barely even, to herself, would be to reveal all she was and had ever been, was but a mirage. To reveal that truth so privately

kept, could, if she believed in a god above, sentence
her to an eternity of damnation.

I know, and have always known.

Oh, she'd tried, spent years endeavouring to force
herself to believe she'd never truly known Sebastian,
or his heart. Years, attempting to force herself to admit
that this unshakeable conviction that he'd been innocent all along was merely her feeble heart's attempt at
reassuring itself; she hadn't loved a murderer. Years,
trying to force her heart to accept that she *had* loved a
murderer; that what it believed was nonsense, that he'd
been guilty, and all was as had been said and done.

Attempting, in vain, to accept what had been declared as inalienable truth: that on the night of December the first, in the year of our Lord 1814, Sebastian
Francis Lloyd, of the village of Barrow Heath, had
murdered a woman known only as Alice, and her
young son, who had been called Bertie. She had been
presumably twenty or so; her son, approximately five.
There had been no obvious motive—at the trial, the
prevailing and condemning theory had been an *intimate* connection between Sebastian and Alice—if
indeed there could ever be a motive to such demonic
savagery as had been seen by those who witnessed
the scene on the hilltop, that snow-laden morning of
December the second.

No one who knew Sebastian believed he could be
such a demon, *would've even thought* to believe it,
had it not been for the undeniable facts of the case,
and the lack of any other suspects. Juliana, who then

had held such certainty in her heart that she knew him better than anyone, wouldn't have believed it if not for all that. Still, there was *belief*, and there was *fact*, and when faced with such evidence and logic as she had...

Perhaps that was the precise time when she'd been forced to truly *grow up*. One might posit, given the harshness of her upbringing, that it would've happened sooner, and in many ways, it had. Then again, perhaps it was precisely *because* of her upbringing that she'd clutched so tightly to such childish notions as love, belief, and faith; the only light in an otherwise stygian existence. However, that light too had been extinguished, those notions abandoned to a well-ended childhood, with the murders. For it didn't matter how loudly her heart screamed that Sebastian could never do as had been done, it didn't matter how tirelessly her mind worked to desperately arrive at another conclusion, *the facts and logic did not lie.*

Such simple words, those: *facts and logic do not lie.* Words she'd clung to, to get her through...everything. The seeds of doubts, they'd sown, before giving her some sense of conviction, some sense of certainty; right up until Sebastian had dropped through the hatch, a noose around his neck. There had been something in his eyes in that fateful moment...

She'd fainted, for the first time in her life. When that *something*, akin to anger, and a plea, had disappeared along with the light in his eyes, and her heart had drummed quicker than any tattoo, and her soul had screamed out in agony: *he was innocent.*

Oh, she'd still clung to those words: *facts and logic do not lie.* Still spent years forcing herself to believe them, to believe that she'd been a girl who knew nothing at all of the true hearts and souls of men, that Sebastian had been guilty, and it was just her *wanting* to believe that she hadn't been so foolish as to be deceived, and love a monster worse even than her father.

But with every passing day, they'd lost their power. The seeds of doubt had never grown, nor been reaped. All that had grown and bloomed for eighteen years on rotten soil, was her instinctual conviction: *he was innocent.*

If she knew this—then, and now—one might wonder: why would she not leap up, rejoice for this mighty miracle, and vow to help him uncover the truth and reclaim his life?

Why would she not thank her lucky stars for a chance to find answers to one of the questions which had gnawed at her for years: *if not him then who?* Why would she not even tell him as much—*I believe you*—and open her heart to all these new possibilities before her?

Questions more complex than readily appeared, and to which the answers were too knotted and incomprehensible to even think on just then. It was taking all Juliana had—which wasn't much, considering the events of these past weeks, *tonight*—to keep her eyes open. She wasn't seemingly lounging in bed because she wished to—all she wanted was to run screaming through the house, and so much more—only it was truly all she could do with the bare amount of strength she had. That, and *project* strength, certainty, and composure, for to lose any semblance of that…

That too would lose me myself.

In truth, she might've had an easier time of it— recovering from the emotional upheaval of Sebastian rising from the dead, his demands, and a fainting spell after weeks of sleeplessness and turmoil—were she not expending so much precious energy *looking* at him. Drinking him in, cataloguing the changes, vaguely imagining what his life had been, and truthfully, revelling in the feeling of having him returned to her. The relief, the joy, of knowing the world had not lost Sebastian Lloyd, intertwined so acutely with pain, fear, and remorse, overwhelming in and of themselves.

He looked…nothing like the boy she'd known once, yet she could see the boy within him, as clearly as if he'd worn a mask painted with that visage. The promise of the man he would become was gone, replaced by the man he'd become instead, and yet she felt as if she knew this stranger as well as she'd known the other.

He'd become harsher. The shape of him shifting from that of a strong young man of middling height, to a lean fighter. Overall the shape of his face remained the same; long, angular, with a proud pointed chin. The rather large ears that stuck out adorably were still there, peeking from the mop of dark blond hair which came to the nape of his neck, and somehow seemed both assaulted by the wintry storm, yet tamed into submission, cleared from his large forehead, and those two thick brows which slashed across it, tipping now into seething disapproval.

There were lines written deep in his tanned skin she didn't know, telling tales of exhaustion and grief, and those lines she did recall perfectly—the ones at the corners of his eyes when he smiled, pronounced even in his early years—had been swallowed by those new tales. His cheekbones were sharper than ever, his lips still fine—though she cared not to dwell on those—and his long, blunt nose had been broken more than once. In better light, or without the hindrance of a shadowed beard, and moustache, she might be able to tell whether or not some of the marks upon his visage were scars; if that shadow peeking from beneath the cravat he wore was a remembrance from his death.

Perhaps the greatest change, yet the most immovable, were his eyes. Dark now, almost black, though she knew they were a rich marble grey. Deep-set, narrow almond eyes, delicately upturned and feline. Those eyes had always had the power to hold her captive, in their intensity, their verve, spark, and depth of...

Love. Soul. Intelligence.

They held her captive still, though they were devoid of love now—*rightly, as is my own heart*—sparkling and arresting with all they'd once held, though now, like the rest of him, there was an added untethered wildness.

Even though...

Wild he'd always been, so perhaps feral was more apt. Dangerous, unsteady. Barely restrained power and ferocity, brimming from him like embers sparking off hot iron. His voice held those qualities too; where once, his low, gentle tones had been a lullaby, now they held the sharp quality of a menace which needed no effort to demonstrate its power and undeniable threat, and it had nothing to do with the clarity and educated ease he'd forced upon his voice. Some part of Juliana recognised the peril of that confident instability; another, more primal and vital part of her was mesmerised by it.

As though I were some pathetic rabbit, caught in the sights of a demon.

'Don't fret, my darling,' Sebastian scoffed, her rabbit-like self waking from hypnosis. 'I shan't shout again. We'll conclude our business, quickly, quietly, and then I shall be on my way.'

'Our business is concluded. You bade me return with you to Barrow Heath to uncover what you call *the truth*, and I said: *no*. Even were I to accept,' Juliana said, further proving to herself she was no frightened leporid. 'What would there be to find? And were there something to find after all this time, I would think competent investigators—of which I know of a few, and of which those in this house know more— would be better apt to such work, than a governess, and a man who should be dead.'

Something flashed across Sebastian's eyes, and Juliana clenched her teeth so tightly they might've chipped, to stop herself shivering from that one look.

'Do you think me a complete dullard, Juliana? Don't,' he added, likely seeing the retort on the edge of her tongue. 'I'm not, and there is a reason it shall be you and I. When I said I was come to take you home, Juliana, I meant it. For your brother was right, it's time for you to return to him. It's time for his truth to be revealed.'

It took a moment—a long one, which she could tell Sebastian enjoyed immensely—to sort out every morsel of information contained in those words.

'You read Rourke's letter…?' she said slowly.

It wasn't the most egregious morsel, nor the most baffling, yet somehow it was the one her mind chose to address first.

How you have changed, Sebastian.

'How dare you—?'

'*Tut, tut, tut*, Juliana. I needed to be certain you would be of use. There are no rules in this game, that was made patently clear eighteen years ago.'

Reining in her anger—which threatened to transform into rage and make her do things she'd regret—she took a breath and focused on the most important morsel.

'If you think Rourke was involved—'

'Involved? Your brother was at the very heart of it!'

'Of course he was, his position demanded—'

'That he be rid of the likes of me before I corrupted you.'

'You believe he'd murder two innocent souls merely to have you blamed and sentenced to death? Those years spent wherever you've been have certainly impaired your abilities to reason if that is the greatest theory you've come up with.'

'Then prove me wrong,' Sebastian challenged, stepping forth, even closer. Though he only now stood just at the end of the bed, it felt *too* close. 'You believe your brother innocent, so vehemently, as you might've me once upon a time…then prove me wrong. For know, if you do not, then I will go back, and do *whatever it takes* to prove my greatest theory. I will have justice, Juliana, one way or another. And do not make the mistake of underestimating me, or the lengths to which I'm prepared to go to free *myself.*'

Juliana held his gaze despite the torture it was to her shredded heart and nerves.

The challenge in those grey eyes she'd once called home was not merely a challenge for her to follow him, *prove him wrong,* nor even a challenge to protect her brother from him. Worse, it was the same challenge he'd always issued her; to be brave. To be courageous beyond what she believed herself capable of, to eschew rationality in favour of following her instincts and heart.

And look at what that got you…

Though she liked to think it had got her nothing but pain, and regret, the reality was, following that lesson had got her to where she was today; a warm house, of love, and friendship. A good life, during which she'd learned the true meaning of *heart,* and *courage,* by herself, and through the trials and tribulations of her friends.

Once, she'd been powerless to preserve innocent lives, and to this day she bore the guilt for that. For years, she'd pushed herself to move *onwards*, ignoring her own heart's pleas, merely allowing herself to wonder *if not him then who*, never taking any action to right what she'd always known in her heart to be an egregious wrong, because…

It matters not. Powerless you are no more. And the guilt of more blood and ruin I won't bear.

Damn you, Sebastian Lloyd.

And so, although there were hundreds of reasons why she couldn't, or shouldn't follow him back to the Hell he so casually called *home*, be it self-preservation, or merely duty to Ginny and this house; thousands of reasons why she should cast him back to the past and move on again with this life she'd built herself from ruin and ash, Juliana knew as surely as if trumpets had sounded that *this* was her day of reckoning.

Therefore she uttered the words that would change her life, transform her in unknown ways, and perhaps there was poetic symmetry to reality as there was to great art, for the last time she'd spoken the simple, yet powerful words, it had been with only Sebastian as witness.

'Very well, then.'

Chapter Three

It was entirely unacceptable that at precisely ten o'clock, when Sebastian saw Juliana emerge from the thick, frosty mists that had descended after a rather promising dawn, sitting atop a cart, looking a dark, severe spectre of imperiousness, that he felt such relief. He attempted to shake it off, stepping away from his carriage, hailing her and the cart's driver—a young man he recognised as one of Yew Park's grooms.

Unfortunately, his attempts at shaking off the feeling of a momentous weight lifting from his shoulders and heart, along with a *smidgen* of joy and pleasure, were fruitless, and so as the cart approached and stopped, he turned to rationalising instead.

He was relieved, and allowed to be, as there was no certainty to her coming. Last night—*early this morning*—she might've agreed to this business in a weakened state, terrified for her brother's safety, only to then renege, confident in her righteousness, and sure of the protection the marquess and marchioness would afford her and her brother if she so pleaded and cried.

No, he had no true way of forcing her. And if she hadn't turned up, well… He would've made do. He didn't *need* her—in any way shape or form—it was only that this task would be easier *with* her.

Precisely.

To boot, he was relieved because today, dressed all in blacks and dark greys, her hair tightly braided and hidden beneath a simple bonnet, her nose turned up as she descended the cart to meet him, she *looked* like the stern, cold, foreboding governess she was. Nothing remained of the Juliana he'd seen last night, so reminiscent of the Juliana he'd known and loved once. Free, wild, generous, yet unbending as an oak. Nothing remained of his Juliana today, and considering she wasn't his any more, that was good.

If she ever was mine.

In fact, I do not think she ever was, and perhaps, that's why I loved her so.

Yes, perhaps.

The point remained, and was strengthened therefore: she was never his, never would be, and he would do well to remember that in the coming days and weeks.

She is a weapon to be wielded; nothing more.

'Juliana,' he greeted flatly as she stood before him in dips of frozen mud in the inn's yard. He glanced over her shoulder to find the groom waiting, watching with a rapt and concerned gaze, so he tipped his head, and turned back to her. 'Is that all?' he asked, noticing the small bag in her hands—likely barely two changes of clothes.

'It's all I need,' she stated simply, her eyes in turn flitting over him—or more specifically, his rich and perfectly tailored clothes, as fine as any toff's, though not near as eccentric as her employer's—then flicking over his shoulder, to examine his extremely well-appointed carriage, which even without crests or marks, was undoubtedly *his*.

'Shall we then? If your attendant is satisfied you are safely delivered?'

Juliana raised a brow, and he knew whatever would leave her mouth next would flay him, however he was spared her sharp tongue, as a keening cry sounded from the back of the cart.

They all turned, and a mass of brown curls emerged from beneath a dirty old blanket, then sprinted towards them. Sebastian's breath was knocked from him as Juliana's was when the girl he recognised as the marchioness's flung herself tightly around her governess—though it was his heart which felt the impact, not his flesh.

Still my flesh feels the blow resounding within every fibre.

'Elizabeth!' Juliana cried, holding the girl tightly. 'What are you doing here?'

'You cannot leave,' the girl whined into the layers of fabric, her comportment belying her age—which he recalled was about thirteen or so—status, and indeed Juliana's own. 'You cannot!'

Juliana's jaw tightened as she sighed, fighting tears, though the rest of her softened as she stroked the girl's hair tenderly, and the latter buried her head further into the crook of her governess's shoulder.

Sebastian turned away, the image of Juliana embracing the girl...reminding him of all they'd dreamt of having, and which had been stolen from them.

For the best. What manner of parents might we have been, given the chance?

He ignored the voice telling him that Juliana obviously would've made a wonderful mother, and listened instead to the voice speaking to him now.

'Why must you take her away?' Elizabeth was asking him fiercely, with wide eyes, yet the unyielding strength of an ancient goddess; inherited from her mother, or Juliana, he couldn't rightly say.

Both, I suspect.

'We spoke of this, Elizabeth,' Juliana said sternly, pulling the girl away from her body, but still holding her hands. 'My friend needs my help. You know that when friends are in need, we stand by their side.'

Elizabeth appeared unconvinced, yet knew the battle was lost; likely before she even emerged from her hiding place.

Fighting for a lost cause, I can only admire you for that.

'But you will come back,' she declared, her eyes meeting Sebastian's in challenge—beseeching a promise he was compelled to make; despite his own better judgement and desires.

So he nodded, ever so slightly.

Damn the miniature witch.

'I promised your mother,' Juliana smiled weakly. 'I promised you. I won't be long. I'll meet you in town well before spring breaks. Now you best get back before they discover you missing, and send out the county to find you.'

The girl hesitated, before looking him over once more, then nodding to Juliana.

As she scampered off towards the looming groom, who sported an anxious look on his face which told of his apprehension at what he'd encounter when he returned the child home, Juliana straightened.

Once the girl and the cart were again swallowed by the mists, she turned back to him, any softness long vanished; a figment of imagination rather than reality, he was sure.

'Shall we?' she asked, raising that brow again, as though he'd been the one to delay their departure.

Clenching his jaw he bit back an acid retort, and instead merely took her bag, handing her into the carriage as quickly and perfunctorily as he could, focusing hard on keeping his mind elsewhere as her hand touched his.

If she felt the lack of attendants she was surely accustomed to now—he had only a driver, a hired hand whose silence he trusted only for he was required to, though he'd not make a confidant of him—Juliana didn't say, simply installed herself neatly in the dark, plush depths of the carriage, which he was grateful was large enough to ensure they could sit opposite in without risking closeness. In fact, he thanked his lucky stars for just that as he installed himself, shut the door, and banged on the roof.

In an instant, they were off, rumbling and bumping slowly despite the quality of his *equipage*, only gaining speed and smoothness once they met the main road. Still, it was a treacherous way, and time of year to be travelling, though if luck was on their side, they would encounter minimal obstacles to slow them.

Thick silence invaded the space, Sebastian forcing himself to not watch Juliana raptly as she stared out the window, watching her familiar surroundings *whoosh* past and slowly disappear. In the grey half-light, she seemed even harsher and icier—another thing he was immensely grateful for.

Still, as he found his eyes flitting to her more often than not, he resolved he needed to do something, so he chose to speak; and it certainly wasn't because he was feeling stifled by the silence, or had a growing compulsion to ask all manner of questions, about her, her life, her…*everything*.

We are nothing to each other now; if we were ever anything true.

'I thought governesses were meant to be severe,' he grumbled, dispensing with some flecks of something which may or may not have existed on the cuff of his sleeve.

'You used to think for yourself, not abide by lazy, tired generalities.'

'She loves you.'

Juliana's eyes met his, and there was so much in them…

It was his own fault; he'd meant the words to sound bitter, cutting, not admirative or longing.

'I heard of your employers' history,' he said, finding a properly distant and judgemental tone. 'How did you come to be involved with them?'

'How did you come to possess a fortune?' Juliana asked in return, glancing at the carriage's decadently comfortable interior meaningfully. 'Best neither of us asks questions we don't require the answers to. I'm only here to save my brother from being hurt by your… delusions and misguided vengeance, so all we need is a plan, so that we may be done with whatever we're calling this useless exercise.'

Once you might've wanted to preserve me from harm too, now we quip and bite as if Napoleon and Nelson.

'I wonder that you even presume to know him after all these years,' Sebastian remarked, unable to prevent himself from adding fuel to the proverbial fire. 'I have it on good authority the only contact you've had is in those letters of yours.'

'He's my brother. I know his soul.'

He tried not to sneer; *tried*.

'You asked for a plan, it is this: we shall pose as husband and wife. A perfect excuse for such a long-awaited return.'

There.

That had quietened her retorts.

She stared at him with wide eyes, and he took some satisfaction from that surprise; at least until she began shaking her head, regarding him as though his skull no longer contained even traces of a brain.

Once, she alone never regarded me thus. Ironic.

'Ludicrous,' she finally managed to get out, as if it had taken that long to decide where to begin, or perhaps the most adequate vocabulary. 'Not only am I not about to go play-acting as your wife—'

'Why not? You were once a masterful actress.'

Though he didn't flinch, something inside him did as he saw the wound his words inflicted, and it was only by anchoring himself to the fierce rage which took its place within seconds that he managed to stop himself from apologising.

This wasn't how any of this was supposed to go, and he couldn't explain it, but dwelling in rage, quips, and anger, it made *this*, being around her again, easier, and so he fed it.

He actually thought she might strike him, and in truth, he would've let her.

'Setting aside for now debates on my talents for the metaphorical stage,' she finally said, still seething, which he welcomed with every breath. 'Does your obviously addled mind honestly think Rourke, nor *anyone else* in Barrow Heath won't recognise you? Especially considering *my* sudden return? Do you not think everyone will wonder at my marrying a man who looks *exactly* like Sebastian Lloyd?'

'My own father didn't recognise me,' he bit back, and *that* finally had her fully quiet.

He again dismissed the hurt he saw in her eyes, declaring it for her own feelings, though deep down, he knew she hurt for him.

She pities me, and I've no use of it.

Just as he had no use for the pain he felt at remembering that day; no use but as fuel for this task ahead of him.

'And yes, before you say anything he was aged, and already dying when I finally stood before him again some months ago. So I tried again. Found the doctor who brought me into this world, and the one who prevented me from leaving it. I tried friends. Acquaintances. Anyone I could find without setting foot in Barrow Heath. I *wanted* to be seen. *Recognised*, no matter the cost. Quite a brace of people I sought out... However eighteen years of being dead to the world, and fine clothes, works miracles apparently. People see what you tell them to see, Juliana, so it shall be with your brother. You alone have recognised me thus far, and I am willing to bet you'll continue being the exception not the rule.'

And that there is the rub.

Juliana felt it too; though luckily for both their sanity, she quickly pushed it aside.

'What am I to call you?' she asked quietly.

'Thomas du Lac Vaugris is my name now.'

The look Juliana gave him then nearly broke him; but it was his own fault yet again.

The mistake however had been made eighteen years ago, when he'd chosen to inhabit that name, still holding a flicker of hope, and love, and sentimentality close to his chest, despite everything. A made-up name they'd imagined as children; the name he'd have when, in another life, he'd not be a shepherd's son, but a man of fortune, power, good standing, able to be her husband. Able to love her, in full view of the world, and her brother, without question, or shame.

That look she gave him now…so full of nostalgia, and grief, made him desire to make it better, to go back to things as they'd been, to forgive; only he couldn't. So instead, he turned the other way, to gaze out, unseeing, from his own window, forcing them back into cloying silence.

This is going to be a long journey indeed…

Though she had a thousand questions—half of which were rational, and important, the other half things she had, in fact, no business being concerned with, such as *when did you come back to England, who was this doctor who saved you, how can I be the only one to recognise you*—Juliana contented herself with the silence that enveloped them.

It was the only thing preventing her from banging on the roof, demanding they turn back, that this had all been a mistake, that Elizabeth had been right, she couldn't go, and that she needed to return to her true home.

I can't do this.

She wasn't prepared for this, any of this; she obviously hadn't slept last again night—even if she'd miraculously had the ability to after everything, there hadn't been time as it had already been well into the early hours by the time Juliana agreed to this quest, a meeting time, and Sebastian finally left, skulking out as he'd come—so obviously her decision-making was severely impaired, and she should've just stayed, and talked to Ginny, and Spencer, and found another way…

I can't do this. Every word, every breath, every moment with him shatters me further.

Closing her eyes to the blurred landscape which reminded her of the ever-growing miles dividing her from Yew Park House, she took a deep breath, forcing herself to remember all she'd left behind, for it was what had given her the strength to believe she *could* do this. She brought back to mind Elizabeth, and her friends, who had, by their own struggles, battles, and courage, inspired her to do this.

And she recalled her parting with Ginny—as heart-wrenching and painful as any might be, particularly since they'd not parted in the decade since they'd known each other; a lifetime considering all they'd faced and overcome together—to remind herself of why she wasn't turning back.

'What do you mean you must leave?' Ginny had asked, perplexed, stunned, and hurt.

'As I said, a friend is in need of help, and so I must go. I am sorry, I appreciate it will be difficult what

*with the return to London, I'll see if Sofia can take
over Elizabeth's lessons—'*

'*Don't be ridiculous, Jules. You know that's not why
I'm upset; you only have duties and are called governess because you wish it. You could lounge around all
day for all we care.*'

Ginny had sighed, shaking her head, and striding
to the study's window.

Outside, dawn had barely been peeking, making the
loch appear a shimmering piece of armour, and Juliana
had vaguely wished she might cloak herself in it to face
every hour of her life that would follow that moment.

She'd thought then how strange it was, that she'd
dared to imagine the most challenging days of her life
had been long since lived. That though not all life's
trials and vicissitudes had lain behind her, that she
might live out the remainder of her days in quietude,
in a warm house, bursting with love; only Sebastian's
reappearance, demands, and threats, had shattered that.

But she'd also felt that the dawn had brought some
strength back to her, at least enough for her to take her
leave from the person who'd saved her in more ways
than one, and whom she loved dearly—without making more of a mess, because of course Ginny wasn't
upset about the girls, but Juliana's vagueness and lack
of explanations. Ginny had never begrudged Juliana
her silence, and lack of sharing much of anything regarding her past life, despite the bond of true sisterhood between them. Still, in that moment, the lack was
a betrayal, which Juliana was well versed in.

Part of Juliana had demanded, as it did now, she throw herself at the feet of all her friends, beg for their help, and counsel, however she simply…couldn't. There were some things she simply couldn't share. She couldn't contaminate Ginny with the sordidness of her own past now become present. Since life had first thrust them together, she and Ginny had been able to continue on, putting one foot in front of the other, by leaving the past where it belonged; behind them. They had, literally and figuratively, moved on. Had either of them dwelled too long on it—beyond during some occasional dark nights—they wouldn't have survived. They would've been swallowed whole by the gleeful fiends of past terrors.

Certes, Ginny had confronted much of it when she'd fallen in love with Spencer, and Juliana knew the two spoke of it frequently, in a quest to heal, and grow. Except that was the crux: Ginny had moved on better in many ways than Juliana ever could. Joined the Spencer family, found happiness, and joy, that neither of them had ever imagined she might; found new friends—who had become Juliana's—built a beautiful loving home, and Juliana couldn't in a thousand millennia, taint that.

As for the others, as much as their courage inspired her to accept Sebastian's demands, challenge, they too were on their own paths to healing, and she couldn't disrupt that, by bringing more death, grief, and sadness into their lives.

And most selfishly of all, she couldn't face changing

who she was in their eyes, for when this was all done, she would return, as if none of it had ever happened; or so she had promised herself then.

No matter that it was an impossible wish, she wasn't ready to relinquish it.

'I always felt you would leave us someday,' Ginny had finally whispered, as dawn lightened the landscape ever more. *'Go find your own happiness. I've been foolish, allowing myself to believe we could always remain as we are. That we should.'*

'It isn't like that,' Juliana had said, going to her friend, and sliding an arm over her shoulders, embracing her as she hadn't in a long time. Ginny had stared up at her with pleading eyes, and she'd nearly relented. *'Would that it was.'*

'You've been out of sorts for weeks, Jules. We've all seen it, felt it. I've not said anything, but we've all been worried. I can see it now, even clearer, something isn't right, and your silence is...'

'Maddening?'

'To put it mildly. All of us in this house, and beyond, have faced trials these past years. Were it not for each other, we wouldn't have got through them. So why won't you allow us to help you now?'

'Because I'm not strong enough to face what I must, and tell you of it all. Someday, perhaps, when it is over. When we sit again, together, as sisters. For I will return, Ginny. I'm not leaving you for ever.'

'Then why does it feel as though you are?'

'Where I must go, to see this done, there is nothing to keep me there. And there is no danger, I'm merely—'

'Helping a friend. A friend we've never heard of, nor are even to meet.'

'I'm sorry, Ginny. If you would speak to Spencer and the others... I would appreciate it. I'll say good-bye to Elizabeth, and find my own way to Aitil; I'd like my leaving to be unmonumental.' Ginny had nodded, and Juliana had sucked in a deep, somewhat calming breath. *'Thank you. I will return, I promise.'*

'Promise that you'll be careful,' Ginny had said desperately, turning and taking Juliana's hands in hers. *'I don't believe whatever this is, is without danger, if only to your heart. There's something in your eyes, Jules, it scares me. Still, I cannot keep you here. You feel you must go, and so you must. But I'll have your promise that you will be careful, and call upon us, should you need anything. Promise, Jules!'*

'I promise,' she'd breathed, tears brimming in her eyes, as there had been in her friend's, and Ginny had wrapped around her, Juliana holding her tight.

It had been achingly bittersweet for, despite her promises, Juliana had known then she was telling one great lie; that she would return.

For though she would, she'd known then that the woman who left Yew Park House, would not be the same who returned in future. She would be a stranger that Juliana dreaded to meet, for all she would have lived.

And so that is what scares me now. However turn-

ing back isn't an option. I can't do this, but I can't go
back and tell them of it all even less.

So onwards into the past we shall go.

Chapter Four

'My apologies, *darling*, I should've asked if you objected to our sharing,' Sebastian said, obsequiously as he could, opening the door to *their* room at tonight's chosen inn, beckoning her to enter with an outstretched arm. Had Juliana paid more attention when they'd arrived, rather than merely waiting for him to make the arrangements, then blindly following him to a table and tucking into some admittedly delicious pie, she might've been prepared for this.

I don't think anything would've prepared me for this.

Though she managed to school her features, and simply gazed on at the Spartan, but comfortable room, featuring a bed, necessary amenities, and sitting area with two chairs and a tiny table beside a roaring fire. Sebastian was goading her, and though she welcomed it, she refused to rise to the occasion, and give him any satisfaction by admitting that actually *yes*, she had *quite a few objections* to this arrangement.

It was *too* much, too quickly.

The hours they'd spent in silence travelling today,

following this morning's *spat* had, beyond allowing her some time to recentre and remind herself why she wasn't fleeing back to Ginny—though she felt that urge again at this unwelcome surprise—had also somewhat allowed her mind, and eyes, to accustom themselves again to Sebastian's presence. To truly realise he was alive; within arm's reach.

And admittedly, the increasingly mind-numbing ride of endless silence had also afforded her rest; she'd even managed a few hours of sleep—deep, dreamless sleep—thus recovering some semblance of wits and strength.

The problem being, as some portion of those returned, so did reality. The emotions, the questions, the fear, seeping back slowly, like poison into heart, and mind. So did the undeniable truth: the time for her to stand tall and get this situation under control was fast approaching, if not arrived. Something which would be much easier if…

If my own body wasn't such a bloody traitor.

For today had shown her that too. Her ability to rest, to sleep, wasn't due to sheer exhaustion, to the shock of Sebastian's reappearance after weeks of believing she was going mad, the prospect of returning to Barrow Heath, or even the loss of all she held dear. She *very* reluctantly had to acknowledge that she was able to rest, and sleep, because shockingly, incomprehensibly, she felt safe with Sebastian.

There were a thousand reasons not to. She was a woman alone, with in essence, a stranger; a hard, volatile man, who'd been changed by life—granted, as she, and everyone else on Earth had, but still. He'd followed her, *haunted* her for weeks. He was seemingly intent on meting out misguided vengeance upon her brother, as he believed *him* guilty, which even with what little Sebastian knew of Rourke, and despite Rourke's long-ago disapproval of him as a potential husband, Sebastian should know was utterly absurd. To only list a few.

However, the fact remained that she'd slept and just *existed* all day in his company without any concern for her well-being, because she knew, with undeniable certainty, that he was there. That he wouldn't harm her; that he would see her taken care of—even if against his own will, considering his general mood—like tonight itself proved. She'd not paid attention because she trusted him; she knew the shared room was for her protection, nothing else. In fact, she couldn't deny… It *felt* just as it had when she'd been a young woman; when Sebastian was home, safety, and comfort, all wrapped into one. Despite it being appallingly preposterous, there was no denying her entire being *felt* at rest in his company.

Appallingly ludicrous indeed.

Especially considering his hostility; and her own. Every word coloured with barely leashed anger, tasting of the bitter bickering of ancient enemies. Except they weren't enemies; or perhaps they were, Juliana was certain of nothing.

It's only going to get worse with all that's to come, which is why you must find certainty in what you can.

'I've slept in worse company,' she said, only half as haughtily as intended, shaking herself back into action by striding into their room.

If bickering and hostility are that certainty, so be it.

'I'm sure you have,' she heard Sebastian scoff, closing the door as she went towards the bed, setting her bag beside it before ridding herself of her bonnet and gloves on the night table.

'Those chairs look comfortable enough, so you shan't suffer much, *darling*,' she said over her shoulder as she continued about her business. Hanging her coat on the screen in the opposite corner, and sliding behind it to pour some water into the waiting basin to wash her hands and face. 'And I'll thank you to take yourself into the corridor when I change into my nightclothes,' she added, emerging once again.

'So you've developed modesty.'

'Perhaps I'm merely hoping you've developed genteel manners to match your fine clothes,' she quipped, her frustration stemming not only from his words—which, in all honesty might've actually garnered a laugh—but mainly from her annoyance at noting just how handsome he was, standing there in the firelight; how her heart instantly felt a jolt at having him near again.

Such observations and feelings in this situation are precisely the reason your sex garners a reputation for idiocy.

'You used not to mind so much my coarseness,' he reminded her, his voice dropping and finding its original tones again; something of a seductive growl laced with bitterness.

His eyes glittered, and he made to take a step towards her—for what purpose, she dared not even think on—but she stopped him.

'Love makes fools of us all.'

'So it does.'

It was more a deflation than a sigh which escaped him, before he shrugged off his coat, and settled in the rather handsome armchair by the fire, rolling up his shirtsleeves, and loosening his cravat.

'We need to talk,' she said seriously after a long moment, debating the words, and wisdom of approaching this now, rather than tomorrow, when they were better rested.

Time is of the essence and I doubt we'll ever be well rested.

Sebastian raised a brow, challenge and contempt once again in full view, and that bolstered her. Unsure whether it was a gesture of avoidance, or invitation, Juliana chose to assume it was the latter, and settled across from him, swallowing hard as she realised the shadow around his neck was indeed the scarred reminder of his execution. Her heart twisted with pain as fresh as the day he'd received the mark, and she promised herself never to gaze away from it. She may be many things, but a coward, that was not one of them.

At least, not for a long time.

'What are we to speak of then, Juliana?' he asked,

meeting her gaze, the grey depths softer than she'd seen since his return; though she wouldn't mistake it for anything but exhaustion.

In fact, the slight drooping of his left eye confirmed that hypothesis; another detail, another part of him that hadn't changed.

Another something which means nothing.

'This plan you purport to have,' she said, gentler than she'd intended. 'Why you believe my brother guilty.'

'The plan, Juliana, is to return to Barrow Heath, and ask those questions which should've been eighteen years ago. To follow the trail further than ever was back then.'

'That isn't a plan, Sebastian. If we're to even *pretend* to be allies in this ghastly game of digging up the past, and the dead who inhabited it... I need a plan,' she told him, as sincerely as she could, appealing to whatever charity he might have left in him. 'I will not be swept up in the currents of your quest for revenge, allow you to behave an Alastor. I spent too many years wandering through life, with no will of my own; I won't be that woman again. No good will come from it. You said you wanted the truth, justice, so convince me that's truly what you're after, and I will help you, with all I have.'

And perhaps we'll all make it through this trial with minimal damage.

Oh, delusion truly is due diligence for the desperate...

The look Sebastian shot her made clear he wasn't convinced by her proclamation, though neither was his silence dismissive, so she continued.

'You know very well that stranger or friend, ask too many questions, and you'll only receive slammed doors, and questions in return. We must therefore be clear on *which* questions to ask, for questions *were* asked eighteen years ago. Just because you didn't like the answers doesn't mean they weren't the truth. Unless you are telling me now you feel there was an intentional miscarriage of justice.'

'No. Those officials involved did their duty, acting on what they believed good information, some rumour, but mostly fact. However, the point is, just because the answers paint a tidy picture doesn't mean they are *the truth*. The painted image is invariably the product of the artist holding the brush.'

'So you believe my brother not only guilty of murder, but of being said artist?'

'That he was the artist was never in question, Juliana,' Sebastian said gently, with enough deadly seriousness to demonstrate his righteousness. That truth was one she'd never wanted to imagine, yet it made some sense, and was easier to accept than the other. *So many reasons for Rourke wanting to...make such a mess tidy.* 'However yes,' he continued, seeing the effect his own certainty had. 'I believe now that it was for more than to merely be rid of me.'

'Why?' she asked again, breathless.

It just…

Doesn't make sense. Never will.

Rourke had no motive, and even if he did…he would never commit such horrors. I know my brother's soul; if I know any one person's on this earth.

Perhaps even better than I know my own at times.

No. She would listen to Sebastian's reasoning, if only to show him the flaws in it, but she would never be convinced her brother capable of what had been done. Sebastian's return, and disavowal of his own guilt, had cemented her instinctual conviction of his innocence, but that didn't mean she hadn't given the case, the facts, the conclusions, any thought over the years. And part of her reluctance to return perhaps stemmed in some ways from her belief that the truth *couldn't* be found after all this time. For in all those moments when she'd tortured herself with *if not him then who*, she'd only come to two unfruitful conclusions: *it was someone we knew who hid their heart and deeds too well, others like Rourke unwittingly aiding in their quest for swift justice*, or *it was a stranger no one noticed and that we could never therefore hope to find.*

And she had thought of it, many times, trying to do what they were now, only…

I was a coward after all.

'I would've brought a drink had I known I'd be faced with such an interrogation,' Sebastian sighed, dropping his head into his hand, and massaging his brow.

'I can wait if you'd like to fetch one.'

'No. Let us be done with this.'

As he turned to stare at the fire, Sebastian knew by the look in Juliana's eyes, that the rapidity and short-ness of his answer betrayed his caution as regarded drink; after quite a few years using it to numb the horrors and pain, he'd given up the stuff for any *rec-reational* purposes. Again, he rethought the wisdom of bringing Juliana along for this quest—of justice, not vengeance; or so he was as certain as one could ever be.

It can still be justice even if I wish for whoever ruined me to suffer that crime too.

He was rethinking bringing her, because…he was admittedly finding it difficult to be around her. When they were nipping at each other, or she was being frost-ily imperious, he was fine—in fact, he rather enjoyed it, for the reassuring and entertaining blanket it was. But when she was…open, vulnerable, *human*; when she saw parts of him she had no business seeing having long lost that right, then things became more difficult to navigate. His mind and heart became less certain; he became less certain of his own strength. To see this done, and yes, if he was *entirely* honest, to resist her.

So find something you are certain of, and hold tight to it.

'You want to know why I believe your brother the true culprit?' he asked, turning back to her, holding tight to his conclusions and what certainty he had regarding this affair.

Juliana had always valued reason, and logic, and he didn't think that much had changed, so though she might not *deserve* answers, giving her some might just assure greater compliance and assistance.

He also couldn't deny that finally being able to make the case of his innocence to her—something he'd attempted at the trial, but which had been disastrous, every weakness in his tale shredded into pieces, and frankly, everyone's minds having already been made up before it even began—held undeniable appeal.

Though I shall not examine why.

'Firstly, his vehement, dogged pursuit to have me found guilty, and condemned.'

'He was attempting to protect me, and the village, from someone he believed dangerous. They were found on your lands, murdered with your own belongings—'

'*Secondly*,' Sebastian continued, forcing Juliana to cease parroting the *facts* which had seen him hang, by their convenient twisting. 'The victim, Alice, was known to have asked for directions to Stag House from the Widow Morel on the morning of November the thirtieth, after declaring she was seeking out family in the area.'

'No one knew her nor claimed any connection. She could've been asking for directions to Stag House for she was related to any of the servants, or merely because it was the closest marker to where she was going.'

'By that I assume you mean, *the closest marker to me*,' he sneered, and regret flashed in Juliana's eyes.

Though this whole conversation had begun at her bidding, she was regretting it, and in some way, he understood.

He'd had nearly two decades to, if not make peace with the past, then find ways to step back into it, without too much injury. Whereas, in a bid to protect her brother, and disprove his theories, she'd just launched herself into the past without care, not fully appreciating all she would have to face to undertake this lamentable task. And despite his understanding, he would give her no quarter.

I too have long-unanswered questions which deserve resolution.

'Do you know, despite everything… I never thought you believed those idiotic fabrications they touted about Alice and I being *involved*. Me being the boy's secret father,' he admitted, true curiosity and surprise mingling with utter grief, as he studied her closely; feeling as if he was only just seeing her truly. 'Foolish of me, to hope that though you may believe me a murderer, you might've at least known my heart to be loyal.'

Cheeks flaming, she bowed her head.

'What was I to believe?' she asked quietly, shrugging before meeting his gaze again. 'So much of you was a mystery to me—we always spoke of the future, not of the past. It made sense, and…'

'Your brother convinced you.'

'Rourke asked me to consider the possibility,' she corrected. 'He'd heard the rumours, knew they would come out at trial, and sought to prepare me. It was part of an ongoing conversation,' she said slowly, delicately, turning once again to the flames, and admittedly, he was grateful to not bear the burden of her gaze, as he didn't...feel entirely *solid*.

Though he would have to sort out his emotions, find solidity again, later; right now, he would hear the answers he'd longed for, and deal with the aftermath in due course.

'Rourke only asked...how well I truly knew you, and your heart. How certain I could be that love hadn't blinded me. That you weren't involved with me to better your position, and line your pockets with my inheritance.'

'And you weren't. I suppose that answers quite a few questions,' he nodded.

'You were my first love. I was young, Sebastian. You gave me no explanations, no reassurances. Why shouldn't I have considered that I was merely the latest to be fooled by pretty words and promises? After all, have you not returned now only to use me to your advantage?' she challenged.

'What was I meant to do? Write you a letter from gaol? Invite you for tea?' Juliana sighed, conceding the point; both ignoring that which she'd won regarding their present circumstances. 'You were my world, Juliana. I had need of nothing else,' he told her, allowing himself the briefest moment of vulnerability.

He thought he caught a glimmer of regret, of unshed tears, but then he posited it was a trick of the fire. 'So whether or not you believe it, the truth is: *no*, I was not the boy's father, nor did I know the woman,' he said, returning to the matter at hand. 'Everything I said then was the truth, before you, and before the God I still believed in. Yes, I was in the village near Widow Morel's house that day; to fetch the collection of journals on Constantinople you so desired, as you well know, since I gave it to you that afternoon. Yes, the implements used to commit the murders were from our farm; I believe they were taken to implicate me as I noticed their absence before I went to the village, but merely thought I'd mislaid them. Yes, those two poor souls were found on our lands, and I should know, for I was the one who found them that godforsaken morning.'

Juliana flinched as his voice cracked, the horror of that sight plain, and Sebastian took a long moment to breathe, and stabilise himself.

'Even if you don't credit my word, you knew my father. I may have been his son, and he may have been away during those fateful days, however at the very least, consider that he might've had some idea if I'd fathered a child at barely fourteen. And you know, he never would've stood by me had he even *thought for one second* I was capable of such monstrosity. No... Everything was designed to make it appear as though I was the murderer, and do not fool yourself—there *was* design. It is one of the reasons I believe it to have been your brother.'

'Anything else?' she asked quietly, albeit slightly defiantly, taking all he said, yet maintaining distance from it.

'Your brother travelled to Scotland immediately after my execution. Allegedly to consult physicians as you were...unwell, however there are gaps in the reports of his travels, and he might've gone to Oxford, or London, or had someone attend you in Barrow Heath, rather than travel to Scotland.'

'You posit there was a more sinister reason for his journey?'

Sebastian inclined his head, the hint of a challenging smirk making it to his lips, though he had *some* decency, and tried concealing it.

'Is that all?'

'One of the investigators I hired found a note, from an interview with the Widow Morel, which was deemed irrelevant, and not presented at trial. The morning of December the first, the widow stated that not long after Alice and Bertie had left—before I was seen anywhere in the vicinity—she saw her husband.'

'Her husband who'd been dead for forty years.'

'Her husband who once possessed a mount which looked remarkably like your brother's old stallion, therefore I believe it was your brother she saw rather than her husband. And lastly, in those same interview notes, my investigator found repeated mentions of *"the pretty gold picture"*, and *"theft?"*, so my hypothesis—

as his, and the interviewer's likely was—is that Alice had upon her some sort of gold frame, or miniature, which was then taken. A planned murder for the theft of that one item makes little sense, but is possible, though arguably Alice spoke of something she'd had to sell along the way, considering their impoverished state. I knew nothing of it, and even had it been presented at trial, it might've been claimed I'd taken it.'

'And that's…all?' Sebastian nodded again. 'So you accuse Rourke with nothing more than breadcrumbs and circumstantial evidence—not even that, circumstantial musings.'

'I was hanged with less,' he reminded her bitterly.

It was Juliana's turn to sigh, and turn to the flames for guidance and wisdom.

Sebastian waited, doing as she did, _breathing deeply_. She may not have been _won over_, but she was listening, _hearing_, and that was something. He could see her wrangling with, if not doubts about her brother, the realisation then that what she'd been sold as irrefutable facts and reason were in fact, nothing more than circumstantial musings.

He saw her wrangling with the holes in the spun tale, the _refutable_, and that was all he supposed he could ask for; for her to finally see that the interpretation of the main facts was as malleable as wet clay.

'These men you engaged to make enquiries, they didn't uncover anything else? No tales of strangers previously unnoted, or movements of inhabitants that didn't match the initial reports?' Juliana asked, meeting his gaze again.

Sebastian braced himself as his heart thumped faster, wondering—*hoping*—the lack of argument meant she might truly be coming to believe him innocent, and a more courageous man would've asked outright.

'I might've mentioned that, Juliana,' he said instead, knowing patience would be required to see her come to his conclusion about where the guilt lay. 'There was nothing so miraculously noteworthy.'

'So no clues as to Alice and Bertie's family name, home, or anything to help us know who they were? I don't suppose they found this *"pretty gold picture"*— for that would be immensely useful.'

'Unfortunately not. They did discover Alice and Bertie had travelled from Oxford, though that wasn't their home, only where what limited means they had ran out. From there, they made their way on foot, and with the kindness of strangers, the very same that saw the Widow Morel take them in, as you know.'

'Obviously that must be our priority,' Juliana nodded, her engagement making him feel *better. Nothing wrong with that*. 'Finding out who they were is the most complex line of enquiry, yet the most vital, as there we likely find motive. I agree, I don't think it was about theft, and Alice wasn't...touched, before. And although there can be opportunity in design, seasoned predators may prepare, I'm not ready to conclude they were murdered without motive beyond sport or unholy urges. I shall think on how to proceed.'

Sebastian didn't mention that he believed the *'pretty gold picture'* held helpful clues as to their identity, and that he intended to search Stag House for it—his investigators having found no trace in any pawnbroker's or the like for thirty miles—but it wasn't out of kindness, merely because he wouldn't alienate his new ally so quickly.

'I'll await your thoughts then.'

'We must also discuss… Well how it is we're meant to have met, and such,' she added, changing the subject, and indeed, the conversation's tone.

'Another time, Juliana,' he said quietly, his own exhaustion, physical and emotional, clearly visible now, though he didn't care, for there was dangerous ground; they both knew it, and had already trodden far enough on such.

There was a moment then, the tiniest, most infinitesimal particle of time, where it felt as though the years melted away, and it was just the two of them, as it had been, and he was *with* her, and they were…

'Write to your brother,' he said, pulling them back to now, where they should be. 'Tell him you're on your way, with a new husband. I'll ply someone with enough coin to see it delivered before we are.' Anything he thought he might've seen in Juliana vanished—*another trick of the firelight*—and she nodded. 'I'll make myself scarce for half an hour or so. Allow you the time for that, and to change and settle for bed.'

Another nod.

Sebastian took a breath, and rose, Juliana following his motion as he went to put his coat back on.

'You said earlier, that you'd help, with all you had,' he said quietly, before opening the door, staring unseeing at the latch. 'Even if it is upon Rourke justice must be meted?'

'Let us hope neither of us have to learn the true answer to that question.'

'Good night, Juliana,' he nodded, grateful for her honesty.

'Good night, Sebastian.'

To hope is not a skill I possess any longer, he thought grimly, making his way from the room.

And so I can only fear we will someday soon be forced to learn the answer.

Chapter Five

Though he felt he needed it as much as Juliana had, and despite the carriage's lulling—well, bumping—tempting him to, Sebastian was unable to sleep. It wasn't that he was unable to find it, like last night, which he'd spent in that armchair, thinking about too many things he had no business thinking on—though he was doing that too—it was that he couldn't; the reason more infuriating than the incessant *thinking*.

If he'd been half as clever as he purported occasionally to be, he might've feigned sleep; the added advantage being that feigning sometimes saw it sweeping you away easily into its embrace. However, this whole endeavour was making one thing inescapably clear: if he truly was half as clever as he occasionally purported, he wasn't in any way behaving thusly. Not because he wasn't feigning sleep as they devoured more of the many miles dividing them and Barrow Heath, but because he wasn't feigning sleep because he couldn't stop studying Juliana, and couldn't rid himself of the need to see her safe at all times. Barely two days in her presence, and already he couldn't properly wrangle his emotions or thoughts; not that he'd been able to before, however last night had made it infinitely worse.

He also wasn't near to half as clever as he occasionally purported, because for all his dreams of vengeance—*justice*—years of planning, and all the rest, well, as Juliana had expertly demonstrated last night, his plans were…*tenuous*, and barely meritorious of the name *plans*. It was infuriating, and troubling, and essentially, he was seething, really. If only the anger he felt now was the same he'd lived with for years— nearly his entire life, actually—he might've managed it better, trouble being, it wasn't.

Before his arrest and execution, he'd been angry against an unjust world, and those who exploited it and its inhabitants for gain. *After,* he'd been angry, with all those who had seen an innocent man convicted and hanged. Those were righteous angers. There were many like him across the world who expressed the same anger at an unjust, exploitative world, and he couldn't think of a single person—beyond perhaps the holiest of the holiest—who could endure such events, and not be angry. Then again, even Christ himself had cried out, wondering if his Father had forsaken him; so perhaps not even the most devout were spared such turmoil.

Point was, Sebastian had spent most of his life filled with anger. The past eighteen years especially, without Juliana nor love for balsam, he'd felt it keener than ever, a poison, devouring him alive. He'd fought hard to keep it at bay, to save what morsel was left of his soul. He'd channelled it, transformed it into something with a speck of good, for that purpose. He'd fought to not be destroyed by it, and instead, *built* with it. To prove, to the world, even though it would never know, that he could build something *good*. To feel anger now seeping in again…made him angrier.

It was a harder beast to combat this time. Not directed towards others—ill-doers, an unjust world—but himself, and though he'd been angry with himself before, it hadn't been anything close to this. He couldn't find a way out of it; mainly because he had too many reasons *to* be angry with himself.

The chief reason obviously being that he'd come into this so *ill-prepared*. He'd felt it the night he'd come for her, and he felt it surer now. For all his planning, and accrual of wealth and means—the latter having originally been to *live his new life and build something good* though that was a jest and a half—he'd returned to this forsaken isle with nothing more than breadcrumbs, a theory, and general intent.

Get Juliana. Return to Stag House. Find the pretty gold picture. Dig up answers about Alice and Bertie. Expose Rourke. One decades-old mystery solved by sheer will and a bit of play-acting. Voilà!

Some part of him had always seen the limitations of such a hare-brained idea—*ideas*—and yet.

Here we are. Nearly twenty years and you've still

*learnt nothing; you're still the uneducated boy who
acts without thought.*

To boot, not only was he angry at himself—that
alone he might've managed—he was also angry at
Juliana. Last night he'd watched her, so closely, as he
did now, not in rapture—though her hypnotic beauty
and presence could never be denied—but in study. He
was searching, *desperately seeking*, some notion, some
indication or sign of what she felt. At his return, at…
his demise, at *anything* or everything.

Those months after his arrest, imprisoned whilst he
awaited trial—even during the trial itself—he'd never
had the chance to see her, speak to her, know how she
felt; what she truly believed. Even if he'd been granted
ink and paper, he'd known no message would ever get
past Rourke, and she'd never come to see him. He'd
only ever spotted her in the gallery during the trial,
and only for seconds at a time as he fought to make the
law see his innocence. Her testimony as regarded his
movements that day had been presented as an anonymous written statement to the court, to preserve her
honour; allowed since there was nothing debatable, and
she could offer no alibi. It had been a simple statement
of facts Sebastian already knew, which revealed nothing of what she thought or felt. Yet through it all, even
at the end, he'd allowed himself to hope, that despite
her silence, despite everything, she *knew*.

Whether that made it better or worse, he couldn't
rightly say. But not knowing her thoughts, being denied her in so many ways, it had been as sure a torture

as any of the flesh might've. So now, given ample opportunity, yes, he attempted to divine her thoughts and feelings through study. Yet infuriatingly, the closer he looked, the less he saw; the more he believed Juliana cold, emotionless, caring—like any of her ilk—only for those of her ilk. Her agreement to help now, wasn't for *him*, because she believed in his innocence, but because it made logical sense to *minimise damage*.

Sebastian had always...felt the pain of her choice back then—what had seemed her choice, considering her silence, and those few glimpses he'd had. He'd felt the pain of her apparent belief of her brother's lies—of all their lies—over his word, *his* love. He'd felt her betrayal, her loss of faith, but over the years he'd found his way to some manner of forgiveness. She'd been young, so many tidy tales spun, her brother... Well, Sebastian had never been blind to Rourke's sway over her, to the hold her love for him had over her, and he'd understood, knowing what they'd suffered together at the hands of their father; how such could forge unalienable bonds.

Only now, none of those excuses or justifications truly held; his forgiveness therefore couldn't hold. She wasn't a child—how could she still doubt him, even in the slightest? She might be helping, *seeming* to believe some manner of his innocence, yet she still unquestionably chose her brother over him? Had there been *no* love at all, for her to merely come on this quest to keep Rourke safe, rather than wishing to perhaps help him, the innocent man condemned to Hell for no reason?

How could she truly feel *nothing* at having him re-appear? He'd thought she might, once she slept, rested, and was better able to fully accept all his return was, and meant, and…

Nothing.

How could she just go back to being rational, and sound of mind when he could barely hold his own skin together, let alone his heart or mind? How could she just *sit* there, when he was here, after eighteen years, the man she'd once pledged to love for all eternity and beyond? And how could he need to demand answers to any of those questions, be so idiotic as to need to know any of it in order to survive? How could he feel the need to restore his name, if only solely in her eyes, so that she would be able to speak the name Sebastian Lloyd once again, with love?

How is it—?

'Judging by the deepening scowl, I wagered I should interrupt whatever hurricane of thought you're engaged in before it drowned you,' Juliana said, startling him—nearly to demonstration. Though he'd been staring *at* her, he'd lost focus, so he let his eyes readjust; his scowl *not* improving at being faced yet again with her aloof, unperturbed demeanour. 'We must discuss our… Well, the story of us, I suppose, and though we've many miles left, I'd rather be done with it.'

'Anything to minimise inconvenience for you. Though I wonder at what better you've to do for those miles left.'

Whatever Juliana wished to say, she bit it back, though the sharpness flashed in her gaze.

'We keep it simple,' he told her, as unaffected as could be. In fact, he relished her bite more with every passing hour; it kept his own emotions in check. 'I met that Walton fellow whose company you all keep regularly on some distant shore, and we became friendly. His shipping business is one such as would otherwise attract my interest, and I've seen enough of the same shores as he to lend that tale further credence. As for us, after our introduction, we had a whirlwind, though quiet romance. The end.'

'Your idea presents one grave problem, Sebastian.'

'Do illuminate me, Juliana.'

'Despite your praises of my talents, given the current state of affairs, I don't believe either of us possess the skill to sell such a tale as a *whirlwind romance*. We'd be better off selling some story of forced nuptials in a bid to preserve my honour or such nonsense.'

'As if anyone could believe you, the unflinching, unyielding Juliana Myles, were forced to wed because your honour was at stake.'

'As if anyone could ever believe you were so swept away with love, you just couldn't wait to marry me. You can barely bring yourself to look at me, and when you do, it's as though you wish to burn me to ash with pure, unfettered hatred.'

'At least I bloody feel *something*, Juliana! Even if it is hate! Because yes, I hate you! I hate you with all the love I once possessed for you! At least I *feel*. You,

you just sit there, and judge me, from atop the throne in your ice palace of nothingness!'

Instantly, Sebastian knew a line had been crossed, not only with his own temper, the harshness of how he spoke to her, but also within himself.

A line he couldn't return from; past self-control. A line which once crossed, meant he could no longer keep words he knew would break whatever fragile, already teetering construction of an alliance between them, from leaving his lips. He could no longer hide his desperation, his pain, and so he felt himself run even further from that point of no return, his heart screaming out for the answers he'd craved more than life at times, for eighteen years. So, with all those pleas and desperation on full display, he slid forward, and somewhat clumsily with the swaying and bumping, dropped to his knees before her.

Still, she sat there, his very own Despoina, the only sign she was in any way affected, her quicker breathing, and stiffening at his gesture of beseechment.

'Did you truly love me so little then, that my return has but spoiled your plans for the new year?' he croaked. 'Was *I* such a fool then, to believe you when you swore our selves, mortal and immortal, coiled and knotted together by forces stronger than God?'

'How dare you ask me that?' she finally seethed, her own temper and nostrils flaring, as she yet again regarded him as though he lacked a brain.

'Finally, some emotion!'

'Eighteen years, Sebastian! Is that how long it takes

to forget someone you claimed to know so well? Not even two decades?' she asked him contemptuously, and the momentary relief he felt at seeing some of what lay in her heart dissipated, for then, he realised he'd been gravely mistaken.

She kept everything for herself, to preserve herself, as she always did.

It was not coldness nor uncaring; only ever hidden depths.

'I thought you saw me, knew me once,' she continued, and the pain he saw in her eyes, a pain of betrayal he knew all too well, struck him down.

As did something else he couldn't see clearly yet for the anger he clung to; this time at her not trusting him as she once had, to speak her mind and heart without reserve, and without being pushed to it.

'I believed you saw the truth in every glance, every touch, every word when apparently that wasn't enough for you. I loved you with everything I was, and I believed every word! You ask me now if I feel anything? I feel more than I have in eighteen years, felt more in an instant at the sight of you! I spent half my life walking through the world with an annihilated heart I couldn't believe still beat! Eighteen years, moving through life, through this world, like a soulless shade for having loved you, and lost you, and I held on to lost dreams, and love, and promises, and refused to live for the guilt and wretchedness and pain I felt. And then you reappear, and expect what? For me to be able to speak of it? Ask you plainly, why you never came for me until you needed something? Until you need me to return to *that* place? I have no words for what I feel, there is no language to describe *any of it*, and I owe you none of what's in my heart, nor mind, not any more. You lost that right when you left me to believe you were dead, and mourn you, and stop living, for eighteen years!'

Juliana's words, her confession, her very being echoed in the resounding silence which followed.

Even if he'd wanted to, he wouldn't have been able to hear the sounds of the carriage, horses, and road; anything but their harsh, stilted breaths. He wouldn't have been able to see anything but her shining fury; feel anything but her, somehow surrounding him, threading into him through every pore again as she once had.

Threading herself back to where she always belonged.

That thought prompted him to do the most foolish thing he'd yet to do in perhaps his entire life. It prompted him to stretch out, rising up towards her, his hand catching and grasping her skirts, to kiss her, and Juliana might've preserved them both, by shying away, striking him, or calling him out for such an unthinkable transgression, only she didn't.

Instead, she met him in his folly, and finished closing the distance; finished making the choice, her hand sliding to cradle his jaw, fingers tangling in his hair, her thumb notching against his earlobe just as their lips met.

Time, reason, a sense of place, everything melted

away. There was no past, no present, only this insatiable need; the one which had never left him. Her taste, her touch, the feel of her, *here*, beneath his fingertips, beneath his skin, rather than merely in his imagination and dreams, ignited a long-slumbering fire he had no hope of extinguishing, not in a thousand millennia. Breathing deeply of her, his body reaching out to get closer, he delved into her mouth, and Juliana met and searched with as much passion as he. The dance of their tongues and lips and teeth was messy, and unbridled, yet retained some familiarity of old.

How I missed you...

They clutched, and clung, and grasped, taking as much as possible in an to attempt to satisfy their long unsated, and insatiable need; just as that fire between them could never be extinguished, no matter how either of them tried. Sweat beaded on his brow, and he smelt Juliana's on the air between them, mingling with the rest of her scent, and he groaned.

More... I need...more...

He dared to open his eyes, breaking away from her mouth, sucking in what air he could; though it was quickly taken from him again when he spied those dark brown eyes of hers, alight and alive with the wild desire that reflected his own. Silently, he asked her to make the decision again; either would damn him to eternal misery, but he didn't care.

Without hesitation, Juliana slid her hands from where they were tangled—one in his hair, the other clutching his shoulder beneath his coat—taking hold instead of his already mussed cravat and placing one over his heart, as she guided him to sit beside her.

Following his movement, her body not releasing him for a second, as she'd never released his heart, she straddled him, mindful to keep her head from hitting the roof as they bumped along, and she adjusted her skirts.

'I... I am healthy,' he managed to breathe, needing her again—*always*—to know she was safe with him. 'But I've no preventive...'

'As am I,' she nodded, leaning in to whisper beside his ear, hear breath catching his earlobe. 'You'll just have to recall how we made do as younglings.'

He made some sort of assertive noise as she leaned back again, and he watched her, breathed with her, fascinated—this time in awe and wonder—in another world suddenly than that of mindless hazy passion as she led the dance. He might've done something then, only she was too quick, too efficient, distracting him by taking perhaps seconds to free him, and readjust herself so she could welcome him once again inside of her.

Taking hold of his shoulders, as he did her waist, she did just that, her eyes steadily meeting his for the briefest moment before they closed in bliss. Sebastian might've succumbed to that sensation which could not be named—beyond bliss, wonder, or pleasure—when he slid inside her once again, except his heart stilted at the sight and feel of her, and he realised the truth.

I love her. Still, always.

He clutched her tighter, his heart straining and pulling, his mind reeling, and he reached out to lose himself in her kiss again, hoping he could...make that realisation disappear. Erase it, send it back from whence it had come, lose himself in her and this slick, sweaty, primal connection, only he couldn't. Their connection only made it worse, and so he sought further, relishing every bite of her fingernails in his flesh, of her teeth against his lips. She rose and fell against him, seeking her peak, driving him faster towards his; old preferences well remembered enough it wouldn't take long.

And as desperately as he tried to lose his mind to it, to simply feel her warmth, and the wool of her dress, and the salt of her kiss, and tickle of her hair, and huffs of her breaths, he couldn't.

I am angry most of all for having loved this woman; for her love drove me to ruin.

I'm angry most of all for loving her still, with all I am.

Angry that we've no future for it was stolen from us by the past.

I'm angry for dragging her back to a place from which I swore once to rescue her.

I should never have abandoned her.

She always deserved better than what I could offer.

I should have come for her years ago, a conquering hero.

I wish I could hate you, my love, but apparently I cannot.

That was his final thought before Juliana threw

her head back, tightening around him, gasping as she reached her summit of pleasure. He held fast, letting his heart race, but holding her steady as he could never be again, until she returned. Then he pulled himself from her, clenching his teeth as relief and pain mingled; in heart and body alike. Only then did Juliana hesitate, perhaps wondering whether she should leave him in his current state, but in the end, with a determined glint in her eye, she chose the greater evil.

Taking him in hand, and seeing him to his own summit of pleasure in a very quick few strokes, all whilst she held his gaze, challenging as ever, as if to say: *love me if you dare.*

Only he'd taken up that challenge over twenty years ago, and as he'd just learned, it was not one which could ever be reneged on.

Would that it were.

Not that it—or any of this—changes anything.

Chapter Six

The silence had returned, which would've been a blessing, had it not been teeming with the unspoken, demanding, clamouring to be given life and breath. Time was running out to say all that needed be; though that didn't make the *saying* any easier. The miles dividing them from Barrow Heath were few now; though Juliana hadn't seen them pass, unable to but stare at the carriage's swinging red velvet curtains for days, but oh, how she'd felt them.

When they'd first set out, she'd welcomed the silence, the rest and respite it had provided. Now she missed that variety of silence; who she'd been briefly living in it. It had been claustrophobic, tense, yes, but so intensely overwhelming it couldn't be battled. Whereas this silence that she and Sebastian had dwelled in for six days and as many nights, it was... sad. A veil of foggy sadness, which could be lifted with mere words; words which required heart *and* will, except Juliana was too heartsick to face them. In the other silence, she'd been fiercer; a resting warrior, mustering strength. In this silence, she was a sad, hurt girl, lost in time and space, and it mightn't have been so terrible had Sebastian not been so quietly solid.

Distantly attentive.

Non-intrusively present; ever ensuring her safety and comfort, yet a shadow, abandoning her to her writhing thoughts, as if afraid of what words would finally emerge.

You and I both...

It was as if their interlude had robbed him of his fight, his ferociousness, his hatred. Changed him into another being, stranger than the last, and faced with the choice again, she wasn't sure she would *indulge*, though at the time it had seemed a boon; much needed relief from tension and pain. Only she too had been changed by their meeting again thus, and now, she wondered if the cost was worth the pleasure and fleeting relief.

But then, hadn't that always been their problem? One poets would describe as love's most delectable outcome; transformation through the act of love. Only to Juliana it was a problem, and perhaps always had been, though once, she'd believed as those idiotic dreamers did—that it was fate, or destiny, or *love*, and not something...else.

When she and Sebastian had first consummated their love, it had felt like stars were aligning; Fates singing of fulfilled destinies. She'd thought: *this is what love feels like.* She'd believed herself a butterfly, emerging from a cocoon, her flesh, organs, skin, tendons, mind, heartstrings, all of it, rearranged by Sebastian's touch; by how they were together. Even in their less earth-shattering encounters, she'd felt a certainty, an otherworldliness she just *knew* meant they were destined to be. That their souls were entwined; not even death capable of killing their love.

Of course, then, she'd not imagined the latter would be tested so soon.

Fate indeed.

The problem was that their recent interlude was all she'd remembered, treasured, and more. Being with him, his skin, the way he touched her, his breath mingling with hers, his taste…all of it transformed her still, as though he were some magician of old, casting spells for bones to break and reassemble; never the same again. Together, the two of them were doubtlessly something extraordinary. *Except,* Juliana saw now that extraordinary quality was but a hallmark of compatibility, lust, and the in sync desires of two beasts who mated well together. There was science to it; the veneer of Fate, love, and all those idiotic beliefs she'd held despite her devotion at the altar of rationality, were gone.

It didn't matter that she'd never found anything comparable to what she and Sebastian had with anyone else. She hadn't exactly tried; there had been a few bland and unremarkable attempts at kissing strangers some years after Sebastian's *death*—a footman here, a visiting friend of this family or that there—after which she'd resigned herself to being alone. Alone wasn't lonely, and she could take matters into her own hands to satisfy biological needs for release. She'd not closed herself off possibly loving again; though she'd not been entirely open to it either. She'd had one great love, and that was what the gods or the universe or nature or chance, had allotted her.

Fine, so she had closed herself off to it; and that too was part of the problem.

Despite her inclinations to the rational, when it came to Sebastian, nothing had ever been rational or logical. She'd entombed herself alive like some queen of old when he died because he'd been her great love, her soul, and her heart, and she'd never love again. It had only ever felt like the truth, except now…

She realised she'd loved the memory of a ghost for eighteen years. Confused Fate, with compatibility. She'd been the romantic, forlorn, idiot she'd scoffed at in books, and wasted her life.

Not wasted. You found so much, and mustn't diminish all you had, lost, and endured.

Nonetheless…

'We were children, Sebastian,' she said quietly, determined to vanquish this burdensome sadness, her eyes affixed on the swaying velvet, unable to look at him *quite yet*. She felt his gaze however, as surely as one might the sun. *A despicably romantic simile.* 'What we called love,' she continued, clarifying though she knew he understood her meaning; as he always had, even when he'd understood not a whit. 'If it was that, it was the love of barely formed beings. What passed between us…is proof we still share the desire we once had, but nothing more.'

Sebastian said nothing, for a long time, and this silence too, was different.

Anticipatory.

A fog both lifting and falling; words disappearing sadness, yet inviting a new gloom, *concealment*, to join them.

Concealing all you cannot say, even to yourself.

Finally, it became too heavy, forcing her to meet Sebastian's gaze. A sliver of sun shone through the window, glinting off his grey eyes, and returning his harshness, previously so comforting, yet remarkably absent for the past six days.

Say something, Sebastian, I beg you.

'You thought I'd not recognise a mindless rut, Juliana?'

'You know that isn't what I meant, Sebastian.'

'Then please, illuminate me. Be my teacher again, as you were once, bringing me your books, and giving me lessons on the world. For to me, you were attempting to remind me of my place, our situation, after a six-day-long deafening silence. Perhaps you've mistaken me for one of your other playthings, who need to be explained their usefulness.'

She stopped her rebuttal from escaping her lips just in time; her personal business, or lack thereof, was none of his.

Besides, indulging in an argument, temptingly distracting though it was, would be a mistake, for this was their last chance at stark, necessary truth.

And we both deserve one moment of it before everything goes to Pandemonium.

'You asked how I felt about your...return,' she said, finding the calm certainty, and straightforwardness necessary to see this done. She found it by anchoring herself in Sebastian's mercurial depths, however if it worked, no use debating the wisdom. 'Rather you accused me of feeling nothing, and I shared...much of the jumbled weave of emotions and thoughts which have been mine since you came back. But there is more to say, and we both know it must be before we return *there*, so that we may be somewhat clear of mind.'

Sebastian inclined his head as if to say: *lead on then, madam*, and so, Juliana did.

'My love for you was so profound,' she began, forcing herself to hold his gaze, and say only what she must, lest she be tempted to... *Be as fanciful as those idiotic heroines and pack in your good sense for a pair of pretty eyes.* 'I believed it could be nothing but everlasting, and so, I still do, for it marked me. I'll always be grateful for it, however... I preserved it, as one might specimens. It remained unchanging, for it could not change with the seasons, with us; and so it is, the love of youth. Perfect, unalienable love. Its threads still hold pieces of me together, and so it is everlasting. So I was grateful, relieved, joyous, when you reappeared, and I thought, *thank whatever powers be above for not forcing the world to be without Sebastian Lloyd.*

I'm still grateful for the miracle, or luck, or whatever spared your life. Know that.'

After a moment, he nodded, infinitesimally, his jaw ticking in time with the carriage's rocking.

'But we are children no longer, Sebastian. We've lived lives, become strangers. The love we had, was for...'

'Other versions of us.'

'Yes. I appreciate you already know this,' she added, sensing an edge in his tone, and hoping to prevent any argument. 'My point is... Hate me if you will. If it makes your life, this endeavour, any of it, easier. I can bear it. What I cannot do, is be...the girl I once was. I cannot change the past, and I cannot continue to bear the weight of what happened to you. I've borne it all these years, Sebastian. Tortured myself with more intricate deviousness than you or any demon of Hell might've. Wondering, what I might've done to try and save you, what I'd done to see you condemned... *If only I'd said something more, something better, found a way to aid an escape, convinced Rourke to help you...* All that, and more. But I must thank you, for you rising from the dead, these days on the road, they've given me peace in that at least. I never truly saw it till now, but... I did what I could. I had many advantages—wealth, wit, strength—and I was older than many who've faced worse, but I was also still a child. A girl, with no true power, or agency. Would my speaking for you, have changed anything? I don't believe—I didn't truly then—it would've. The law wouldn't have batted an eyelid at the assurances of a foolish little girl in love, even had I been able to provide a true alibi. And *yes*, I tried to assuage that guilt at my powerlessness by convincing myself what they said was true, but I...'

Juliana stopped herself, unable to say...*everything* quite yet.

Taking another deep breath, she glanced out at the sunlit sea of colour whooshing past, then turned back to Sebastian, who looked either ready to leap from his seat, or be absorbed into it.

'I won't bear the weight of what happened to you any longer. Hate me for whatever role you believe I played, whatever faithlessness you think I demonstrated, because I know now... The guilt I felt, it isn't mine. I don't know whose it is, but I won't carry it. I will aid you in this, for no, I won't see my brother, or you, or anyone else hurt, and I believe that yes, Alice and Bertie deserve for their truths to be told. For justice to be truly served, if it can be. But that's all.'

'We might've had a love for the ages, once,' Sebastian said quietly, after a moment long enough to convince her he wouldn't say anything, turning to watch the passing palette of colour. 'I should've come back for you long ago. Some nights, in those moments the stars seem to extinguish for the night being so dark, though they likely shine brighter, I imagined I did. Even in my imagination, our life was...one of fear, in shadow and poverty. You deserved better, I always knew that. However I see now, it was wrong of me to abandon you.'

A tear trickled down her cheek; she hadn't even felt it, nor the tightness in her throat or heart appear.

But, oh, how I feel them now.

'I wouldn't be myself had you not,' she breathed, meaning it not as accusation, but as *thank you*. 'So I'm glad you never came for me.'

Juliana saw him nod out of the corner of her eye; but nothing more.

Both of them continued to stare unseeing out of the windows, as the miles separating them from Barrow Heath diminished evermore.

A tale of love for the ages we might've had, once.

Chapter Seven

Even had Juliana wished to, she wouldn't have been able to stop herself from balancing on the edge of her seat, to peer like an anxious child as they neared Barrow Heath—or more aptly, Stag House, for they wouldn't be traversing the village. They'd made exceptional time today; roads, horses, weather, *everything*, conspiring to speed them along on their final stretch, and with every mile, Juliana's nerves increased, until she was a tight bundle of them, ready to implode.

Eighteen years...

Eighteen years since she'd travelled these roads—seen those trees there, age—old oak, ash, chestnut, and beech popping up from the hedgerows, marking the way, then opening up as the drive to Stag House came up on the left.

Eighteen years since she'd been so close to the place which had seen her birth, seen her grow; a place which had seen immense sorrow, and snippets of joy, which she was ever loath to call *home*. Her fingers tightened in her skirts, knuckles white, surely, beneath the gloves, and she forced herself to breathe as the carriage slowed, turning onto the drive.

There were no gates, no walls, nothing to keep it contained from the world; anyone without knew there was nothing good to be found within, and those within knew a punishment worse than death awaited if they attempted escape. The drive too was lined with trees—tamed beech these—the house's grounds, and surrounding fields barely visible just beyond, before all opened as the way rose, climbing the mound on which Stag House had been erected less than a century before by her father, with their mother's fortune.

From there, the drive was bare to the elements, though judging by the smoothness, it was well maintained, opening out onto the rolling hills and fields and forests on every side; save of course, for the house right at the end. Juliana couldn't see it yet, so she focused on the surrounding vistas, breathtaking, and full of memory, even as half was dissimulated in the thick curtain of icy rain and greyness which blocked out what little sun was left to shine today. Then finally, before she could prepare—though centuries wouldn't be long enough—it was there.

Stag House.

The carriage slowed before stopping in the immense, empty circle before the house, leaving a view of the latter framed in the window, like a tiny painted card. Juliana's breath shallowed and quickened, and she found that despite her best efforts, she couldn't make use of the steadying tricks she'd once taught Ginny.

Memories ebbed and flowed—snatches and scraps of
the tapestry of her youth—as the imposing grey stone
filled her view. The three-storeyed Palladian construction—as symmetrical, bland, and starkly ostentatious
as could be—hadn't changed or aged. Its grimness remained—and wasn't the weather's doing; more than
once she'd thought how apt the foreboding grimness
was, for wasn't it a prison?

Why have I returned here?

Her body revolted, begging her to scream, demand
Sebastian take her far away, and there were bodies
moving outside, emerging from the house like blurry
ants, and someone was speaking, but she couldn't—

Breathe.

'Juliana,' Sebastian said gently, his warmth surrounding her.

She startled, finding him beside her, watching her
with undeniable concern, as his hand held hers tightly.

His eyes flicked to the window, and that muscle in
his jaw ticked again; she mused that he'd wear it out
at this rate of usage.

'I should never have brought you back.'

The words were the shock she needed; a jump into
the loch on the coldest day.

*Yes, remember the loch. Yew Park House, Ginny,
Elizabeth...life beyond here.*

*Your friends, their strength which must now be
yours.*

Removing her hand from his, Juliana fixed herself,

straightening into the strongest, most detached version of herself she could manage.

'Save the false kindness for spectators,' she said flatly, sitting back, making room for him to leave. 'I've no need of it.'

A bitter nod, and Sebastian emerged, smoothly putting his hat on as a blast of frosty humid air swept inside.

Another deep breath, and, squaring her shoulders, Juliana descended, noting despite herself that Sebastian handed her down, not the anxiously waiting footman. For the sake of appearances, and because the winds were most destabilising, Juliana didn't recoil, but instead slid her hand onto his arm, and let him lead her towards the gathered bodies standing before the few stairs leading up to forbidding oak doors.

She refused to acknowledge that without him, his warmth and steadiness, she wouldn't have taken a single step; though she didn't take many before Rourke was there, leaping towards her, excitement, and joy barely contained. Her heart melted, relief and love washing away the ill for now, and she released Sebastian's arm, throwing herself into her brother's tight embrace instead, barely seeing him. He smelled the same—like these lands—and bergamot and wet wool. He felt the same too, mighty, tight, warm and loving—strong yet delicate. She buried herself into his chest, and held on dearly, even the gale seemingly disappearing.

How I've missed you, brother.

And oh, how she had. Even despite her complicated feelings towards him as regarded the *Sebastian affair* and the role he'd played—to protect her—in seeing what he believed justice done, Rourke was never why she'd left, and she loved him more than words could express. He'd been…her world, her protector, her friend, her teacher, her joy. So of course, after so long, it would be good to see him again. Of course she'd missed him; just as she'd wondered if *he* would be cross at her for…*everything.* For disappearing into the world mere months after Sebastian's execution, abandoning him. In all the letters they'd exchanged, she'd never once felt anger, or resentment, yet still, she hadn't been certain she wouldn't feel any once they were together again.

But I feel none, and all that matters is that I've returned.

I may not have found the path back myself, and I cannot say there isn't regret in my heart, but I am here, Juliana thought, slowly pulling away to look at him.

He looked well; the years having barely taken a toll, though she knew he'd faced his fair share of trials. Grey streaks peppered his thick dark locks—even more visible for the wind sweeping them into a Byronic coiffure. Lines had deepened at the corners of his eyes, and along his cheeks and brows, but the fineness of his elfin features remained, promising those creatures' eternal youth. The pout of his mouth remained too—adding to the youthfulness—though the cleft in his chin had deepened.

It was in his eyes Juliana remarked the most change; or rather she found they finally demonstrated his age. Those sharp blue depths—wide and bright, a contrast to her own—had always held a wisdom beyond his years. Now that maturity appeared less brutal, less heartbreaking, more settled and natural. Though as ever, along with the wisdom, there stood an ocean of precious and infernal memories, which stole her breath.

Lifting his hand, he swiped his thumb beneath her eyes, smiling that crooked smile of his which once had every woman for miles swooning; and perhaps still did.

'Don't cry, sweetling,' he whispered, wiping tears she hadn't even noticed.

'I didn't realise I was.'

My brother isn't a murderer.

If you saw, felt what I do now, you would know that too, Sebastian.

'Come, let us get out of this gale, before it blows us away, and you can introduce me to your husband properly,' he chuckled, glancing briefly over her shoulder at Sebastian, before tucking her arm, her entire self, into his side, and leading her up into the house she'd sworn never to set foot in again.

All at once the world made itself known anew.

The rain, pelting and biting; the wind, howling and swirling. The others moving around them; the whispers and motion. Her purpose; Sebastian at her back. The memories soaked into every stone, every hill surrounding her; the loss of all she'd left behind.

Momentary loss. You will see them again; find home again.

Steeling herself with that hope, *wish*, *promise*, she let Rourke guide her up into the hall, with its chequered tiles, grand staircase, columns, and mouldings, and... seemingly everything as it had once been; down to the very last vase. The stillness, severity, and piercing bitterness remained, as it likely would throughout the house—wickedness not easily expunged from anything infused so profoundly with it.

Not long after Juliana had left, Rourke had begun to make changes—or so he'd told her—slowly, but consciously. Before then... The most he'd managed whilst still wearing the controlling shackles of their dead father, had been changing their entire household staff—from Father's minions, to strangers who cared not a whit if something other than religious hymns were sung in the house. Rourke's late wife—a Cambridge woman Juliana had only known through his letters, whom he'd married a decade ago, but had sadly passed two years after the wedding from fever, having borne no children—had aided in his attempts to shake some of the evil from this place. For those vases, pictures, and pieces, though *seemingly* the same, were new; an attempt to bring light, and change.

Still the ghosts of the past assail me with cries and shrieks, as steps sound closer and doors slam...

'Ma'am?' said a voice beside her, and Juliana startled, realising a maid was attempting to take her things, and the only slamming doors were those behind her; the steps, those around her.

'Thank you,' she said, allowing the woman to do her work, as she glanced across at Rourke, currently wiping the rain from himself with a towel.

'I'm sure you're in need of rest; to change, and settle in, and are likely famished,' he said, handing the towel back to the butler at his side—Collins, if she remembered correctly, the only one she recognised though perhaps more servants from years ago remained. 'However, you must introduce me to your husband before I let you escape again,' he smiled, striding across the tiles to them.

Moment of truth.

'Rourke, may I present my husband, Thomas du Lac Vaugris,' she smiled, hoping nothing showed of her apprehension, as the two turned to each other. 'Thomas, my brother, Rourke Myles.'

Juliana held her breath, watching them so closely she thought her eyes were bulging as they shook hands, studying each other with the barely leashed intensity and hostility of opposing conquerors.

Am I then the land they've fought over?

'So you're the man who has at once stolen my sister away, and returned her to me,' Rourke finally said, a glint in his eye that almost looked like recognition, but which Juliana realised was merely *mischief* when he grinned, and she could breathe again. 'I'm unsure of whether to make you feel unwelcome, or thank you.'

'I'm quite certain you can manage both,' Sebastian

drawled, that vibrant, dismissive confidence she'd first spied, then which had dissipated these past days, in full view again.

Yes, I'm certain my eyes are bulging now.

She was tempted to thwack Sebastian's arm, but instead she settled for a glare—knowing he could feel it despite patently refusing to look anywhere but in Rourke's eyes.

The moment held, suspended, like some manner of balloon, until finally it broke, lightening, as Rourke chuckled; Sebastian chiming in—falsely, but not unconvincingly.

'A pleasure to meet you,' he added, sounding almost genuine. *So he is become the better performer. Another reason to be mindful; to remain objective.* 'I've heard much about you.'

'All terrible, I'm sure,' Rourke quipped with a wink, releasing Sebastian's hand. 'Mere pleasantries aside, I'm glad to have you both here. It's been quiet for too long, and hopefully, we will fill it with laughter imminently. I look forward to knowing you better, as I'll admit, I'd never heard a word of you until Juliana wrote saying she was returning home with her husband.'

'I am sorry for that Rourke.'

'Nonsense, Jules. You're here now, that's all that matters. Now go, both of you, follow David there,' he smiled, waving at one of the loitering footmen. 'He'll see you situated, and introduce you to those you need know. I'll see you at dinner, so rest up, for there will be no trays tonight. I cannot dine alone knowing you are back at Stag House. Also, I hope you don't mind, but they were rather insistent, and I negotiated a few days' respite, however John and Celia will be joining us on Monday.'

'It will be lovely to see them,' Juliana smiled, longing for a tray—*and a magic carpet to take us all away from here.*

However she would regret locking herself away from Rourke just as they reunited, and as for the upcoming evening with their neighbours, and friends of old— *yes,* friends, *that is the word*—that couldn't be helped, and might actually be an occasion to begin discreet inquiries.

Lest we forget why we are truly here.

'Excellent,' Rourke grinned. 'Now, off with you,' he shooed, laughing, and Juliana kissed his cheek before taking Sebastian's arm again, and following him across to the stairs.

They followed David up, and she glanced down at her brother, and though the chill and glaciality loomed, she felt warmer, for seeing him there, smiling up at her again.

It will be all right; this need not be the trial you believed.

Chapter Eight

Though he'd told himself he would not only face, but welcome an eventuality where Rourke recognised him, called him out, and destroyed any hope of redemption, when the last of the attending servants finally left them in peace—having made it clear he and Juliana required no assistance unless otherwise specified—Sebastian let out a long sigh, realising then, just how relieved he was that everything was going according to plan.

Or rather, that they still had a chance, and that they could rest, though there would be little of that here.

Never was nor ever will be.

He was reassured that he hadn't made one great and grave miscalculation, and that Rourke was precisely the man he'd thought. A man with too much money, privilege, and self-importance, who never looked beyond what was presented to him.

It will make this much easier.

What wouldn't, was Juliana. He'd known returning here would be difficult. He'd known her childhood here had been...*bad*, to say the least. He'd known she loved Rourke immensely; hadn't he even been jealous that her love for her brother exceeded that which she'd ever held for him? Yes, he'd *known* all that, only…he hadn't allowed himself to care.

To see, truly understand what all this meant for her. He'd just dragged her along because he needed her— but then *that* was the crux, wasn't it? He needed her more profoundly than merely *requiring her assistance*, only he'd been too dull, stubborn, angry or *something* to recognise that. To boot, he saw now, he'd underestimated, miscalculated, missed something, for there was more hurt and discomfort in Juliana than he'd ever imagined, and he…

Hated it.

Screwing his courage tight, praying for inspiration, he strode over to stand beside her at the window. She'd been there, staring out at the nearly invisible landscape, swallowed by twilight and storm, since they'd been shown in here. Lost in her own thoughts whilst around her the world bustled; quite as she'd been when they'd arrived. Lights flickered in the gloom below, the only sign that the view included not only a fair portion of the eastern grounds, but the village itself. Though he'd never been *inside* Stag House—he and Juliana had been some manner of reckless, but not *so* reckless—he did know this was likely the best guest room; yet still, a *guest room*.

It was large, well-appointed, obviously boasting a good view when one was visible, and decorated in a blend of neoclassicism and that fashion of about fifteen years ago. Simple lines, glossy pieces; taste-ful, sparse vases, lamps, and other assorted ameni-ties; pale-lavender-and-pink-lined wall-hangings, and plain upholstery and bedding, the latter ever so deli-cately embroidered. Few pictures—one pastoral scene above the mantel—all remarkably soulless. All new, Sebastian knew somehow. As if someone had stripped what was before, replacing it with what was *de rigueur* rather than any thought or care.

I fear I have indeed made a grave miscalculation after all.

Sebastian's heart tugged as he glanced over at Ju-liana, a creature of shadow in the barely illuminated space she occupied. He reached out, to touch her gen-tly, perhaps even ensure that she was real—for Lord knew he'd imagined her so many times, seen her, nearly as tangibly, beside him, it wasn't so distinctly impossible that she wasn't now—then thought better of it, and lowered his hand.

Her eyes flicked in the glass before them, and if he couldn't touch her, well, he could bloody well *say* something comforting, only he couldn't seem to think of how, *what*—

'We should prepare for dinner,' she said quietly, un-moving despite her words.

'We've time. You could rest a while, if you like. It's been a long day, and one whose end we haven't quite reached.'

'I'm fine.'

'You don't seem it, Juliana,' he told her, gently as he could.

'I'm well enough to play the role I'm required to. It seems you were correct, about Rourke not recognising you.'

'Were you hoping he would?'

'No. Were you?'

'I thought... I feel only relief, so I suppose not. There's still dinner to get through,' he added, a smile in his voice, attempting to lighten the mood. *Lamentably.* 'The room is handsome. Most comfortable-looking chairs. And we won't have to be concerned about proximity to your brother's room, being in the guest quarters.'

'It was a kindness Rourke did me, sparing me from the sharpest memories alive here, despite his redecorating.'

So I was right, and see something clearer now.

'I never... You never said, Juliana. I knew it was bad, but I see now...'

'What? More reasons to believe my brother guilty?'

'We can leave,' he breathed, his body leaning in ever so slightly, hoping she could feel him, and all he sought to offer. *Which in this moment, is everything, even an end to this quest if you were to ask...* Though a second later, feeling her disbelief, he added something to make his offer more palatable. 'Stay at the inn—'

'You wanted this, Sebastian,' she bit back, not bitterly, but as a steely reminder. 'You never knew the extent of it, for... We only ever spoke of the future, never the past, nor even often the present. We made plans to escape, to live new lives, but I see something now too,' she laughed mirthlessly, and Sebastian gritted his teeth, the onslaught of regretful realisation writhing his insides. 'We never...truly knew each other. Spoke of who we were, what we'd lived before we met. Only who we wished to be. As I said. The love of children.'

'Juliana—'

'We need to prepare for dinner,' she said, turning away to do just that.

'My kindness isn't false,' he said, hoping all he couldn't bear to say, and she couldn't bear to hear, was audible. 'I cannot but be kind to you.'

'And I cannot but refuse it.'

He nodded, not that she saw, as she continued on her way, to refresh herself, and likely change into the cleaner, slightly finer of her remaining two gowns.

Sebastian made himself scarce, adjoining to the dressing room to do the same, for it was time to en-sure the mask of du Lac Vaugris was well affixed.

You've made it in; now get what you came for, so we can leave this place for ever.

'Thomas—I hope you don't mind me using your Christian name as we're family now, and manners may separate us from the animals, however too much for-mality stifles—do tell me more of yourself, what it is you do, and how you came to meet my sister,' Rourke said jovially, without preamble nor breath, but with an edge, once they were settled at the massive mahogany table dominating the dining room.

A room, which like the bedroom—they'd been spared any pre-dinner socialising, so Sebastian had only those two rooms for comparison—was tastefully, but impersonally furnished, though here, gloom, and darkness pervaded more tangibly. He would blame it on the dark woods used to appoint the comfortably sized space, the lack of windows, and the fact only three of them sat at the table, however he knew it wasn't *only* any of that.

The number of candles burning vigorously in the various sparkling candelabra and sconces alone soundly did away with that theory.

Bringing his attention back to the table, he glanced across it at Juliana, who appeared utterly absorbed by the overflowing feast of meats, fish, and vegetables on her plate, though he knew she missed nothing. Again, he longed to reach out, hold her hand, give her strength—she looked as subdued as she had years ago—only he refrained, taking a bite of his own food, and nodding, acknowledging Rourke before silence became rudeness.

Here come words I might've dreamt of saying once but now taste of ash.

'As you say, Rourke, we are family now.'

'Excellent,' Rourke grinned, though the smile didn't quite reach his eyes. He looked over at Juliana, as it was her turn to nod, which she did, throwing him a weak smile. 'So yes, tell me everything.'

Some might describe Rourke's air as *casually yet fully attentive*, however Sebastian would've called it: *challenging and perniciously manipulative*.

Then again, perhaps his bias coloured his view of the man; and despite his *near* certainty that Rourke had been the master puppeteer of his demise, they were here to find answers, so he must keep an open mind. They'd not discussed it again, but if Juliana wasn't crying out that *yes,* she saw it now, her brother was the killer—and Sebastian saw nothing but longing and love in her—then he should entertain the possibility his conjectures were erroneous.

Proof this time. No more innocent men shall be condemned for personal reasons, with only circumstantial evidence.

Likely, Rourke was being…protective. They'd never liked each other before, but they'd never known each other, and then, Sebastian had been but a farmer, far from good enough for Juliana. Now he was Thomas, with means and such as men like Rourke valued, however that didn't mean innate and instantaneous acceptance. Wouldn't he be wary if he'd a sister, and she returned after nearly twenty years with a stranger for a husband?

Absolutely.

'I began in trade, though speculation is where I made my first, and subsequent, fortunes,' he answered, with only a hint of obsequiousness.

'And your people, Thomas,' Rourke continued, unfazed. 'French?'

'Titled, before the revolution—from Dordogne. However my grandfather—God rest his soul—was not so attached to it, and played the hand dealt. Made something of a name for us in Lichtenstein,' he said casually, not daring to look at Juliana as he recited the old tale they'd concocted years ago, though he hoped it brought a smile to her face. *Might it too if she knew the truth woven into the lies?* 'My parents emigrated to London when I was a child. I suppose the city birthed too my interest in both trade and finance.'

'They are still in London, your parents?'

'With God, after swift illness some years ago.'

'My condolences.'

'Thank you,' Sebastian said, dutifully bowing his head—though he doubted Rourke's authenticity.

Behave.

'So it is in London you met Juliana?'

'Only recently, having left for the Continent on business years ago, and having only returned this past autumn. A friend of hers, Walton, with whom I'd had dealings, introduced us, and I cannot but say I fell under Juliana's spell.'

Sebastian dared to glance at the aforementioned; needing her to know…

It isn't all a lie; there's truth, as in all the best dissimulations, in what I say, and feel.

She must've felt his gaze, for she raised her own, and he dared go even further, and let the smile threatening to reach his lips. It revived her, light flashing briefly in her eyes, the hint of a smile of her own making his heart skip a beat—*or three.*

Then Rourke reached over, taking her free hand, resting beside her glass, into his, along with her attention.

'Our Juliana is most enchanting,' he smiled, raising her hand to his lips, and there was something…about the way he looked at her, it niggled, though Sebastian couldn't quite formulate his thoughts just then. 'She only ever deserved the very best, and I'm sure you'll prove yourself worthy, and appreciative of that. Either way, now that she's come home, all will be as it should be.'

'Yes, it will,' Sebastian agreed.

It is bloody well time.

Another smile, and Rourke released Juliana's hand, as they returned to their meal.

It was then Sebastian realised, even as he kept the conversation going, enquiring about the estate, the area, Rourke's own business—light and simple things which allowed Juliana to keep as quiet as she wished to—what about Rourke bothered him so. It was a possessiveness, in the way he looked at Juliana, touched her, spoke of her, that he'd never seen before, for not having had the opportunity. All those years ago, he'd believed his lack of station, of means, had made Rourke dislike him, *hate* him, and want to separate him from Juliana. Now he saw, it was only that Sebastian had been loved by Juliana.

But then Rourke had raised Juliana for years after

their father died, before all the rest, so perhaps it was merely misplaced protectiveness, like that of parents who believed no one ever possibly good enough for their children. Still, Sebastian knew additional wariness was required moving forward, as not only must he preserve his secret, apparently he would also need fight to keep his place at Juliana's side.

Ensuring she isn't caught in the crossfire...

Chapter Nine

'An interminable sermon, however I find them all thus, and that he isn't of the fire and brimstone variety like his predecessor must be counted in his favour,' Rourke said as they made their way down the church path lined with yews, thankfully out of earshot of the vicar, and congregation.

Juliana nodded, entirely at a loss, and not solely because readjusting to being here, returning to Stag House, having Rourke within arm's reach, was much more than she'd bargained for; not that she'd bargained for any of it.

If not for Sebastian keeping conversation flowing during dinner last night—though she might've done without them crowing like roosters, perhaps inevitable yet still infuriating—it would've been *very* quiet, considering she'd only had enough in her to be present and accounted for. She had a thousand questions for Rourke, however everything including *conversation*, was…a little much just now. She just needed to find her feet, and soon would.

All the quicker for Sebastian's steady presence, though I'll not admit to it even in my own thoughts, just as I'll not admit...how it feels to be seen as his wife.

No, she certainly wouldn't tread on such treacherous ground.

As for Rourke's thoughts on today's sermon... She had nothing much to contribute; they both harboured the same general sentiments on religion, and certainly the same disgusted hatred of the old vicar, who'd been of the same ilk, and rather a *good chum* of their father's.

Which says it all.

In fact, Juliana might've questioned Rourke's presence at services had she not known that it was merely an obligation considering his station and position as a respected, land-owning gentleman. Though she'd sorely wished to avoid attending, Sebastian had pointed out it could serve as their reintroduction into Barrow Heath society, and afford a *lie of the land.*

Besides, it got us out of that house, whose walls exhale painful memories, infecting the very air we breathe. Perhaps I should've accepted to stay at—

'Juliana?' Rourke asked, interrupting her thoughts, thankfully.

Do cease getting so lost in them.

Blinking, she returned to the moment, realising they'd stopped at the lych-gate, and both men stared at her, expecting an answer, or contribution.

'Apologies, I was distracted.'

'I was saying you'd promised to show me the village,' Sebastian offered gently. 'As it turned out such a fine day.'

'Yes,' she smiled, turning to Rourke. 'Help Thomas get his bearings. We'll rejoin you for lunch.'

'Of course. One never knows how long sunshine will last, so one must enjoy it,' her brother smiled, albeit slightly disappointed. 'Shall I send the carriage to collect you at the inn, say around one?'

'Perfect, thank you.'

'Well then, enjoy your walk. I'll look forward to your thoughts on our corner of the world, Thomas.'

Sebastian nodded, and Rourke shot him a look she'd neither the desire, nor the will to decipher—though she noted chats with them were in order, about behaving like children—before making his way out of the lych-gate, and into the awaiting carriage.

'Thank you,' Juliana said, once it disappeared.

'We agreed on getting a lie of the land,' he nodded, clearing his throat, doing his best to pretend that was why he'd suggested the walk. 'And we've a day for it, beyond the mud, but I can survive such travails if you can.'

'I've encountered my fair share of perilous mud, therefore I should survive. I would like...' Juliana trailed off, glancing around at the now near-empty churchyard, save for the few hangers-on chatting with the vicar and his family. 'I would like to visit their graves.'

Sebastian said nothing, simply held out his arm, turning them back towards the church, though she felt his solemnity as she slid her arm onto his, and followed him.

Halfway up the main path, they veered right, taking a similarly yew-strewn, but less travelled path which circled around the graveyard, to the north side of Barrow Heath's squat Norman-style church. Along the way, the history of centuries of inhabitants was told through the headstones, wooden markers, sarcophagi, crosses, sculptures, vaults, and chest tombs.

Though he said nothing, Juliana felt Sebastian hold her closer as they passed her parents' sickeningly majestic, yet severe, sharp-lined chest tomb, and she examined it only enough to note how well-kept it was; likely Rourke not wanting their mother to bear any shame beyond having to lie beside their father for eternity.

Perhaps I might've told you everything we endured, Sebastian. Only it was our burden, our wounds, Rourke's and mine.

She wondered if…perhaps there were things to be said now, but decided she would ponder that at a later time. For now, they had another purpose, and so on they went, to the quiet, open north side of the grounds, where the graves were sparser, newer, and simpler. No trees shaded the building or its silent neighbours, leaving the sun and other elements free rein; leaving the eternal sleepers and their visitors a picturesque view of the fields, then woods and river below the ancient stone wall marking the boundary of life and death. The sky had cleared, immense, cerulean blue peppered with wisps of white; only the chill remaining to remind them that inclement weather was never far off.

Sebastian led them to the far north-western corner, where Alice and Bertie had been laid to rest, far from anyone, as though someone had been afraid closeness might somehow carry their misfortune unto others. That had always rankled Juliana, and though she'd been unable to see that wrong rectified, she had convinced Rourke they should take care of all the arrangements, and ensure they had a proper headstone.

And the view is lovely; not that they can see it.

Juliana shook her head, reminding herself that along with ghosts, she didn't believe the dead rose daily to enjoy some gentle sightseeing.

'Wait,' she said, as they stopped before the grave, the headstone Rourke had chosen, covered in moss and in need of a clean. 'How did you know where they were?'

'I asked one of my investigators,' Sebastian told her, untangling their arms, and going to tidy up. He removed some weeds, and took out a pen knife to scrape the most marred spots on the sandstone marker. 'I hoped to pay my respects.'

Juliana glanced around, spotting a patch of snowdrops beside the wall, and went to collect a few, thinking she would return soon to plant some, along with other blooms for Alice and Bertie.

Kneeling down, she laid the flowers beneath the headstone, as Sebastian sat back on his haunches to admire his work—effective for the short time he'd been at it, especially on the names.

'I'll come back, do a better job. I wouldn't have thought they'd leave it like this, that someone would at least make a show of charity. Take care of them.'

'Superstition and fear too often get in the way of doing what's right.' Gently, Juliana passed her gloved fingers over the blank, scratchy space between *Alice and Bertie*, and *Died December 1st, 1814*. 'I'd always hoped to someday fill this space with their full names, and birthdays. I made Rourke order it thus, so it could be completed. I suppose even then I knew they deserved more than for this to be all that was left of them in this world.'

Even then I knew there was more to the tale; that truth mattered even if it couldn't bring back the dead.

'I used to dream of them almost every night,' Sebastian breathed. She glanced over at him, harshness more profoundly etched; pain in his unfocused eyes. 'I had nightmares of the rest too, feeling that rope around my neck, but... Often my dreams of them were worse. I'd see her, all dressed in those pale rags, wandering the fields and hills, the babe in her arms. Spirits yet to be, come from the earth, destined to return to it, no matter how fast I ran, screaming, trying to stop it from happening... The winds would take them too far, and then... I saw them as they were that morning. And my heart broke for them over and over again.'

There was so much to say...

That she knew that pain, those dreams, that guilt, all too well, for she'd suffered them too—and others—for eighteen years.

That they would find answers.
That...
Instead, Juliana merely she slid her hand into Sebastian's, and held tight.

Having paid their respects, and reminded themselves of their purpose—*the truth*—Juliana and Sebastian slowly made their way into the village proper. They ambled along the short way downhill, past rows of squat stone cottages and houses, each extremely well-kept; Barrow Heath needing always to be known as a *proper* place. One of means, and *good* people, not like those dirty, crumbling cities, or dilapidated villages elsewhere.

Naturally, that didn't mean there was no delinquency, or poverty, only such things were hidden, very well; another reason why Alice and Bertie's murders had caused such outcry and shock: things like that didn't happen here.

So much allegedly never happens here...
Lunacy.
Luckily, they didn't encounter many other souls as they ambled, though more were about as they arrived on the high street proper—naturally the serviceable selection of shops were closed, so it was merely people making their way from one house to the next, attending to Sunday chores, or enjoying the clement weather—at the very end of which stood the inn.

'Every stone still in place,' Sebastian commented thoughtfully. 'Every speck of dirt seemingly too, yet

I'll admit, it feels more foreign than the most distant shores.'

'I know what you mean,' she said, avoiding what she longed to ask: *what distant shores, tell me more*, though she hoped he might…share, if she waited.

So, he did, almost absentmindedly, as if the sun's warmth, the simplicity of their walk, caught him unawares…

As I feel so often these days, with you.

'I never felt connected to this place,' he mused quietly, frowning, as if only just realising. 'I never felt its loss, as some do, in the marrow of their bones. You were my connection to it. My home. And then, I lost you, and there was no home to be found again, though I did find beauty. Wonder.'

There was again so much to say, feel, and ask, but perhaps the sun was playing tricks on her, evaporating her better judgement and good sense, for she merely waited for more, with bated breath, taking every morsel he offered as one might blooms for a treasured posy.

'Even in the darkest times, there was beauty, and I suppose that's something remarkably, inherently human, isn't it?' he asked, and she nodded, gently, afraid to spook him; and herself. 'Finding connection to places, to people, through beauty and wonder. I felt more connected to the land, to its inhabitants, in the great markets of Constantinople, or atop the highest peaks of the Carpathians, than I do—did—here. Felt closer to Sasha—an old sailor I met in Casablanca— or Antoinette, the composer who took me on the most delightful culinary tour of Vienna, than I ever did to anyone here. Once, I thought it was because of what happened, but now I see…it's because of who I am, and always was, and never could be, and…'

He paused, in his tales and ambling, and Juliana was glad for the reprieve, overwhelmed too, and not solely because this was all so starkly opposite to the harsh quips, and safe, bitter distance of their beginnings which she'd blanketed herself in.

His openness was overwhelming, her relishing of it was—*why, let us not think on*—and *what* he shared was too. She longed to ask about his travels, his life, yet those snippets he mentioned so casually, about where he'd been, the wonders he'd seen, the friends he'd met…

I'm jealous, for you lived the life we'd planned, whilst I stopped living.

A young couple passed them by, and Sebastian touched the brim of his hat, bringing them both back to the here and now.

The woman smiled at Juliana in complicity, as if to say: *see we are both married now*, and both the smile, and Juliana's recognition of the couple as the grocer's daughter, and haberdasher's son, threw her just enough to combat the acidity in her heart.

'The faces are familiar, yet I know them less than strangers in London,' Juliana commented as they began walking again. 'Then again I'm allowed to meet the gaze of strangers now, so perhaps that's the difference.'

A muscle tightened in Sebastian's arm, and she realised she'd revealed something she hadn't meant to.

This damned sun, is it some strange serum of truth?

Regardless of what loosened her lips, the choice was now to either be as open as Sebastian had been, or steer back to safer waters. To keep believing as she had, that these burdens and wounds were hers and Rourke's alone; or to take a page from her friends' books, and share.

To better heal.

'We weren't to make connections, Rourke and I,' she said, against her better judgement, yet feeling something in her soul unlock, creaking and unwillingly, but necessary. 'I imagine you thought like the others, that we Myles children were entitled brats. But it was Father who ordered we not engage with anyone *unworthy*; do anything *unworthy*, lest we jeopardise our position as *wealthy, educated, God-abiding* folk. We weren't to speak to anyone, do anything, unless he allowed it, like those damned hours I spent embroidering church cushions with the vicar's wife. Rourke was lucky, he was allowed John as a friend. Otherwise…considering neither he nor I were prepared to face punishment for transgressing Father's greatest edicts—even be it by greeting a farmer—we kept to ourselves.'

She shook her head, and followed Sebastian's lead, pausing at the stone bridge over the river that traversed the town almost perfectly at the halfway mark—the same river which wound around below the church, and eventually, came onto Stag House lands.

He hesitated, then pulled her closer, leaning one arm on the bridge, and sliding his other around her waist. It was forward, kind, and nothing she needed indulge in; except she did need it, and was quickly growing tired of fighting his kindness, despite last night's proclamations.

Kindness, comfort, right now, I can accept them and call them: illusion.

'I barely remember your father,' he said, relaxing as she didn't pull away. 'Merely impressions... Sharpness, hardness. My father didn't like him, but then he only ever dealt with your father's man, before Rourke dismissed him.'

'All of them, Father's people...were just as bad as he was. His watchers, his fiends. When Father passed, we didn't know how to be free again, but Rourke found the courage to do that much, free us of them too. Paid them handsomely to never be seen within a hundred miles of Stag House. I don't know that I would've ever been brave enough to pick up a book Father would've otherwise burnt if not.'

'And then you picked them all up, and shared them with me.'

'The celebration of my freedom,' she smiled up at him, brighter than she had in a long time. 'Learning all I'd been denied, then spending time with you.'

'I never... Thought you spoiled, or entitled,' he said seriously, and she shouldn't keep staring at him, only she couldn't stop. 'I was fascinated, as far back as I can remember. I only ever thought…how fierce you seemed. Sad sometimes, but mostly fierce.'

Juliana swallowed hard, trying to reconcile with this new unseen piece of herself.

In those days, she'd always felt sad, estranged from the world, save for Rourke. To know he'd seen her, thought of her, believed her fierce, it…

Rearranges parts of me I don't fully understand.

'I remember you raising your eyes to me, sheep farmer's son that I was, in church one Sunday, before your father passed,' he continued, and she froze. They'd never spoken of that day, she'd never told him… 'As I said, fierce.'

Breathing a sigh of relief, though her heart knotted itself quite thoroughly, she smiled unconvincingly, gazing out onto the sparkling waters, letting that useless memory tumble out and be swept away by the current.

Dangerous territory.

Too easy to forget who you and he are now; why you're here.

'Unfortunately I fear Barrow Heath doesn't share such gracious recollections,' she said, in a voice so flat she barely recognised it. 'They kept a wide berth then, and I fear it won't have changed much. It will add difficulty to our enquiries. As will my tendency to *not* ask questions, lest I be asked any in return.'

Up on the hill behind them, the church rang quarter to one.

Tapping her waist lightly, Sebastian straightened and slid his arm away, and though she bemoaned the loss of warmth, she found it anew when she tucked her arm into his, and they set off towards the inn again.

'Make yourself known at what shops you can,' he suggested. 'You left shortly after…everything, so perhaps some will be eager to gossip. I'll take the inn, Tuesday, maybe, once we've made it through that dinner tomorrow. I'll find some excuse, not that Rourke will mind having you to himself.' Juliana glanced at him, wondering at the venom, but he didn't expand, and she wasn't in the mood to push. *They're just being competitive and protective.* 'Outright questions will come better from me, the curious newcomer, who must hear everyone's retelling of the grim story. And lest we forget, alcoholic incentive is always useful.'

'I assume that as well as examining the paper trail, your hired hands spoke to anyone involved in an official capacity?' Sebastian nodded. 'And besides them, the Widow Morel was the only one to have contact with Alice and Bertie by all accounts.'

'It was a blow to discover she'd passed, before even my men could reach her. See if she recalled anything more.'

'Do you have copies of all the papers?' Sebastian nodded again. 'I should like to read them, another pair of eyes couldn't hurt.'

'They are not easy, Juliana.'

'I don't imagine they would be,' she said, side-stepping his mark of concern. 'Beyond that...we can only hope someone recalls some detail that will lead us to knowing more about Alice and Bertie, for I've no clue how we're to unravel this mystery otherwise.

'There is something else,' Sebastian said seriously, almost ashamed.

Juliana frowned, and they stopped, having passed along the rows of closed shops, houses, and cottages constituting the rest of the main street, and now stood a little ways from the inn, where the road opened up onto the borders of Barrow Heath, the fields and farms that kept it alive, then, the greater world around it.

It was quieter here, and Juliana realised they hadn't encountered anyone in a while; though she doubted there weren't avid faces and ears at windows.

As there are in every village, town, and city I suspect.

'I want to search Stag House for the picture,' Sebastian admitted sheepishly, not meeting her eye. 'My investigators found no trace of anything close to that description being sold, so it must still be here somewhere.'

Taking a deep breath, she resisted her inclination to tear her arm away, stomp about, and refuse him, and not because of the potential spectacle she might offer but because...

'Fine,' she said, and Sebastian was satisfyingly surprised. 'It's an idiotic idea, but I shan't dissuade you, and if it helps you see Rourke is innocent, and gets us moving on to better ideas, then why not. Though had he done it, he'd be far too clever to keep such damning evidence.' Raising a brow, she rather enjoyed the dumbfounded understanding that preceded his nod. 'It'll be a few days, but I'm sure he'll visit John, or have some business in town, granting us time.'

'Juliana—'

Rourke's carriage passed them, going to wait at the inn, and she made to get them moving again, but Sebastian didn't budge.

'I'm sorry,' he sighed, and those three words were perhaps the greatest shock thus far on this journey. Though she wished sorely to dismiss them, *him*, along with his kindness, make everything less complicated again…she couldn't. If only because, lost as they both were, they'd be doomed if she did. 'I dragged you back here, purporting you were the key, ripping you from your new life, and I… I am sorry.'

There was more he didn't say, she knew, but that was…

Enough.

Now your turn, for without honesty, we'll never find the truth.

'We both have much to be sorry for, Sebastian. You bringing me back here… Don't apologise for that. The manner of my enlistment could've been more delicate,' she grinned conspiratorially, gaining a dangerously warming smile from him. 'I've seen too many secrets emerge of late, friends uncovering long-lost pasts, confronting long-escaped demons, to believe I'd be spared my reckoning. It was my time to pay the piper. Come now, best not be late,' she said, before mountains could be made of molehills.

Collaboration, honesty, kindness…

Those were something; anything more was quite another.

Chapter Ten

Having two additional people at dinner didn't dispel the house's ever-present gloom, though it did chase it back, so that it was bearable. Since his and Juliana's walk in the village, their time had been spent indoors—because of inclement weather, a lack of threads to follow, and a need to visit with Rourke—and both he and Juliana were feeling the *entrapment*.

At least, to Sebastian these walls weren't painted with painful memories he was only now realising the true extent of; in fact, they were strangely protective, preserving him from the memories waiting *out there*.

Keeping up the charade of du Lac Vaugris, behaving normally around Rourke, and mainly, keeping an eye on Juliana, were also shielding him from his own past's assault. He longed to ask her about everything, how she was, what she felt, if she would share more of what he saw dancing in her eyes—be it good or ill—yet he refrained. Their complicity, her trust, only newly gained, were as fragile as snowflakes, and he wouldn't risk them. Though part of him relished the openness she'd demonstrated yesterday, the tokens of herself she'd given him, he knew to relish any of it was…

Inadvisable. Informative yet useless.

Understanding more about her helped put many things from his past into better perspective, answering long unacknowledged doubts and questions, however yesterday's closeness—metaphorical and physical—had been too comfortable. He needed to remember that while they might have a small chance at friendship again, they weren't what they now presented themselves as to the world.

We are not husband and wife. Never could be. I did not come back for her.

He hadn't years ago, when he might've in every sense of those words, and perhaps his return now was in part to exonerate himself in her eyes, however that was all. He could love her still, yet know their time had long passed; there would never be a future for them together again, for too many reasons to list, including that he didn't want one.

Quite.

Regardless, his watchfulness of Juliana, and Rourke, had prompted him to notice some things, be it in regards to either, or both as they were together; ungentlemanly though it perhaps was, he hadn't yet left them alone. Not because he still believed Rourke guilty, and didn't trust him generally—they'd be alone tomorrow whilst he went to the inn—but because with every passing hour he saw the trial it was for Juliana to be here, ever clearer. So he resolved to be her bulwark, if only from memories or conversations she wasn't ready for; undoubtedly there were some, despite all her correspondence with Rourke. That had been one thing he'd noticed, a sense of unbroken familiarity and ease between them, coupled with hesitancy, and awkwardness; the pains of regrowing a relationship changed by life and time.

I know those well; she and I face that too, in a very different manner.

He'd noticed too, the way Juliana's eyes flitted sometimes towards the family wing, or searched for various objects; her avoidance of certain places. Her growing quiet and reserve; the subtle loss of strength and verve. Equally, he'd not missed the way Rourke went about his business efficiently, always *doing something* as gentlemen not at leisure were wont to; then tiny cracks, sharded moments when Sebastian would glimpse him, standing in a corridor looking utterly lost. Unaware almost, of where he was, and what he was supposed to do. He would glimpse the boy Juliana had told him of; the one who'd shared her heartbreak and joys. And though learning more of their childhood wounds did in some ways lend credence to Sebastian's suspicions—which he would never admit to Juliana—it also further eroded them. A conflict began to brew inside, as Rourke transformed in Sebastian's eyes from a calculating, controlling, cape-wearing villain pulling the strings of those around him, murdering innocents in the darkness, into nothing but a man.

A man of flesh and blood whom she loves.

A man of flesh and blood who was currently laughing with his friends—those same friends who aided in pushing back the gloom of this place, John and Celia Winter.

Sebastian had known *of* them, seen them around in his youth—John's estate bordering Stag House's, whilst Celia's father owned lands on the other side of Barrow Heath—but naturally never *knew* them. They'd always seemed nice people—and he'd never heard word spoken against them or their families—bright, jovial souls. They were closer in age to Rourke than Juliana, about the only ones nearby who fit that description and were of *respectable families*; likely why John and Rourke's acquaintance had been allowed by the not dearly departed Mr Myles, even if they didn't share the same faith, hence their absence on Sunday.

Celia and John looked somewhat alike, Sebastian mused, glancing between them as they entertained Rourke and Juliana—and admittedly, himself—with tales of their boating expedition on a semi-frozen lake this morning, which nearly ended with a swim. Both were of middling height, with light brown hair, and hazel eyes; faces and dispositions of understated, plain gentility. Well-to-do country folk, whose smiles and *bonne humeur* elevated them to remarkable people; or so he'd observed during the blessedly short introductory pre-dinner drinks they'd shared.

Hell, they even elevate Rourke's disposition to inviting.

'If you're still here when the perilous ice finally departs, we should have a day on the lake, even a picnic,' Celia said brightly, her excited gaze flicking between him and Juliana.

Throwing her a non-committal smile, Sebastian glanced to Juliana, at his right, and found her doing much the same.

'We aren't entirely sure of our plans as of yet,' she added, Celia's brightness threatening to be extinguished by an approaching awkward silence. 'However, if we are here, that sounds lovely.'

'You'd both enjoy it,' John said, half encouraging, half placating. 'Rourke has amply made up for those times in our youth he couldn't avail himself of that delight, so might you.' Juliana nodded graciously, and John's eyes flashed with remorse when he realised the effect his reminder of her restricted youth had. 'Of course it isn't so mighty a vessel as you've surely seen and travelled upon,' he added, turning his attention to Sebastian, and the conversation to more pleasant waters. 'I wager you've seen many marvels over the years.'

'I have been very fortunate. As I've been supremely fortunate to meet people from all walks of life, and share such pleasant meals as this.'

He inclined his head, even going so far as to raise a glass to his host, who bore the mark of respect with a gracious smile.

'Hear, hear!' John agreed.

'You must find Barrow Heath so dull, and unsophisticated,' Celia commented, and Sebastian quickly shook his head.

'Not at all. Different, but then every place has its virtues, its intricacies, which may not be to everyone's tastes. I'm certainly finding Barrow Heath more charming by the minute.'

It was Celia's turn to incline her head, smiling before she turned to Juliana.

'Charming though your husband claims this place to be, and good as it must be to return home, I wager you'll be gone well before spring. You were always so clever, always interested in the world, and with a husband such as yours, I doubt you'll resist the call of exploration long. Though if you do leave, you must promise to write. We may not have been close as girls, but I hope we can forge a stronger connection now. We love your brother so, it feels as though we're family rather than friends.'

Whether it was a blessing or a curse that Rourke spoke before Juliana, Sebastian doubted he'd ever be able to say; though he'd put good money on the latter being the safer wager.

'My sister is but two days returned, and now you'd have her set sail before breakfast!' Rourke jested, though there was undeniable bite in his tone. 'Juliana spent many years away from home,' he continued, gentler, holding out his hand, and Juliana took it, sporting the rarity of a genuine smile. 'Years exploring this great country, paving her way in a manner most incredible. We must allow her time to rest, and decide what to do next. If we're lucky, and clever, we may convince her and Thomas to settle down. A home, close to family, and time to enjoy married life, cannot be but tempting to a man who's spent years travelling, building his success. Why else would he marry now?'

Why else indeed? Sebastian thought bitterly, as Rourke's attention focused on him, an expression on his face halfway between *cat who got the cream*, and *checkmate*.

What rankled most, was how tempting the picture Rourke painted was.

When they'd made their plans, long ago, he and Juliana had imagined a life of adventure, and exploration, building something worthy. Building too, a warm, loving home, for themselves, and the family they hoped. A home not necessarily anywhere but with each other; still, there would be a sense of having *arrived*. A settledness, even in continued motion.

So yes, some part of Sebastian, right then, had the audacity to imagine a future such as Rourke painted— here, in Stag House, and Barrow Heath. A future where none of them were who they truly were, but instead painted figures, acting out a happy play of home, family, laughter, boating trips, and—

Stop. We are who we are; such a life was made impossible.

'As you say,' Sebastian said, diplomatically, with surprisingly little bite, *for Juliana's sake*. 'We have time to make plans. For now, we're enjoying this time to rest, and truly get to know each other.'

He felt Juliana's eyes on him, sensing the double meaning, but he ignored her, raising a brow, then his glass, with what could only be described as a saccharinely taunting smile.

The conversation resumed, John and Celia having the grace and wit to turn to nonsense parcels of local news, and talk of London politics.

Luckily for everyone, Juliana soon after released Rourke's hand.

Only Sebastian couldn't help but wonder, if he was so easily tempted by such shiny impossible futures, what it must be like for Juliana.

What a strangely cursed house this is, with its enchanting power to conceal the foundations of malevolence by at once offering memory, then disappearing it with alluring promises of perfection and joy.

Without caution, it will consume us in ways we never saw coming.

'Does he make you happy, Juliana?' Rourke asked, pulling her from a delightful interlude, where she thought of nothing, was tempted by no imaginary futures, nor raked over hot coals of past remembrances, merely sat by the enveloping fire, enjoying the jolly tunes Celia played.

Glancing over, she found him standing beside her near the hearth, and smiled, buying herself time. She then turned to the man in question, finding him in lively discussion with John, though she knew as invested as he appeared, he was aware of everything;

she prayed he'd fight his instincts, and afford her a moment alone with Rourke as he hadn't yet.

Not that she didn't feel profoundly Sebastian's vigilance, for all it kept some of the conflicting stimuli at bay, giving her time to find some footing, though she thought it unlikely she'd ever find solid ground again. However, she could find some navigable path, no matter how daunting a task it was, particularly as she was contending with long-buried secrets, pain, *and* dissimulation.

Juliana was acquainted with the latter—Sebastian hadn't missed his mark about her skills as a performer—but then in her experience many who'd suffered harrowing events did. They learned, as she had, to conceal the truth of their minds and hearts. That being said…she was no actress, and had no real knowledge of how to be at once herself, yet another beast entirely; one made not of hope and delusion, but of pure falsity and imagination.

A self, who had married for love. Moved on, to build a new life.

A self who had not been consumed by her past; with a bright, clear future—not fixed, but certainly *good*.

Though unsure whether it was the best course of action, Juliana called back to mind and body how she'd felt once about Sebastian, about life, in those precious moments of pure happiness and hope, drawing on them to feed the illusion she had to sell.

Anchoring herself in Sebastian's steady gaze, she breathed in a host of recollections—*eyes glinting in summer sun, grey depths full of love, darkening eyes when he'd...*

'He does,' she told her brother, turning back to him with a genuine smile, and Rourke nodded, his eyes flitting to Sebastian briefly. 'I wouldn't have married him without love, or kindness.'

'Then, that's all that matters. I just wanted to ensure you hadn't settled for less,' Rourke said seriously, but with the same look he'd have when he'd check on her after one of Father's lessons. That connection might've chilled her, had it not warmed her heart so. 'I know you had a good life with your last family, yet I appreciate not everything is so easily said in a letter, and there have been scandals. You know that were there ever to be...a situation you thought impossible to solve alone, you could come to me.'

'I know, Rourke. I would. I did have a good life, and remain close to those I left. However, Thomas gave me a chance at something I'd long discarded, and his strength, his conviction... I wouldn't have returned here without them,' she told him, the unimpeachable truth resounding profoundly. 'And so I beg you, love him, as I do. Welcome him, get to know him. Show him what a wonderful brother you are, for my sake.'

Show him who you are so that he'll know you could never do what he says you did.

So we can find the true culprit, and have a chance, all of us.

'For your sake, Juliana,' Rourke agreed, leaning down to kiss the top of her head.

Closing her eyes, she lost herself in that touch, years of such kisses, flooding back in her mind; from those he'd given as she lay in bed, destroyed in the aftermath of Sebastian's death, all the way back to the cradle.

Though she couldn't recall it, she knew that from her first cry he'd been there, and would remain so as long as there was breath in his body.

I—

'Juliana!' Celia called. 'Join me for a duet!'

Opening her eyes, Juliana grinned, nodding and rising to do as she was bid, for perhaps music was just the distracting divertissement she needed.

With one last look at her brother, she joined Celia before the pianoforte, and together they sang of luscious summers and happy maidens.

All the while she felt both Rourke and Sebastian's eyes, and could only think: *when all masks fall, I hope we've a chance such as I can almost believe we might tonight.*

Chapter Eleven

'Have you partaken of too much of Barrow Heath's hospitality at the inn?' Rourke asked, peeking his head from the shadows. Sebastian startled—he was already on edge, having felt *watched* the whole walk back through the frosty, foggy night—then recovered, shirking off the cold, eerie night along with his coat, hat, and gloves, handing them to a waiting David. 'Or would you join me for a nightcap?'

Though he could think of few things—if any—he wouldn't rather do, he nodded, knowing not only that it might prove useful, but that, perhaps, Rourke was... extending an olive branch.

It didn't matter that Sebastian had spent the better part of the two decades believing Rourke his enemy, for Juliana's sake, he'd accept the damned olive branch; though he told himself it was merely to know his enemy better.

Even if with every passing day he feels less of an enemy.

'Barrow Heath's hospitality is generous, however

it was more the atmosphere I sought,' he said, shaking off that queer thought, and striding over to where Rourke waited, smiling surprisingly genuinely, at the study door.

'An inn's atmosphere must feel rather familiar. With all your travels, I'm certain you must be quite at home in them.'

If that was meant as a pique, Sebastian didn't feel it; instead it seemed meant kindly, which absolutely threw him.

As did the study into which he was ushered, and which in its redecoration, had become overly bright. The typically masculine lines or dark woods had been replaced with white painted bookshelves, floral upholstery, and lavender armchairs, and Rourke was currently standing at an intricately forged wrought iron drinks trolley beside the hearth that might've looked more at home on the lawn during a garden party.

Concealing his shock, he joined Rourke before the fireplace.

'Indeed I am,' he finally said, as he was handed a whisky, and they clinked their glasses. 'I've always found such establishments the best locale to get to know a place. And I've struck more deals over scratched-up, ale-soaked tables than in proper offices.'

A nod, a smile that again, held no bite, and spoke only of camaraderie, and Rourke went and settled in one of those lavender armchairs before the fire, Sebastian joining him.

He wondered if the ale he'd had perhaps two tan-

kards of earlier had been brewed with strange mush-
rooms or herbs, for he felt as if he'd left Stag House,
and returned to some fever dream facsimile of it.

*Or perhaps that's Rourke's intention—to put you
off guard.*

Except it didn't...*feel* like it.

Earlier, when Sebastian had left, he'd felt an irratio-
nal hatred at the thought of leaving Juliana alone with
Rourke all evening. He'd known it made no sense, especially considering the moment the two had shared
after dinner last night, which had settled, and revived
Juliana's spirit. To boot, last night had also shown that
Rourke had *friends*. And John was a good man, with
a brain in his head, and empathy in his heart; as was
his wife. They were good people, whose judgement
of others seemed sound, and reliable; therefore if they
were friends with Rourke, had been for years, Rourke
had to have redeeming qualities Sebastian couldn't see
because of his own bias; and despite that he was *trying* to keep an open mind.

So to the inn he'd gone, not only out of necessity,
but by dismissing his concerns, and reminding himself
that no matter how hard he tried to convince himself
otherwise, he wasn't a rational man. Oh, he had reason,
common sense, the ability to follow logic, however he
acted on emotion. Once, Juliana had even confessed
it was something she'd always admired: his ability,
his freedom, to feel, and just *do*. Of course, he'd told
her then, and knew better than ever now, just how
many dire consequences could stem from that *ability*,

however that was beyond the point. The point was, he hadn't liked leaving her alone here with Rourke tonight, for some inexplicable, emotional reason.

It also hadn't helped that Rourke had been almost gleeful when Sebastian announced he fancied an evening alone, but then he'd told himself likely he just wanted an evening with his sister. All night, the thought of them alone had still rankled—and he'd reassured himself with all those prior reasons, and that his evening at the inn was necessary, and really, he just didn't like leaving Juliana alone in the house which leeched the life from her with every passing hour, ever so perniciously.

But then Barrow Heath was always suffocating; everything about appearances and small-mindedness. It always sucked the joy, wonder, and freedom from us, so we couldn't ever breathe here.

Juliana's spirit, her love, was my air, my life, my freedom, and truth.

Yes, she—

'I wanted to apologise,' Rourke said, and had Sebastian not been sitting, he might've fallen over, the man's sincerity making him blink, trying to wake himself from the fever dream he'd stumbled into. Meeting the steely blue eyes, he frowned inquiringly. 'My sister pointed out I haven't been...entirely welcoming.'

'It was a shock, I'm sure, to have her return so suddenly, and with a husband you'd heard not a whit of in tow,' Sebastian managed to say diplomatically, his mind taunting him: *why again were you so concerned to leave this man alone with Juliana?* 'Had I a sister, I too would seek to know the measure of a man before I welcomed him into my home. No apology is necessary.'

'Thank you,' Rourke nodded, sipping his whisky, turning his gaze to the fire as he swirled the rest of the amber liquid hypnotically, and mindlessly in his hands.

'I hope you two enjoyed your evening,' Sebastian said after a moment.

Was he trying to get information?

Should he be trying to discover other information?

He wasn't entirely sure—actually, yes he was.

Apparently I'm trying to make conversation, as I've no idea how to be with this man I hated with every fibre, and couldn't trust but hours ago, yet whom now I cannot seem to hate despite all I try.

Swallowing hard, he sipped his whisky, attempting to focus on using this time wisely, rather than sorting through a useless jumble of emotions.

'We did,' Rourke smiled brightly, meeting his gaze, though there was a flash of disappointment in his eyes. 'Quiet, dinner and a few rounds of cards. Juliana told me some of this last family she was with.'

'They are good people. She was sad to leave them when we married, but hopefully we shall all meet again soon.'

She shall. I'll never make friends of them as I purport to have already; that future less possible than the one we imagined years ago.

'So she tells me,' Rourke agreed. 'They always

seemed to value her greatly, and she'll surely miss them. Teaching too, unless she finds another path to it.'

'She is an excellent teacher.'

Always was, he only just managed not to say.

It was odd, sitting here with a man he couldn't claim to know, yet who'd been such an integral part of his life, speaking of another who'd been too, and having to remember that he wasn't Sebastian. He was Thomas, starting anew; only just learning of Barrow Heath, and the Myles children.

He wasn't Sebastian, who might've laughed, and smiled with Rourke, remembering fondly the days when Juliana had squirrelled the new books her brother had bought out to the Lloyds' cottage, to share all this knowledge she was finally allowed to acquire, with the sheep farmer's son. He couldn't say: *yes, your sister always believed me more than a brainless farmer, but someone who could achieve anything*. He couldn't admit that Juliana had given him his early education, taught him so much—in many ways—and given him the tools to survive and thrive these past eighteen years. He wasn't Sebastian, who'd made plans with Juliana, for a grander life; dreams which had kept him going in the darkest times, though they now seemed so fantastical and childish.

I am Thomas du Lac Vaugris, who cannot make plans or dream with your sister for I'm as fantastical and childish an illusion.

'The world is hers,' Sebastian added in the strangely pensive, and comfortable silence. Lying, acting as

Thomas, despite years of experience, became more cumbersome and distasteful with every passing day, and so he had to remember to infuse the lies with truth. 'I'll never stand in her way.'

'I'm glad to hear it. I only want to see Juliana happy. Always have, always will.' Sebastian nodded, waiting, some hesitation in Rourke speaking of a desire to say more. 'It's strange, having her back. I'm glad of course, I've long hoped she would return however…' Rourke's eyes narrowed, searching Sebastian's, debating his next words, and he had to admit, it was oddly confronting to meet *this* man's gaze, and feel only as if they were two men, without a past, getting to know each other. 'Has she…told you much, of her life here, before? Our life?'

'A little.'

'It isn't something so easy to speak on,' Rourke nodded, turning back to the fire with another sip of whisky. 'Much happened here, which we don't speak of, for it is passed. I've tried… Well, you cannot have failed to notice this room,' he laughed. 'My late wife was of great help in here especially. I've tried to make this house somewhere Juliana would feel at home in, somewhere she could return to.'

'These armchairs are most comfortable,' Sebastian noted, and Rourke laughed again.

'They are, aren't they?'

When Rourke met his gaze again, Sebastian even found himself smiling, as though they were two old comrades, sharing tales of pranks long past, and…

Stop.

'A most excellent choice, I commend your late wife.'

They toasted to that, and Rourke hesitated again.

'I made choices, long ago, that…injured Juliana,' he said finally, and Sebastian held his breath, wondering…

Is this the moment I've been waiting for? A confession?

Can I see in his eyes now proof of his past misdeeds?

Strangest of all…he wasn't sure what he wanted to see; if indeed he wanted to see proof of past misdeeds to convince him of Rourke's guilt.

Bloody Hell.

'If she hasn't already, perhaps she might tell you someday,' Rourke continued, quieter, yet less seriously, nothing in his eyes but regret—of having hurt someone he loved. 'Suffice it to say, she lost someone she cared for, who was unworthy of her, and though she may not blame me, I believe it will always strain our relationship. But that's the difficulty when we love someone, isn't it? We must do things to protect them, to pave their way to happiness, which hurt them. I was so alone before my sister came along. So very alone,' he said, his voice becoming distant as he turned back to the fire. 'And then along came Juliana, so small and fragile… I swore, that I would always protect her. She saved me from a life of solitary torment, my baby sister, and so I owe her a world and life of happiness.'

He fell silent for a long moment, and Sebastian watched every memory, every doubt, every fear, every care, and every wish dance in the shadows cast by the flames in the lines of Rourke's face.

And his heart felt...*sad.*

'But I'm glad you are here,' Rourke said, shaking himself, straightening, as he wrestled his demons back into their lockbox. 'Both of you. It feels so natural to have you, bringing some life back into this house, and though I know your plans aren't set, I do wish for us to be happy however long you stay.'

'Thank you,' Sebastian said, his heart, truthfully, full of gratitude, and longing. It was enough to prompt him to move, raising his drink before emptying the contents, and rising. 'I should get to bed, lest Juliana wait up, worrying that I've been lost to fog. Thank you for the drink.'

'Any time, Thomas.'

A nod, and Sebastian saw himself out, glancing back one last time before he did.

Truly, we should never have returned. This house is cursed in so many devious ways.

Chapter Twelve

'Considering your mood since breakfast, and the loss of your Thomas du Lac Vaugris swagger,' Juliana said, indulging in what Sebastian could only describe as an off-balance and exaggerated impression of a strutting peacock, that admittedly had him grinning widely—not least of all for the gentle mocking returned some verve and play to Juliana, something he'd not seen for a while. 'I presume the inn yielded no miraculous revelations.'

'I fear not.'

Juliana nodded, continuing down the corridor, as they made their way towards the family wing; Rourke was out on business, and they'd refused his offer to accompany him, so they could tour—*search*—the house.

Sebastian trailed behind, much more sombre today than she, even despite their current occupation, which might've seen their moods reversed. She was right; he was *pensive*, less confident, and somewhat dismal this morning. He'd spent what remained of last night in his bed—the armchair in their room—tossing and turning as questions, doubts, and *feelings* swirled. About Rourke, the past, her, and what he felt for her; about the future, so opaque and impossible to even imagine. Though perhaps that was nothing new to someone who'd often pictured this future they were currently living, only for it to turn out nothing at all like he'd imagined.

As all my once dreams, plans, and imagined futures were shattered by reality.

For eighteen years under foreign skies, he'd grappled with the past, but returning here—despite Stag House's walls preserving him thus far from the more virulent memories—had shown him how much he *hadn't* been grappling with the loss of everything; particularly those once dreams. For so long, he'd been so consumed by anger, and regret, at the *loss* of his youthful dreams and hope, that he'd forgotten the dreams and hope themselves. Their beauty, innocence, and splendour. How infallibly they'd kept him, his spirit, and heart alive; up until he'd lost them.

Dreams were so often dashed by life; it was a tale told the world over a thousandfold. And yet in a sense, wasn't this whole return, this dream of justice, and revelation, but another youthful, innocent, and childish dream, as sure to be dashed on the rocks as the others? Finding the truth, his freedom, it was all he'd dreamt of, for so long, but now that he—*they*—were here, searching for it... He couldn't see the end of the road. Imagine what life would be, how it would change, if they did solve this grim mystery, and right old wrongs.

Perhaps the most troubling realisation, was that his life *wouldn't* likely change much. Once, he'd dreamt it would become all he'd ever wanted, that he would live with a bright, open heart...turn back time, perhaps. Now he saw with unprecedented clarity the idiocy, and impossibility of that. One couldn't turn back time, and change who they'd become. Truth or no truth, free, exonerated man or not, he couldn't stay in England. He'd seen too much, become too much, to remain in one place. Perhaps he'd always been thus; hence those dreams of adventure he'd long ago concocted with Juliana. And as for Juliana...

Once, in his most exuberant fantasies, he'd imagined she could be his again; and he, hers. That, if the truth came to light, and he was exonerated, they could begin again. Have the life they'd dreamt of, be happy together, be...as they now presented themselves to the world: a happy, loving couple with a long, joyous future before them. Now he couldn't even dare to imagine such a thing. Too much life had passed, they were too different, wanting different things, and though his love for her would never die—try as he had to kill it— and she was, and for ever would be, his one chance at great love, time couldn't be turned back. He may love her still, yearn to know this new Juliana as he'd known the old—though he felt he did—they could only ever be partners *in this endeavour*. Perhaps, eventually, something close to *friends*. But they couldn't have what they once had.

Though he would never agree that theirs had been a

childish love, a love of youth—he'd gained some clarity the past few days, and knew it to be lasting, and true; an unbreakable connection—he accepted that no amount of love meant that they, like those in the fairy stories, were destined to have a happy ending.

Though I pray her ending will have happiness; as it did in all those lives I saw her live in my dreams. Some part of me prays I was wrong about Rourke, for—

'So that's all I get?' Juliana asked him, arms crossed, and he realised they'd stopped at the edge of the corridor leading towards the family bedrooms.

His mind took a moment to return to their conversation—*rather than somewhere it has no business being.*

'The only thing notable at the inn was how improved the ale is since Young Bernard took over for his father. There was as ever, a good mix of locals and travellers—some frequent apparently—and great conversations to be had about the rain, the snow, and the price of cotton. We also featured as a new, favoured topic— apparently you, *the Myles girl*, have returned with a husband *rich as Croesus*—and though I made some friends and pointed enquiries, the most I can tell you is that Jonesy the Postman plants his daffodils too early, and give you every detail of every marriage celebrated in the past twenty years.'

He didn't explicitly share his frustration at such failure—though it was in his voice—and made no mention of his walk back; of the promise he'd made as the icy fingers of night attempted to choke him: that he would find answers, at the very least so Juliana could be free to leave again.

Neither did he mention his feeling of having been watched though he'd seen, nor recalled now, no trace—sound or sight—that he had been. No use worrying her, and considering the chill in his spine had lessened when he'd turned onto Stag House's drive...

Likely some young, bored miscreant—though I forget, we've none in Barrow Heath.

Lastly, he certainly didn't mention that Juliana remained the only person able to see past the mask it had taken him nearly two decades to create; since he wasn't being dragged from the house in irons, it went without saying.

'I'll try again in a couple days,' he said instead, trying to infuse optimism into his tone. 'Perhaps try some of the surrounding villages too.'

Slowly, Juliana nodded, unconvinced, or perhaps just as frustrated as he when faced with failure, and turned to look down the corridor.

'I know I agreed to this,' she sighed, shaking her head. 'However now...'

'You regret your assent.'

'Yes. No. I...' Sighing again, she turned back to him, her eyes at once confused, and honest. A look he remembered well, which meant he could deny her nothing; fail to do nothing which might bring light back to her. *Oh, dear.* 'Now that we're standing here, I once again fail to see the use of this exercise. Rourke didn't do this, and *even if*...he wouldn't have kept it.

Besides, with the house so changed… It would've been long disposed of.'

'I can search alone,' he said gently, tempting his own fate, ignoring his good sense again, as he stepped closer, brushing his fingers along the back of her hand. 'I understand you wouldn't wish to visit the past contained within those rooms.'

'It isn't only that,' she breathed, her eyes searching his, trying to decipher the meaning of his care; or perhaps an excuse to reject it again. 'Search Rourke's room, if you must,' she continued, stronger. 'It's the only place it would be were it here. That or the attic, and I spoke to Collins last night, who advised it had been emptied when the redecorating began. We can check if you like, but it will be quick work.'

'There is no other secret place, a hiding spot, that Rourke might've—'

'Any such places, he wouldn't desecrate like that,' she told him harshly.

Sighing himself this time, he nodded, his eyes travelling to the doors beyond her shoulder.

Part of him wanted to point out that if Rourke was capable of what had been done, then desecrating a sentimental hiding spot would comparatively be nothing, but another part of him knew she had herself considered this, and was right.

This was indeed an idiotic idea; Rourke is no fool and wouldn't have kept such evidence, if he even—

'I'll search his room quickly,' he said flatly, deciding not to waste this opportunity—no matter how fruitless it might be. 'If you'd indicate which it is, and perhaps stand guard, we'll be done with this ever so swiftly.'

'Last on the left.'

Stepping around her, Sebastian made his way to it, hearing her soft footfalls on the rug behind him, but otherwise merely getting on with it.

So it may be done swiftly, and we can move on to better ideas, if there are any.

He ignored the queer feeling in his gut as he opened the door to Rourke's room, unable to acknowledge it yet; that he truly hoped he would find nothing, today, or any other day.

After one quick glance when Sebastian opened the door, Juliana turned away, leaning on the wall beside Rourke's room, and staring out the window whilst he did what he felt he had to. In some way, she was glad, knowing he would find nothing. She only wished then he would finally give up this notion he had about her brother's guilt, though she knew he wouldn't; as she said herself, even were Rourke guilty, the absence of such an artefact of violence merely meant he was no fool.

As she stood there waiting, she was mindful of her breathing, rapidly beating heart, and general discomfiture. Being in this house was bad enough; being back in their once quarters was another matter entirely, and Sebastian for all his growing kindness, for this new rapport that grew between them against their will, wasn't helping.

Not one whit.

Were that you were still the biting ghost I first met... was it only a fortnight ago?

This new Sebastian, so like that she'd fallen in love with, troubled her, almost as much as this house, this place, their purpose. Those days on the road, of silence, of bickering—and even of *that* incident—had been cold comfort, a distraction to all that awaited and must be confronted. This new Sebastian, who she had to play happy wife to, and whose presence was steadfastly comforting and solid, this new Sebastian with whom she shared a room as though it were nothing, when really, it was something, smelling his scent permeating her clothes, hearing him snore, seeing him, if not in *undress*, then in various states of simple intimacy and almost leisure... Well he was driving her a bit mad.

It was a whole, sweet, delectable torture she hadn't counted on, which made her even less capable of facing Stag House whilst at the same time making it bearable.

How do you do it, Rourke? she wondered again, turning her head slightly, so she could hear the rustling in his room.

How can you live here? You'd be better off tearing it down, building something new far from these rotten foundations.

Stag House had always held the power to drain any hope or joy; and that hadn't changed despite all Rourke had attempted to bring some light into the place, and succeeded in *some* respects, if only by his influence and presence.

How can you sleep in that room...

Their father's once, which Rourke had surely made his own given her earlier glimpse—bright blues and whites, full of naval pictures, but thankfully lacking in crosses and biblical quotations—but which nonetheless had been *Father's*. A place they were never to tread, of evil, darkness, and...

I hate this house.

Juliana sighed, her head tipping back against the wall. Once, before their tacit agreement never to broach the subject, she'd asked Rourke, why he remained here. He'd written that Stag House, the estate, was their heritage, and so it was his duty to preserve and better it. That it was the charge appointed to him, like it or not, and he wouldn't shirk it. Some part of her had understood, but now...

If she'd had any courage, she might've asked him outright, what he was thinking, how he felt, if that conviction remained after years living here alone again. Only she'd not had the courage to disturb their quiet peace as they got to know each other again, braving the gulf carved between them by the past, and time. Though conversations were difficult, somewhat stilted, and tainted with shards of bitter memories, she was happy to spend time with him, to have him again within reach. It was *good*. Healing. Yet undeniably, despite their reunion's joy, there was, even beyond their shared terrible past, a sense that... The small talk, and the games, were all just...

Avoidant pleasantness.

Juliana shook her head, her eyes falling, and holding upon, the doors across the corridor; Rourke's and her old rooms. Inadvisable and unnecessary though it may be, she found herself moving towards them, opening the door just before her—*Rourke's*—and wandering into the space as transformed as the rest, but which like the rest, emanated a sad, suffocating vibrancy.

There hadn't been much to strip—their rooms, away from prying public eyes, could be as stark as God commanded—and yet it had been, replaced with an ostentatiously yellow, floral theme, which might've been amusing had it not been...

'Juliana...'

'You might've thought this was a monastery considering what our rooms looked like before,' she said quietly. Not wanting to share, yet ever unable to stop herself, needing Sebastian to see, not only those parts she'd never revealed, but also her brother. 'That was the point, naturally, and so I suppose it apt monks' rooms are called *cells*. Our rooms above in the nursery weren't any better, and soon as we could walk we were moved here to *grow up.*'

Glancing to her right, she found the interconnecting door which they'd been forbidden to use, yet always had—*we transgressed and rebelled sometimes despite the cost*—and went through to her own room, once a copy of Rourke's, now a purple and green fantasia of vines and Grecian scenes.

Purple...my favourite colour.

'No matter how many times Rourke was punished for using that door, forbidden to us,' she told Sebastian, or perhaps reminded herself. 'He never stopped. It took longer for me to be so rebellious, but not him. It was always to check on me. To remind me that no matter how bad it got, I wasn't alone.'

Striding to the window, she looked out onto the hills, fields, and forest which had once made her dream, and now brought only sorrow.

From here, she could see the Lloyds' old cottage, and the hill where...

'I hate this house. I can't breathe here,' she said, her strength failing.

With no idea of what else to do, or where to go, or how to make it better, or what to say, she just plopped into one of the chairs by the window.

'I know,' Sebastian finally said, coming to sit beside her, his own gaze avoiding the window's view.

'We've both tried to move on, best we could; but in here, I feel as if I've not moved an inch. It took me years to be rid of the fear that informed who I was,' she admitted, almost whispering. Feeling it was somehow unwise to open the drawbridge into her own heart; yet unable to *not. Perhaps it is a gift to myself, to heal, and to Sebastian; so he may understand all I did, and couldn't.* 'To not be terrified that life would end should I make the tiniest mistake, or say the wrong thing.

Some days, it still returns, and I must try so hard to be rid of it, but I *can*, because I'm not that little girl any more. Except in this house… It's as though I haven't lived a lifetime. As if I'm the same Juliana I was, and I know for Rourke it's the same, and I…don't know who I am any more.'

Taking a breath, she fell silent, watching as the sun peeked overhead from behind a grey cloud, making the coverlet's gold fringes shimmer on the bed.

When Sebastian did nothing, she continued, saying things she'd never thought to, yet that were necessary to say aloud, in this, once prison; for all truths must be revealed.

For all our sakes.

'Ginny, *the marchioness*, I don't know what you heard, but she was married to a similar son of a demon as my father before Spencer. She told me once that she was jealous, and wary of me, for a long time, because I knew how to handle him, and I was…*so proud*. I had been, before then, of surviving a Hell others had left in droves, and then, a while after she said it I thought: *what a strange thing to be proud of.* I suppose Father prepared us well for the world in the end.'

'They don't know, do they? Your friends.'

'I never told anyone what happened here. Of who my father truly was. You said you never knew how bad it was… There are no words to describe the torture we endured. But it was ours, Rourke's and mine, our secret, our burden. Our victory at surviving it. He protected me, with every breath, every heartbeat, and

A few after that too.

'I wanted so many things,' Sebastian added, bringing her back to the present.

'I know,' she breathed, finally finding the courage to turn and look at him.

I still do, his eyes seemed to say, and so she felt hers did too.

She felt as if everything else which tore them apart had melted away, including the years, and she—

'Let's get out of this house,' he said, not breaking the moment, but preserving them from it. 'We've toured the house,' he jested, managing to extricate a wet laugh from her. 'Time for the gardens, and perhaps,' he trailed off, glancing outside, and nodding to himself. 'Perhaps I've just had a brilliant idea. Or a terrible one, we shall see.'

'How enticing,' she laughed, taking his proffered hand, and rising.

Truly; though I daren't let my tone betray my heart.

Chapter Thirteen

Giggling like naughty schoolchildren, having evaded the servants whilst they made their way from the family wing, and collected coats, gloves, and scarves, dispensing with hats despite the iciness of the bright winter day, for no other reason than they could—dispense with hats, and somehow giggle—and wished to preserve the vulnerable bubble of truth and connection they'd created, Sebastian and Juliana peeked out of the drawing room's French doors, and reassured no one was about, slipped out onto the back terrace.

Juliana led the way, using the old route she had as a girl—*along the wall, down the stairs, tuck to the terrace wall and turn the corner, follow it around to the back lawn*—though unlike in years past, there was no reason to remain unseen, beyond preserving the spirit of the game they'd engaged in.

We're here to find terrible truths, and you engage in games...

Perhaps there was truth in that, however Juliana

needed an ounce of freedom, joy, thoughtless adventure, and connection just now.

Having made it to the back lawn, Juliana continued on her old route, remembering how tricky it had been to remain unseen from here, yet quickly sweeping that memory away, with less difficulty than she might've had her hand not been wrapped tightly in Sebastian's. She was having trouble understanding him, making out the game he was engaged in with this behaviour, only that too, she swiped away.

Just breathe now that you can somewhat.

So she did, leading him through the gardens that Father had always ensured were well maintained, worthy of an *esteemed gentleman*, though devoid of anything which might resemble ostentation. She'd often thought she'd give her kingdom for a folly, in more ways than one, but of course, here were none. Merely a few sparse ancient oaks—*'a true Englishman's ornament'*—and some holly-lined paths to her right, leading down to the river, and woods. Juliana noted that Rourke had tried to make pleasant changes here too—adding rose bushes, other flower beds, benches, and *frivolities*, however she wouldn't fully see his efforts until spring bloomed, and she hoped to be long gone by then.

Such a strange hope, to leave he who I've found again.

'Where to?' she asked Sebastian, stopping. 'You mentioned a terrible, brilliant idea.'

Glancing around, his breath coming out in short breaths whilst his eyes glinted every time the sun escaped from behind a cloud, he got his bearings before finally turning towards the holly hedge–lined paths.

A brilliant, terrible idea, she thought, following him. Onwards, treading the paths she knew by heart, but he had to guess at. Past hidden markers she'd mapped out in her earliest years, now without any regard of who might spy them; all the way until they were once again in the humid quiet of the thick, ancient woods at the edge of the grounds. Grim, and dead though they might seem, at once, they brought her peace, lifting some of the mighty weight from her shoulders.

Slowly, the birds and other creatures living in the confines of gnarly, raindrop-speckled branches too re-laxed, the chirps, squeaks, and rustles of their lives a gentle comfort. On they went, her following Sebastian though she might've her own feet, or the sound of im-patient water over well-worn rocks, all the way to the nook with the old boulder, set a few feet higher than the riverbank, above which clung a gnarly ancient wil-low, its roots tangling and loosening the dirt it stood on with every passing year, as it sought to make its way closer to the river.

Our sanctuary.

Hers first, then hers and Sebastian's—a place marked with some of their best memories. The place that had seen her accept his proposal all those years ago—to share a life, and escape to see the world. The answer she'd given him; the same nearly two decades earlier as it had been but a fortnight ago.

'Very well then.'

They stopped before the boulder, and she closed her eyes, then inhaled deeply, before letting out a long breath, picturing the poison that had seeped into her since her return, being expelled; just as she had years ago.

'Thank you,' she whispered, opening her eyes again to meet his.

He nodded, smiling almost sheepishly, before straightening, the swagger of du Lac Vaugris once again in full view as he accompanied her to their boulder.

'*Madame,*' he said with a bow, and she beamed, taking a seat as primly as a queen.

Still she beamed as he wandered about, cataloguing the changes of their spot, down to the whitecaps of the river below, sparkling silver and sapphire.

'Do you know, I imagined many things over the years, but being here again... I never dared,' he said, picking up some pebbles, then tossing them into the water as he used to, while she'd sit right here, and read him the latest treatise on something or other. 'I imagined you finding me a thousand times,' he breathed after a long while, turning back from the river to her. She felt, rather than sadness, or regret, the ghost of a smile tweak her lips, as she pictured such an outcome; how beautiful it might've been. 'I always hoped, *knew*, you wouldn't stay in Barrow Heath, however I did think...you'd wait. Come into your inheritance, take the money, and run far away. Travel everywhere we'd spoken of, and that I would meet you there. See you, disembarking a ship in Genoa, or crossing the street in Hamburg. Our eyes would meet, and you would know, and all would be well again. Life would make sense. I never…'

'Imagined I would lose myself on this island and forget how to live?' Juliana shrugged, her smile turning sad, and he took a step to comfort her, but she shook her head. 'I like this Juliana you imagined. She sounds…like someone I would've liked to be, but don't misunderstand me, I'm glad you saw much of what we dreamt of. Though I may not have lived that life, and mishandled my grief, I had a good life. I was lucky; I learned I could face the world, young as I was, and that isn't to say I didn't face trying times, however I met wonderful people, learned a trade, and taught children to open their minds… I've been lucky.'

'You made your own luck,' he corrected, reminding her of her beliefs on chance, fate, and higher powers.

'I suppose I did.'

'Would your dreams be the same now, Juliana? If you could leave, no restraints, no past, naught but freedom what would you do?'

'Don't ask me that. We've trodden on dangerous ground of late, but I beg you, do not ask me that.'

'Why not?' he challenged, in that way, that just…

'Because we aren't children, Sebastian. And though I appreciate your kindness, and distraction today, I do not like this game any more. We should—'

Sebastian's eyes sharpened, as his head quirked, and he put a finger to his lips. Whatever he'd heard, she hadn't, so lost in him, but there was something; he was an attuned predator. And just as the latter would, Sebastian was up in a trice, bounding up the short embankment to the willow's trunk.

It seems we have been followed.

The last thing Sebastian wished to do was run off, leave Juliana, not address *anything* of what she'd said or shared today—none of which he bloody well knew was easy—or debate childish games, and dreaming, which he shouldn't, considering he'd already arrived at similar conclusions as her, unfortunately, whoever was following them, *spying* on them, made giving chase the only option.

At least, he consoled himself as he scrambled up towards the willow where he'd heard the blasted intruder, and even spied a corner of a shoulder, now he knew he wasn't going mad. That he hadn't imagined being watched, or followed.

Good good, now concentrate, and don't let this chance at answers slip through your fingers!

Right, he was chasing down a nasty little spy.

One who isn't even fleeing...

Though Sebastian prided himself on having taken the spy by surprise; it appeared the man had been concerned with *hiding*, and not so much with *watching*. Therefore, Sebastian made it up to him just as the man processed the sound of pounding footsteps coming his way.

He saw a flash of surprise just before he launched

himself at the man, though he truly wasn't in top form, or perhaps too upset at the interruption, for he dove slightly *too* vigorously, and sent them both tumbling to around the tree, then back down the slope. Roots, rocks, and mud cut and slid into them as they rolled together, grappling for supremacy, until they finally stopped, just before they hit the boulder. Sebastian managed to get the upper hand, pinning the other man beneath him, and vaguely registered two things before he raised his hand to strike and end any resistance.

First, the man *wasn't* resisting.

Second, there was something familiar about the slightly rough, weathered face, silver-streaked russet hair, and onyx eyes peering up at him.

'Stop!' Juliana yelled.

Sebastian glanced over his shoulder, and the concern in her gaze added to his growing perplexity.

'I know you,' he said, glancing back down at the man, and frowning.

The man shrugged best he could, and Sebastian sighed, releasing him, and rising.

Juliana approached whilst he brushed himself off, and stretched out what pains and kinks he could, to help the man to his feet.

'This, is Josiah Meadows, the Marquess of Clairborne's valet,' she told him, affection laced with the frustration in her voice, the former rankling him, as his recognition of the man did. *Rankling which resembles jealousy.* 'I'd ask what you're doing here, Josiah, however I've a feeling I know the answer. Did Ginny or Spencer send you?'

Or did you follow her yourself?

'His lordship and her ladyship *both* felt more at ease knowing that should aid be required, it would be close at hand.'

'Your employers sent a spy,' Sebastian spat, shaking his head.

To some degree, he was aware of his own petulance, and idiocy; that despite all Juliana had revealed of them, all he'd seen, the *rankling resembling jealousy* was making him slightly unreasonable.

Slightly; comparatively.

'He was sent to keep an eye on me, not spy, Sebastian.' His brows raised, and he glared at Juliana meaningfully, his resentment ratcheting up. 'There's no use dissimulating the truth from Josiah. I trust him,' she said, sincerity in her which should've helped calm him, yet did the opposite.

'With my life apparently,' he therefore bit back.

'Yes.'

The three of them shared a long look, and some measure of Sebastian's anger faded.

He'd trusted Juliana all his life, despite what he'd said, and from what little he'd seen of Josiah, even just at first glance, he seemed a decent enough fellow.

Either way the die is cast now.

'Besides, as Josiah is here,' she continued, once they were on more peaceful ground. 'Perhaps he can help.

Assist with our inquiries; be an outside, objective pair of eyes as we are at a loss of how to progress.'

'We've not even been here a week, Juliana. This was never going to be solved in a day, and I wonder at what great aid a valet could be when the finest investigators money can buy barely were.'

'I'd forgotten that you employed *all* of them in the kingdom and beyond, Sebastian. And as I recall, you were quite fervent about having this *governess* as your Sancho Panza.'

'If I may,' Josiah interceded, and Sebastian glared at him, though the man merely smiled gently, otherwise unaffected. 'I happen to have a talent for ferreting out information. And whilst I would offer to depart, you're aware, Miss Myles, that my life would be in jeopardy were I to attempt it. So perhaps we could take this discussion somewhere more comfortable, and you can both advise how precisely I may be of assistance.'

The steel in the otherwise gentleness of the man's voice told Sebastian they wouldn't be rid of him, and he threw up his hands; literally.

Juliana trusts him, and her employers obviously care for her, better than you ever could, so accept this boon, and cease behaving like a child.

'Are you staying at the inn?' Juliana asked, tearing Sebastian from the cycle of his thoughts before he could plunge back into: *most irregular, I don't like him, he's no business here*, and Josiah nodded. 'I shouldn't be seen there, and though I could explain your arrival to my brother, it would be preferable for you to avoid the house. This afternoon, after tea, we can slip out and meet...'

'At the old shepherd's cottage,' Sebastian said flatly before he could argue with himself. Juliana gave him a look of pure compassion, asking silently if he was certain, and he ignored her. 'It wasn't torched as the locals feared my ghost would haunt them in retribution, and from what I've heard, it's in disrepair, bore the brunt of everyone's outrage, but it stands, and not many dare go there.'

Juliana nodded, her trepidation mirroring his own, though she was polite enough not to make any more of the matter.

For which I'm grateful.

'The cottage on the edge of the western grazing lands,' she told Josiah.

'I'll find it.'

'Until later then,' she smiled.

The valet—or whatever this Josiah truly was beneath that seemingly fitting, yet also ill-fitting mantle—smiled in return, and nodded at Sebastian, before taking his leave.

'Are you certain?' Juliana asked quietly, slowly approaching, as if he were some dangerously wounded animal.

Perhaps I am.

'I wouldn't have said it otherwise,' he said, stopping her in her tracks, the concern in her gaze, chafing as his own kindness had her. He sighed, glancing around as he raked his fingers through his hair, loosening some leaves and twigs caught in it. 'So this... Josiah.'

'Can be trusted.' He raised a brow, *more information please, Juliana*, and she continued. 'He has served the marquess loyally for years, and since I became part of that household, he's been a steady friend.'

'What else do you know of him?'

'He's about as private as I am. I know...he is indeed talented at ferreting out information, but beyond that only that he's a good man. Clever, and kind; someone I believe can help us.'

'A long way for someone to travel merely out of the goodness of their heart,' he noted, knowing absolutely *no good* would come of his remarks, yet needing to know.

'What are you implying?'

'I don't care for how he looked at you,' Sebastian said, with far too much pout, and not enough substance.

'I beg your pardon?'

'It was—'

'Oh, no,' Juliana retorted, devouring the remaining steps which divided them, her annoyance, and affront blindingly apparent. 'You won't even dare *think* of finishing that thought. Even had you *any* right to be jealous—which you patently *do not*—I wouldn't indulge it. Though, for the sake of us moving forward in some version of harmony, I will say this: the love of my friends—his care for me as a friend—brought him here, not that you'd know anything about that, which is likely why this situation is so utterly *baffling*.'

'What's that supposed to mean?' he sneered, her words prodding him back into some manner of spiky hedgehog; while also, reminding him of his place and idiocy.

'What happened to you shattered both our lives, Sebastian,' she said fiercely, coming toe to toe with him, until there was barely a breath between them. 'I've no idea what you did for eighteen years beyond *make money*, but I suspect that for all your travelling the world, there was just as much wandering through it without hope nor heart as there was for me. I at least, was open enough to those still living to find people who became family. Ginny is a sister to me, and I've watched her daughter grow, and love her as though she were mine. I love her newborn just the same, and I may not have much when trumpets sound, but I will have that. What will you?'

With that, and tears shimmering in her eyes, Juli-ana stormed off.

Had her words—these and those from earlier—not pierced him so profoundly, he might've found his voice and feet again, and gone after her, to try and heal the injuries he'd caused, through carelessness, idiocy, temptation, and uncertainty. Only as he stood there, he felt the cutting truth, of being ever and always, very much alone.

Though she seems to believe perhaps there is still time for me yet.

Not that he believed it himself, he admitted.

Chapter Fourteen

Winter's chill clung to the spring night air, the icy wind carrying bright blooms and fresh grasses, but inside the tiny stone cottage was another world altogether. A sanctuary, a hidden paradise, of warmth, safety, and simplicity.

Juliana knew none of it was right; the winter's chill, the scent of blooms, the warmth of the cottage…none of them were real. They were mere remembrances, yet she couldn't stop feeling, seeing, and experiencing themas though she a mage's power to travel through time. She couldn't prevent her own transportation; couldn't but smell Sebastian's scent, along with burning wood, stew, lavender, and their love. She couldn't force her heart to stop wishing, as it had that night, and every time since her first escape to this Eden, that she could lift the cottage, shrink it, and carry it with her always, as nomads did their tents. Except that was impossible, and Juliana knew what feeble currency dreams and wishes truly were.

The cottage may feel real—safe, warm, idyllic—but it was a mirage.

Sebastian's skin, flesh, and breath may feel real, but their love was a mirage.

It must be, for it was intangible. The feelings in her heart, her longing…living creatures couldn't live on such stuff, despite what any poets said; or how it felt otherwise. Their love was as impossible as time travel and shrinking cottages. Perhaps she was still a girl in many ways, however she wouldn't allow her head to be filled with idiotic, romantic notions. Love at first sight didn't exist, and love couldn't defeat reality; no matter what the storybooks said.

That spring night clung to her, begging to differ. A night, full of transformation, which had always felt like life's attempt to preserve her from losing the ability to love and dream. It was perhaps a month into their *dalliance*, two years before *the terrible night*. One of few she and Sebastian shared in the cottage—his father staying in the pastures—and already Juliana had known it was *love* they shared. Already then, she'd expended much energy trying to convince herself otherwise, for her own sanity, and safety. And that night, Sebastian had shattered those attempts, by confessing *his* love. His own uncertainty, his own wishes that they could have something lasting. She'd called them fine, pretty words, and he'd said: *'in time, you'll believe in my steadfastness, when all I do is continue to love you.'*

So she had.

So I did.

But that night, like all others, will fade from memory, and I'll move on, and so will he, and—

'Juliana...'

Forcing time into its proper place, and course, Juliana chased the memory—*memories*—away, back from whence they came, and forced herself to see the cottage as it was now. She couldn't afford to keep getting lost in days long past; only they kept assailing her, forcing her to relive good days and bad. If she'd thought Stag House full of memory, it was nothing compared to this place; the only saving grace that the cottage held more good, though the good was always tinged with bitterness, and regret.

So it was; so it is now.

Sebastian had been right—the single-room, squat, grey stone cottage which had once been his home, had seen the violence of angry neighbours, and likely bored, troublesome children, but was mostly intact. Lacking doors and windows, with rotting, holey thatch, and a floor covered in...well, she didn't want to know, it still had walls. Covered in variously faded obscenities—the lesser of being *murderer!*—however they still stood, and that was all that was needed to keep their conversation private.

She was glad to have arrived before Sebastian saw what had become of his once home. She'd thought he might precede her, having disappeared after tea, and she'd wondered if he would be here, making his own peace with this place.

Apparently not.

Likely, he was avoiding her, and considering her earlier words, it was entirely understandable. There was no excuse for her viciousness, though Josiah's surprise arrival, her vulnerability after sharing all she had thus far with Sebastian—so much, so quickly, especially being so unused to the exercise—then Sebastian's astounding jealousy... Suffice it to say she'd been raw, her nerves frayed to their finest point, so she'd *attacked*.

There's no excuse. Returning is hard for you; imagine what it's like for him.

Only she'd got lost in the past, her memories, feathers of an unalienable love; lost too in the present, Sebastian as Thomas, her husband, this new, strange, strong creature, who protected her, infuriated her, wanted to know her, and was at once familiar yet foreign. She'd lost herself in fanciful new mirages, just as terrible and torturous as her long-lost dreams.

Much may be mirage, but no matter his chosen form, Sebastian Lloyd has informed too many pieces of your soul to be rooted out.

So he had. With his own life, friendship, love, wisdom, courage, and yes, death and rebirth, Sebastian had impacted her life in a manner which defied definition. And in her heart she'd known since she was thirteen it would be thus.

Since that day I first met your gaze, truly...

Sensing him, Juliana turned to the doorway to find Sebastian stepping through it, looking slightly haggard, and windswept. He stiffened when he made it inside, though not because of her.

The memories assail him too, though I wonder which.

You could just ask...

'I'm sorry, for what I said,' she said instead, as Sebastian came to stand beside her before the empty fireplace. 'I know nothing of the life you've lived, or left behind, and I had no right.' He nodded, searching her gaze, her soul, and she... 'These past days, being back here, being around you... I think you know, I don't share, as I have recently, and while it feels natural, it's also...'

'Eviscerating,' he offered quietly.

'Yes. Confusing too.' He nodded again, slowly, and some of the tension within her released; while his mere presence again coaxed confessions. 'When you asked, if my dreams would be the same now—and understand, I mean none of this as an excuse for my behaviour—I wanted to answer. To imagine...so much, and I realised stepping in here, that so much of these past days with you have been full of that same confrontation between reality, and fantasy. When you asked me, I realised how angry I was, at myself, for not living at least some of the dreams we'd imagined. I could've,' she shrugged weakly, tears brimming again. *Damned things.* 'I could've met you in Hamburg, or Constantinople, only I gave up on the Juliana who might've been, and now I've no idea who I might be. I especially fear how little say I'll have on who that is when we reach the end of all this.'

'I rather like the Juliana who is,' he said, a small smile teasing, and she couldn't help but mirror it. 'And I for one, trust her to find a way to becoming whoever she wishes; to tell life it is her choice, entirely. But you should know, though I appreciate your apology, you were quite on the mark, as always. As ever, you saw straight through me,' he admitted quietly. 'I wanted to, you know, be happy, make friends, be part of the worlds I encountered. There were so many incredible people I wanted to know, but I... I would sit down, share a meal with them, and think: *you've no idea of who I am nor could you ever. You've no idea of the evil in the world, or what suffering is.* And I knew, *I know,* I'm far from the only one to have ever faced such tribulations, and that a fair few of those I encountered might've understood; even been worthy of the truth. However, as I'm sure you understand acutely, it's easier to be alone. Pain, loneliness, fear, are all more easily borne if of your own making.'

'I do,' she breathed, giving into the moment in which time held; granting them another piece with which to heal some part of themselves. 'I lied earlier. I wasn't open to anyone or anything. I certainly never wanted to love Ginny, or Elizabeth. Never wanted to be swept up into some ridiculously joyous and strange bunch as the Spencers, and their friends.' She huffed a laugh, recalling just how she'd tried to remain impervious; even as she encouraged Ginny and Elizabeth to give into joy. 'I took the position in Ginny's old house, thinking it would just be another to tide me over for a while. But the moment I stepped foot in there, I knew. It felt like Stag House on the worst days, and the look in Ginny's eyes… I *knew* it well, having seen it so often in Rourke's, or my own. I'd been in unfriendly houses, but nothing like that. I had no idea what I could do… All I knew was, I was there for a reason. It was the first time in a very long time, that I believed in a higher power. Because Ginny was right; I knew that man who was her husband. How to work around him, keep that woman and child alive. How to survive there, and protect them, even if only a little. So I did.'

'And they became your family.'

'Yes,' Juliana nodded. 'Ginny got free, facing challenges with a grace and dignity I'd never seen, nor am likely to again. And together, we built a good life, quiet, and full of love. Then Spencer came along, and…'

'Ruined it?' Sebastian finished, and she glanced over to find him smiling wryly.

'If only,' she chuckled, rather wetly, emotion colouring every part of her. 'No, he made Ginny, all of us really, believe in love, and apparently it's contagious, because ever since they've all been pairing up in that circle, trying to make as many scandals as possible along the way.'

'How unfashionable.'

'Quite,' Juliana smiled.

'You never…?'

Oh, dear.

He shouldn't ask. Not only was it *none of his bloody business*, it was exceedingly reckless. Stupid. Fanciful. Unimportant in the grand scheme of things. Yet as Juliana had said, he was finding it every day—*every hour*—more difficult to, at once remember, and forget.

To remember what they were—*allies*—and weren't—*lovers, friends, confidants*.

To forget, not why they were here, but why they weren't—*to become as we were.*

He was finding it harder to remember that he hadn't come back for her, and that sharing their lives, their hearts, was not part of the bargain they'd struck a fortnight that felt a lifetime ago. For years, he'd believed his second chance at life was the miracle, and maybe that was truer than he'd fathomed, because though he would never have, and didn't want—*certainly*—a second chance with Juliana, perhaps they could have a second chance at honesty, and answers.

Closure, so we might move on.

'I have love aplenty, however… I had my great love,' she told him, not unhesitatingly, but courageously. 'That day you spoke of, when I raised my eyes to you in church was the beginning of my rebellion, my questioning, and so as Lucifer before me, it was my downfall. I was experimenting,' she laughed gently, and he just couldn't stop *looking* at her. Fascinated, as he'd ever been; waiting with bated breath, for her next words. 'Evil was a mighty subject in our house, and I wanted to know if I could see it. For all the evil at Stag House, it seemed invisible to any who dared look, and so I wondered if it could be seen. If I might have a special talent for spotting it. I'd never looked, never been seen, and maybe that is what this comes down to, a need to be seen.'

It was strange to feel so close to her during all this talk of evil, to feel himself leaning closer, to shield her; unsettling to know this lesson's conclusion would be one he wouldn't recover from.

Lifting his hand, he coaxed the rest from her by softly sliding his fingers along the lines of her face, from temple to chin.

Tell me it all.

'My logic then was sound, if flawed, and I soon realised that evil cannot always be seen,' she continued, and was it wrong to feel so mighty a man merely because he could give her strength, and coax such confessions from his otherwise aloof Juliana? 'A conclusion oft confirmed over the years. Yet that experiment was the reason I met your gaze for the first time; perhaps even why we're here today. Tall, gangly, with features you hadn't grown into yet,' she smiled, almost *lovingly*, brushing her own fingers along his ear. 'Your eyes were a rainbow of colour in the morning sun. And I knew, in that second that stretched out for eternity, that you would inform my life. It felt so queer; like having prescience without belief. I tried to convince myself I was lonely, and you were handsome in your own way, seemed a good man... Even after we grew close, I dismissed it as fanciful longings of a romantic girl I'd never be. Turns out I am that girl, always was, because I know now that was the first of many times I fell in love with you. If there is a secret to loving again after a love like that, I've not learned it.'

A chilly breeze swept through them, unfortunately not clearing out the charged silence.

'I think you know the answer, Juliana,' Sebastian said softly, answering her unspoken question.

You're my great love; always were, and always will be.

Though some might be lucky enough to find another, the two of them were cursed with being each other's; and once, soulmates.

Some might be able to settle for else after that, unfortunately we are not of that kind.

And why would there be need for another, when...

When she looked at him thus, and perhaps there was a chance, one he wanted to seize.

He wanted to lean in, feel her breath on his lips, and—

A knock sounded, and they both jumped, separating as they turned to find Josiah smiling at them from the doorway. The apology in that smile suggested he'd heard more than either of them would feel comfortable with, however, there were more important things to worry about.

Wrongs to right. So that she may return home to her family.

For that reminder, of all Juliana had waiting for her, he was oddly grateful for Josiah's arrival.

She has her talisman, her reminder of what awaits; but what awaits me?

He knew well the answer, but more than ever, found he disliked it.

Chapter Fifteen

It had been over two weeks since that day in the cottage. Since she and Sebastian had *both* taken Josiah into their confidence, relating everything about Alice, Bertie, and Sebastian himself; what they knew, and sought to do. If Josiah had been surprised, he hadn't shown it, merely nodding thoughtfully, and asking for clarification on various points; Juliana suspected, he'd already put quite a few pieces together.

He is not a dull man.

No, he certainly wasn't, not that it came as a surprise, as his soothing manner, and steadiness of spirit, weren't; yet in the short time she'd been away, she'd allowed herself to forget everyone. Oh, she'd held on to all she'd left behind, as it kept her steady and strong, however they'd all become almost mythical beings, existing in a land far far away. They'd lost their realness, their tangibility, as the world, and herself, were coated in the thick, dreary mists of memory and regret that pervaded here. But Josiah's presence had cut through, making the path home clearer.

And, good sport that he is, he agreed to keep this whole affair to himself.

That had been a harder bargain—his immediate re-action to Juliana and Sebastian's tale to convince them a marquess would be handy—however he'd eventu-ally relented, admitting it wasn't his story to tell. Un-derstanding also, perhaps, that Juliana needed the life she'd left behind, to remain untainted.

She would also say his help was a relief, a boon, and it was, though unfortunately, thus far it hadn't jolted any great revelations into the light. Perhaps she had hoped that it would be a matter of days after all. That she and Sebastian—then Josiah—would find de-cades old answers within minutes, freeing themselves promptly, to live...

Happily ever after—or at least, happily in our own new lives.

So you're still the girl who believes in intangible things.

Unfortunately, redemption and truth weren't so swiftly found, and now it felt as if they'd been trapped in limbo for centuries awaiting salvation. None of them had discovered anything. Not in Barrow Heath, nor the surrounding villages for miles. Each of them had made as overt or discreet enquiries as possible. Each of them had poured over the papers Sebastian had gath-ered—which for Juliana, had been excruciating, but necessary—and they'd had several meetings to discuss options and the chains of events. The most they could agree on was that there had been design—the weapons having gone missing earlier that day—but they couldn't even agree as to whether it had been planned, or opportunistic design, intending to incriminate Sebastian or merely *anyone*. Other than that, nothing. Juliana would torture herself, trying to spot some detail, some clue that would point them in the direction of some stranger—near or far—or stare remorselessly at her once neighbours and wonder: *could it have been you?* Yet still, she gained no insight, no clue or found trail to follow; nothing to prove to the others what she knew in her heart: *it wasn't Rourke.*

Nothing but pain is gained from these excursions into the past.

They made her question everything as she hadn't ever before; made her realise things she hadn't been ready to accept before. That she'd wanted to believe Sebastian guilty at times, for it assuaged her guilt at not even speaking for him at trial; merely giving an anonymous written account of his movements. Rourke had deemed it best, to protect herself, and though she knew the court likely wouldn't have listened to the fervent promises of a young girl that he couldn't be guilty, and that as she'd told Sebastian, she would bear the weight of his conviction no more, understanding the nuances of her own past reasoning was confronting, to say the least.

As was admitting that despite her protestations, she was a coward, for not having searched for the truth earlier, even as she knew Sebastian innocent. She'd convinced herself that she hadn't the means, then that there was no truth to be found, the dead were dead, so it mattered not, and would only make her guilt worse, but now, she wondered if she might've found something, had she the courage to search earlier.

And so new guilts replace the old.

It was that too, along with the lack of breakthroughs, which were proving trying. In truth, Juliana had hoped that perhaps Josiah's arrival was a sign. The key they'd waited for; the man to get the job done. Beyond his cleverness—which she'd thought would bring much needed new perspective—having previously witnessed his skills and talents, she knew he had a quiet, forceful way about him, that could sway an otherwise reluctant, tight-lipped soul. Not for the first time, she wondered about his past; then pushed those interrogations aside, respecting his privacy, as he'd always hers. Still, the point was, grateful as she was for Josiah's presence, and despite all their shared efforts they were...

At an impasse.

And though losing hope was damning, and unproductive, Juliana found it increasingly hard to resist.

As many things are...

Sebastian being the greatest temptation of all. After that day in the cottage—and all those moments of truth preceding it—everything...settled, between them. Nothing resolved, nor perfect, but lovely. If there was a word to describe what they were now, Juliana didn't know it; in fact she doubted its existence. Though in truth, she didn't care, for she could exist in it; in its loveliness, safety, and otherworldliness. Lose herself in the illusion, and the intimacy; the camaraderie, and tenderness, of the mirage, no matter how dangerous. She even treasured this pleasant loss of reason, and bearings—save for Sebastian—for she knew soon, she would feel the loss of these days, more precious than perhaps those which had come before, because there was an honesty and knowledge between them, that they couldn't have as children.

Some dissimulation remained; notably she'd yet to gain a backbone, and confess outright to Sebastian that she'd known him innocent for a long time. In some ways, she liked to think he knew, her actions saying enough; yet even if he did, she knew full well in time he deserved to hear the words. Selfishly, and somewhat cowardly, she remained silent however, needing the beautiful mirage to remain intact, if only a little longer.

Sebastian himself remained tight-lipped about his life, sharing only the occasional snippet about this distant town, or that amusing anecdote about a stranger, though admittedly she no longer felt a wall between them. His silence was merely a pause, a rest, after such soul-scraping sharing as they'd had, before...

What? Now that is the question.

Whatever it may be, for now, she knew what she needed to. Despite her desire to, she may not know the precise timeline of his life, but she knew the man he was. He was still the Sebastian she'd known, in the most profound, meaningful ways; fierce, gentle, kind, with the moral compass of a saint—though his vices

meant there would be no hagiography. Tender, courageous, and when he looked at her…

I am myself as I am now.

They'd become united, a team, synchronised to each
other's needs, and those of the whole. With him in
her life, everything was easier, which was maddening when it wasn't comforting. Being at Stag House,
was easier. Sleeping with him in the room, was more
restful. Knowing he was there to pass her the damned
salt made eating easier. Their days together were full
of a promise that couldn't ever be fulfilled but in the
mirage, and fantasy they dwelled in. That of a husband
and wife, happy, in love, with a whole life ahead of
them, surrounded by family and friends.

For yes, Rourke tempted her too—as to a lesser degree, did John and Celia.

Rourke who had changed his tune, welcoming Sebastian with open arms, for her sake; who tried to
laugh with him, accept him, and love them both. Once,
she might've disparaged Rourke's fantasies—of them
living out their days here, all together—but lately, his
excitement, joy, and exuberance such as she'd never
seen before, made it so she was swept into them. She
loved him, so very dearly, wanted him to be happy, and
though his happiness in many ways came at the cost
of forgetting the past entirely, and imagining her to be
someone she wasn't…she was tempted. They would
be riding, and Rourke would point out some empty
house needing new tenants, and she'd catch herself,
imagining it—her and Sebastian, free, Rourke as their

neighbour, some evil villain finally punished for his crimes—yet she couldn't stop herself. They'd meet for tea, and Rourke would speak of the future as though she would always be *right there* to see it pass with him.

'You'll love it in the summer.'

'We must go boating soon with Celia and John.'

And then…she would remember.

That was the torturous part of this limbo—remembering, who she was. How much life separated her from Sebastian, and Rourke. For despite all the loveliness, her love for Sebastian was in the past, born in the heart of the girl she'd been, for the Sebastian she'd known. For all the temptation, her brother saw a Juliana who was no longer, and could never be again. Though Rourke *was* trying to know her, beyond what they'd shared in letters, it was as if her return had somehow wiped all memory of previous lives; lives which made the dreams of them all ending their days as happy neighbours in a place so accursed with putrid memory, just that.

Dreams. Mirage and illusion; as much as I am now.

But when this is over, I'll tell him the whole truth, and we'll all find a way to make peace with the past, and find new paths. Father's curse, the curse of this place, shall not devour us; as I believed it had, and would always.

Indeed, she would see to it they all found a way forward, for if there was one thing this time had given her, it was renewed, infallible certainty that Rourke hadn't done what Sebastian posited. Whether Sebastian still believed it was something else she hadn't dared confront; though given how he was around Rourke, she doubted his continued conviction.

Told you—

'I thought I might find you here,' Rourke said, a smile in his voice, and Juliana glanced up, finding him indeed smiling at the library's door. He looked frayed at the edges, and she wondered if he'd been sleeping; how he slept at all here, with no such comforting presence as Sebastian's to aid him. 'Ever your favourite place.'

Ever the only place with life, or escape; our refuge.

'I'm enjoying some of the volumes you've added to the collection.'

He strode over to where she sat at the window, watching raindrops snake down the glass as winds lashed their fellows across the landscape, and glanced at the book on her knees, which she'd barely looked at, too preoccupied thinking.

'Father would've disapproved immensely,' he agreed, nodding at Lucretius's work. 'So naturally I had to have it.'

'Indeed,' she grinned.

'Where's Thomas?'

'He had some business, and fancied a ride. That was before the rain descended, so I hope he's found a warm refuge.'

Rourke nodded, and gestured over his shoulder at the chessboard, set up as ever beside the fire.

'Fancy a game?'

'Always.'

He took the book, setting it on the seat beside her before taking her hand, and helping her up.

They settled across from each other at the chessboard, Rourke ceding her white, as she'd won their last bout.

'You've been asking questions,' he said, after they'd played their first few moves. If it was meant to destabilise, it worked, though she'd rather been expecting such a remark eventually; knowing he would hear of hers and Sebastian's poking around. And there were questions she needed to ask him, having thus far avoided them... *Perhaps now is the time, when we're alone, in our safe place.* 'It isn't good for you, Juliana, and I don't see what you seek to gain; the matter was settled eighteen years ago. Frankly, Thomas should know better than to indulge this morbid inclination.'

'He's helping me heal old wounds. Don't you ever think about them?'

'I don't dwell on the past,' he said bitterly, seizing one of her rooks.

'Neither can we simply forget it. What was done to us, what was done here...it runs too deep; it forged us.'

'Why shouldn't we move on? Isn't that what life is all about?'

'Moving forward. Not forgetting,' she said gently. 'What about your wife? You never speak of her, yet you married her—'

'And then fever took her, and I lost her as I had you. It was sad, but all things must die. One of Father's few worthwhile lessons. I thought you might come back for the wedding,' he added quietly after a moment, pondering his next move as one of his knights was escorted away.

Something struck Juliana as intensely queer about how he said it, but she dismissed it, knowing he'd been disappointed.

'I thought about it. Were you happy?'

'We were well suited. But you're the only one who ever truly loved me, Juliana.'

There was no viciousness, no regret, not even any jealousy in his voice, yet Juliana felt the sting of sheer truth nonetheless.

She'd always known, yet never allowed herself to acknowledge how hard it must've been, how lonely his life must've been, despite his friends, and the quiet peace of it. She'd had Sebastian, then Ginny, Elizabeth, and the others, and she'd convinced herself he'd found happiness only now she saw…

He hasn't felt love in a long time.

'Why did you come back?' Rourke asked, before she could say, promise something she wasn't certain she ever could. 'It wasn't for me.'

'Of course it was,' she told him vehemently, for wasn't it the truth? She'd come back, to protect him, and the other man she loved, from destroying each other or themselves? 'I love you. You've been with me wherever I've gone.'

'Only you won't stay,' he stated, taking one of her bishops. Now she was just being careless. 'You hate me, and will never forgive me the role you believe I played in the murderer's demise. For taking him from you.'

'I could never hate you, Rourke. I know... It took years to reconcile, but I always knew, you were only doing what you believed best. You always took such good care of me, I wouldn't be who I am without you,' she told him, placing her hand on his for a moment. 'However, no,' she said, seeing the mirages dance and disappear before her eyes, breaking her heart. 'You may be able to live here, surrounded by the past, but I cannot. I must start my life afresh.'

'With Thomas.'

'You could come with me.'

'No,' he said, shaking his head, a sad smile on his lips as he took his hand from under hers, then seized her queen.

Checkmate.

Silently, they reset the board, and as they did, Juliana remembered those times they'd spent here together. Reading, learning—only what Father allowed—united. Safe; for a moment, at least.

She recalled sliding a book over to him, when she'd been nine or so. A book full of maps, littered with ancient battles. She'd told him she wanted to visit those places, the whole world, and see what it looked like after the passing of centuries. He'd smiled, a sad smile, much like that he'd just given her, and told her there was nothing in the world which couldn't be found here. The same evil, the same ugliness, and the same terror.

And he'd told her that someday, he would make this place a world as she'd never seen; of beauty, good, and peace.

As they began another game, Rourke taking white, Juliana realised that his curse was that he could never leave, even after all this time; even with all the world could offer him.

It broke her heart.

You tried, Rourke, only this house has seen too much to ever be such a world.

And then, as if the day had not already brought enough, as they played, her mind returned to that book of ancient battles, to those tales of people picking bodies clean after battles—everything from shoes to trinkets, and even, perhaps...

Pretty gold pictures.

Assumptions have been blinding us.

Chapter Sixteen

'Now, behave, both of you,' Juliana instructed him and Josiah, as they stood before the undertaker's door, on the outer fringe of Barrow Heath; whether its location was by superstition or choice, Sebastian wasn't sure. It was like the rest, a small, plain stone house, except there was peeling paint on the door, a lack of flourishing greenery, and windows darkened with grime. The lack of reprimand the house's inhabitant incurred for such faults, *that* he posited was due to superstition.

It had been two days since Juliana had come to them with her idea—he wouldn't call it a revelation, as it had yielded nothing yet, and he couldn't bring himself to hope for a miracle—that though the murders and theft of the *'pretty gold picture'* were connected, there was no correlation. That the murderer hadn't taken it—perhaps hadn't even know of it—a possibility so simple and obvious he couldn't believe they'd missed it; but then there were many cautions about *assuming* certain facts or perspectives.

It had felt strange, having a new theory to explore, a new pathway to potential answers, after a fortnight of nothingness; well, nothing save for odd tranquillity, loveliness, and simplicity. A time during which he'd had to work hard to remember his anger, and purpose, and not fall prey to the hypnotic comfort. Of being around Juliana, finding a gentle intimacy and beauty in how they were—without expectation, merely acknowledgment, of their continued, and unshakeable connection. There was trepidation too, a sense, of *what if*, yet also just enjoyment of the present; of all that had been given and taken.

And if he was honest, Rourke too had played his part in making these past weeks tranquil, and pleasant. He'd held good to his word, welcoming Thomas into the fold, and though they didn't *get to know each other*, they did to some degree, and with every passing day Sebastian undeniably found himself hoping, that perhaps, he'd been wrong all these years. That he'd misjudged Rourke, and that any possessiveness, coldness, desperation, or emptiness he spied on occasion was nothing but a trick of the light; or a remnant of age-old demons.

Like Juliana—he knew, for he could see it plainly despite Stag House's impact on her—Sebastian was tempted by this idyllic picture; a future which could never be, yet that they could dream on safely, if only for a time.

But that time will soon be ending. For we've been

reminded of our purpose—not that we'd forgotten,
merely doubted its success.

So he still did, despite Juliana's clever idea. He, Josiah, and Juliana had spent the past days visiting those who'd been close to Alice and Bertie after their deaths, asking in no uncertain terms, what had been seen; what might've been taken. They heard much that they had to steel themselves against, and Sebastian, had it not been for Juliana holding his hand tightly, might've been swallowed by his own memories of that morning. They'd also heard much about the chaos, and confusion, but thus far nothing of real use, beyond that Mr Tynes—the undertaker and their last stop—had been out of sorts that winter, which Sebastian had recalled then. So now here they were, and though Sebastian refused to hope; he knew this was their last.

Then why don't I hope?

Juliana knocked on the door, giving them one last look of warning. He or Josiah might've argued, except that by all accounts, Mr Tynes required more gentleness than either of them had demonstrated of late, and out of the three, admittedly Juliana was the better wager on that.

Whether those who ever called her cold would agree...

Feet shuffled, and the door creaked open to reveal a red-faced, lumbering and blinking Mr Tynes.

'Yes?'

Like most in the village, Sebastian wouldn't have

said he had any particular feelings on Tynes, particularly since he'd never had much to do with the man.

His father had when his mother had died in childbirth, and he'd only ever heard that Tynes was a good man, with a reassuring presence for those faced with the timely, or untimely, misfortune of one of their loved ones. He'd learned his trade from his father, and before his son's death from fever when Sebastian was about twelve, he'd been teaching it to him. Afterwards, though he remained a solid presence in the village, always present for the great rite of passage which was death, he'd become dishevelled, and increasingly prone to drink; though Sebastian wouldn't ever hold that against him. He'd remained professional and caring, been there for Juliana and Rourke; and been the one to take care of Alice and Bertie.

It appeared however the years and sorrows had caught up with Tynes, now somewhere in his late sixties, dressed in a rather untidy, but serviceable black suit and coat.

'Good day, Mr Tynes,' Juliana said, as the man frowned, his eyes darting between the three of them. 'Do you remember me?'

'Miss Myles—now Mrs…something or other.'

'Mrs du Lac Vaugris,' she said with a smile, and dammit if Sebastian's heart didn't flip-flop—it being perhaps the first time she'd introduced herself thus. *Nonsense, really.* 'This is my husband, and a friend, Mr Meadows.'

'Thought you'd left it in the past, as you should've,'

he said before Juliana could engage in further pleasantries, and the three of them stood there blinking at the harshness; rather more cutting than one might expect him able to be. 'Oh, I heard—the whole village has. 'Twas bad business, and the lot of you, digging it back up, is making it worse. 'Twas done and sorted eighteen years ago.'

'That is exceedingly euphemistic, Mr Tynes. 'Twas more than *bad business*, and none of us should ever forget. Particularly not if an innocent man was hanged; and given that you aren't saying his name, I don't think you believe him guilty either.'

Sebastian's heart swelled at Juliana's fierce championing; at the most overt declaration she'd made thus far that she believed him.

Oh, she'd intimated, by her actions, and some of her words, but never *said* it.

So I am redeemed in her eyes at least.

'You've no idea what's best for Barrow Heath,' Tynes spat, clutching to the door, but not closing it. Sebastian glanced to Josiah, wondering if they should intervene, but Josiah shook his head. *She's handling this.* 'You're not part of it, never were. Why do you even care?' he asked, desperately, as though her answer could bring either salvation or doom.

Perhaps it can to us all.

'I'm the only one left to care, therefore I've no choice but to do so.'

We're the only ones left to care for the dead.

Sebastian felt those words as deeply as Tynes, who,

in the long moment which followed, looked at once aghast, angry, and defeated; tempted to smite her from the earth, yet having expected her answer all his life.

Finally, deflated, curling in on himself, having lost his will, he sighed so heavily, Sebastian felt the weight which had been tying him down, come sit on all their shoulders.

'You hold tighter to those you have when you've lost. 'Twas a bitter winter. Bitter, but not busy enough. And you know what it's like, when bread and meat are scarce and dear, and there's doctors to pay,' he said, raising his eyes, begging her to understand. 'Then again, perhaps you don't. 'Tis a blessing.'

'I understand, Mr Tynes. I've lived hard times, despite knowing I had help to call upon if needed.'

'Yes,' he nodded, lost in a hundred memories. 'I was their help, my sister, and nephew. He was sick, and I couldn't bring them, and I deserved more, for what I cleaned up that day. Anyone who saw that morning, deserved more than life ever gave 'em.'

'What did you take, Mr Tynes?' Juliana asked.

'A gold locket and chain,' he confessed, bowing his head, and shaking it. *A pretty gold picture—a locket...* ''Twas in the grass, nearby, glinting...a miracle, so I thought. Sold it in Burndsey. He died anyway, my nephew, not four months after, his mother not far behind. Matthew he was. A curse, in the end.'

'You tried, Mr Tynes,' Juliana said gently, as they all felt the blow. *Ripples of horror.* 'To make something good of something terrible. I'm sorry you lost them, but you cannot blame yourself. I don't believe in curses, and neither should you.'

Not lying; for she didn't believe in such curses as *that*; though he knew they both believed in those of another sort.

Tynes nodded, half-heartedly.

Perhaps it was Fate you took it, Sebastian thought. *For another mightn't have told us.*

Perhaps it is just a trail with no end; perhaps there is a chance.

Burndsey, though a large market town, wasn't a city, or even so big a shop might not still be there; a shop-keeper not still have records to share, given the right price or tale.

'Have you still the receipt?' Juliana asked, showing more forethought than he.

'Aye.'

He shuffled off to get it, leaving the door open, the sights and smells of a life lived alone, in grief, reaching them.

Eventually, he returned, handing her a neatly folded paper.

'Thank you, Mr Tynes.'

He nodded, again, half-heartedly, and they all made to leave, nothing more to be done for him; it was with himself he had to wrestle, as he likely had for years.

'Mind yourself, Miss Myles,' he warned before they even turned, resoluteness returning him to his old self. 'Whoever killed those poor souls… 'Twas savagery that should never been seen.'

She nodded, and they all turned, his fear permeating their own hearts.

As they made their way slowly back into the village, Sebastian wondered if perhaps…

Danger lurks after all.

Perhaps we shouldn't have come. I shouldn't have risked her.

Still, we must stay the course; at least now we have one.

Is it miracle or curse?

Had his mind and heart not been so full of questions, doubts, and fear, Sebastian might've lost himself in the normality and pleasantness of the day. He might've let himself imagine for the briefest sliver of time, that he and Juliana were merely a happy couple, strolling through the busy streets of Burndsey with a friend, shopping for unnecessary frivolities and delights.

He might've enjoyed the picturesque town's cobbled streets, and half-timbered, leaning houses and shops that hadn't changed since it had boomed in the Middle Ages, having been granted its market licence.

He might've seen the beauty, felt the joy, of wandering about as gentle snowflakes tumbled from a strangely sunny sky; even just felt the change in vibrancy from Barrow Heath.

He might've enjoyed feeling Juliana tucked into his side, even felt her confidence and hope beating in his own heart; as once he'd felt every breath of hers in his own bones. He did feel her warmth, her steadiness—

it alone kept him upright and moving—however he also felt miles away, unable to truly hope, as she did.

As even Josiah, steadily keeping pace yet remaining non-intrusive, hoped.

Whereas he *couldn't* bring himself to hope. That they would find this mysterious locket, after eighteen years, in a place his investigators had already searched; or that in the unlikely event they did, it would lead any further. Of late—since he'd been in Juliana's orbit again—he'd let himself forget too many things. Imagine too many things. But hoping, *truly*, with all his might and heart, that remained an impossible feat, for the dashing of that hope onto the rocks, like every other hope he'd had, would surely kill him.

More soundly than the rope might've.

'Here,' Juliana said, rather too excitedly.

They all stopped and glanced at the shop before them, the bottom half of a squat and time-worn timber building, whose diamond-paned windows were packed full of shining gold, silver, and jewels—from necklaces to platters and watches.

Beside the doorway, a plaque read *Hunter & Parker*; it too, was worn, and looked as if someone had botched the last repainting. Taking a breath, he made to enter, but Juliana held fast, prompting him to wait.

He turned, finding her cheeks fresh and rosy, alive with a long-absent light which he was loath to extinguish; though he knew the look on his face had a good chance of doing so.

'Tell me,' she entreated, and for a second, he considered it. Then his eyes flicked to Josiah standing vigil behind her, and he was reminded of who they were. *Our burdens are our own to bear; not each other's any more.* 'I'm scared to hope too,' she said, at his silence.

'Not so scared hope isn't alive in you,' he breathed, smiling at the sight of her despite the imbecility of it. Nearly as daft as running his knuckles along her cheek, and chucking her chin lightly as he did next; though not quite as foolhardy as what he longed to do—*kiss her, steal some hope from her lips*—which he didn't do. 'It shines in your eyes, Juliana, and I won't extinguish it, not for the world, even if it only lasts a breath of time.'

With that, he turned away, though he felt her tightly against him still, as he led them all inside.

Half an hour later, they emerged from the cramped, dusty cavern of wonders, with a sliver of paper that held, if not *the* answer, then directions to the next path. Though he still couldn't bring himself to hope, Sebastian was stunned as his boots hit the wet cobbles again; larger snowflakes prickling his warm cheeks as they descended from a now bright grey sky. The three of them stopped, glancing up at the snow's birthplace, trying to *realise* precisely what they now held. Reminding themselves, it was nothing but an aged old invoice, with the name and the address of the person who'd bought the locket Tynes had taken.

Too easy.

Much too easy. One didn't walk into a shop, bribe— then gently threaten with Tynes's own receipt as proof—a jeweller for information on a simple gold locket sold two decades prior, and *get something useful*.

Life wasn't that simple, or easy; they all knew that damn well.

'They're likely dead,' Sebastian said flatly, daring the others to disagree. 'Or sold it years ago.'

'Or have it, except there's nothing on or in it to help us learn more of Alice and Bertie,' Josiah agreed. 'Or there is something, but it won't aid us in any way.'

'Or they have it, and moved to America,' Juliana said, a smile in her voice.

Sebastian turned to her, and...

How do you still hope, my love?

How is it I feel hope creeping into my heart despite our proclamations?

'Mr Hunter mightn't have removed the likenesses,' he added, wondering again if it had been superstition, not just laziness, prompting such an otherwise stark businessman to *not* strip the piece. 'That doesn't mean the new owners didn't.'

'A lost cause, really,' Juliana grinned, and he found himself doing the very same.

How dare you make me smile so?

'Then we've not a moment left to lose to prove it so,' Josiah decreed, a smile on *his* face, and so off they went again.

This time, despite himself, Sebastian began to believe that perhaps, there was hope to be had; and it wasn't such a bad thing.

* * *

At least, it wasn't while it lasted. When it was dashed *yet again* upon the rocks of disappointment— especially such a freshly restored version of hope— well, then hope *was* a bad thing. Or so Sebastian was brutally reminded as they stood beside the carriage, waiting for Josiah to accept their fate as he and Juliana already had.

Won't be but a moment.

Personally, Sebastian was pleased at losing hope again, for now he could return to who he'd been.

Who I am; the man I recognise rather than he I cannot begin to fathom.

They'd found it. They'd bloody well found that damned locket.

Come to this house—this address given to them by Mr Hunter—a few towns over. Spoken to the woman living here; a widow who'd been given the locket by her late husband. A superstitious, sentimental woman of faith, who, for those very reasons, had kept the thing; neither wearing it nor removing the tiny miniatures from inside it.

If they'd not been already sitting, sipping tea when she'd brought it out and placed it in Sebastian's hands, he might've fallen over at the impossibility, so dizzying had the rush of hope and surprise been. His heart had beat wildly, as the world turned into silence, but for a strange buzzing.

It was such a small thing, yet so monumental. So important. He couldn't stop touching it reverently, stroking it, inspecting it; searching, yet afraid to disturb. It was a simple thing, perhaps two inches, plain gold, on a plain gold band. Worn by time, though the engraved initials remained—a delicately woven *AN*—which he'd run his fingertips over countless times, ensuring they were real. Even Juliana, Josiah, and the widow had quietened, and he'd thought... It all *meant* something.

That you were losing your mind; that's what hope does to you.

The others had begun speaking again, and he'd recovered his hearing. The widow—Amelia Norton—had said that when her husband had given her the locket for their tenth anniversary, she'd immediately known it was destined to be hers; to safekeep, yet never possess fully. Her husband had never fully understood; the initials had caught his eye, and he'd immediately known he should get it for her, though something had prevented him from removing the miniatures within.

'Seemed wrong to be rid of them before we had something to replace them with,' he'd apparently grunted as he'd given it to her.

Over the years, he'd been variably understanding of her refusal to make it her own, until finally he'd given up, a year or so before he'd passed last spring.

'I always knew someday, someone would come,' she'd told them then, certainty in her eyes that could make the staunchest atheist believe in a higher power. *'It came to me so I could keep it safe, and so I have. I look on their faces every so often, wonder who they were.'*

Sebastian had opened it then, carefully, almost expecting those faces to have disappeared with the years; only they hadn't. There she'd been, staring up at him, smiling, and radiant, as he'd never seen her, but often imagined her.

Alice.

It had taken a deep breath, and long moment for him to will away the twist in his heart at seeing her tiny face, in his hands, as it had been...

Don't.

He'd eventually returned to the present, his eyes drifting to the other face; a young man who seemed at once a stranger, yet familiar, dressed in military regalia.

So this was your sweetheart, Alice? Bertie's father...

He'd smiled to himself, feeling like he was meeting old friends again, but then he'd remembered the truth, and shut the locket.

The widow had seemingly understood, for she'd nodded, and wished them well, and it was then Sebastian realised she'd never asked what they knew of the people in the locket, or what their purpose was. Likely for the best, though if they did find the truth, he would come back, and tell her of it all, so she could know what her safekeeping truly meant.

Someday, perhaps.

And with that thought, he'd followed the others out, and Juliana had asked to see it, and it was then another, more desperate realisation had dawned. There was nothing there; nothing to identify either Alice or her sweetheart. Nothing to give them a clue as to where to search next, just *nothing*.

Nothing but their faces to haunt me for years to come.

Sebastian had dared hope, and yet again it had failed him. They'd reached the end of the road. Might as well just go now, back to Barrow Heath, and be done with it all. He wasn't entirely sure what Josiah was playing at, drawing it out by taking out a magnifying glass, and hunkering over the locket to examine the portraits like a child who'd discovered an excellent pebble, but Sebastian was done with this hoping business.

Now we all go back to our lives, and—

'I know these colours,' Josiah muttered, and it was surprise, *not* hope, that made Sebastian straighten, and stare. 'Sixty-Third, West Suffolk.'

Sebastian's eyes widened, and Juliana glanced at him, but he refused still to be taken in with hope or excitement.

'Are you certain?' Juliana asked.

'As certain as I can be,' Josiah admitted cautiously, throwing Sebastian a look which said: *I understand your reluctance.*

Everything within him wanted to rage; to shout: *what's the point, just another useless clue to chase, like some will o' the wisp in the dark of night.*

He wanted to cast that locket into flames, demand everyone return where they belonged, and forget this quixotic quest, but instead, he controlled his impulses, and nodded.

'Searching records would be searching for the pro-verbial needle,' he said carefully. 'We have her name, but not his. That's if we could even access records, and they were complete. As for the chance of anyone recognising him…'

Josiah and Juliana exchanged a glance, which Se-bastian fought hard not to be jealous of, complicit, and conversational as it was.

'His lordship will help, unquestionably,' Josiah said finally, and Juliana nodded.

'Spencer could get us access.'

Clenching his jaw, Sebastian pondered his options, of which there were two: *allow another to help, end it here.*

'We've no idea where the trail will lead. If there's even a trail to be found. Rourke will wonder at a sud-den departure, and I won't leave you here alone,' he said, and a small smile graced Juliana's face.

'I'll go,' Josiah said. 'I told you, I'm talented at un-earthing things. Wherever the trail leads, *if* there's one to be found, I'll keep you informed, and you can decide whether to join me. If you discover anything here, you can keep me informed,' he added lightly, and for the slightest second, Sebastian almost felt he had a friend, and that they were merely three jolly companions, off on an adventure.

If only this tale were of that sort.

'Thank you,' he nodded, and if Josiah was surprised by the overt gratitude, he didn't say.

'I'll ride with you to Barrow Heath, then depart immediately.'

Sebastian and Juliana nodded, and Sebastian opened the carriage door, helping Juliana in, before he and Josiah followed suit.

'Anything I should pass on to his lordship, or her ladyship?' Josiah asked Juliana once they'd set off again, the mood ever so strange.

'That I am well. Tell Elizabeth I miss her.'

'Of course.'

'Thank you, Josiah.'

They fell silent after that, the strange mood thickening in the air.

As they arrived at Barrow Heath, dropping Josiah at the inn, then setting off again, Sebastian realised it was disbelief, mingling with hope; it had trickled back into him, despite everything.

Apparently none of us have learned our lesson.

Only the next time the hope was killed, he knew it would be a thousandfold more devastating.

Chapter Seventeen

Staring at herself in the looking glass as she brushed her hair, preparing for bed, Juliana spied precisely what she'd seen in Sebastian earlier: *wariness of hope.* It was easily recognisable; she knew it very well, having seen it in the eyes of countless people over the years. Ginny, Spencer, Elizabeth, their family, their friends, and so many more.

All people who had suffered the misfortunes and vicissitudes of life, who, when offered a chance to hope for something *wonderful*, found they couldn't believe. Not hoping, not believing, was safer, kinder, than facing likely inevitable disappointment; a return to the unsatisfying status quo.

Juliana had spent nearly two decades forcing herself to believe that the past was past. Choices had been made; truths lost for ever. What was done was done; the dead were dead. Sebastian's reappearance, her agreement to join this search for the truth, hadn't changed that belief; merely increased her discomfiture of acceptance. Her friends' strength might've inspired her to return, and confront the past; search for the truth, protect Rourke—and Sebastian—from harm. However, though she'd given this investigation her all, she'd never truly believed they could *actually* succeed.

Until the locket.

It felt like another moment tangled by Fate; whom she lent no credence to yet couldn't dismiss. When that locket had been placed in Sebastian's hand, preserved for nearly twenty years, it had felt like every other moment Fate had tangled in her life.

When I first saw Sebastian in church.

When I first set foot in Hadley Hall.

When Ginny met Spencer.

Monumental moments, when she'd sensed her life changing course; or perhaps simply find its proper one. Fate crying out: *here is your chance, seize it!*

Hope felt undeniable now; something thrust upon her unwillingly. She *had to* hope Josiah would find the key to unlock this mystery. Not for herself, and perhaps not even for Sebastian, but for Alice, and Bertie. Two innocent souls, who deserved to be more than grim footnotes; to have more than a headstone mark their brief spells on this earth. She had to hope she would *know* them, so she could remember them for the people they were, not those she'd imagined. They deserved to be more than their deaths, and for that alone, she had to hope they could actually succeed. Though she also had to fear the hope, the answers they would find, because somehow she knew, they would be…

Terrible.

She had to fear arriving at the end of this journey, triumphantly holding those answers up to the world, because *what next?* What came after? What would become of her, Sebastian, Rourke, this place?

It was what she'd feared from the beginning: the unknown Juliana. An unknown version of herself, with an unknown path to travel. She yearned to return to Ginny, to them all, to her life; she yearned for everything to return to how it was, because she'd been *all right*, had moments of happiness, and been content. Yet she also didn't want to go back.

Being back here, for all the dreadful, atrocious memories, had also reminded her of all the good memories, and those dreams she'd once had. Of everything she'd wanted from life, who she'd wanted to be; regardless of Sebastian. Dreams had kept her spirit alive, even before she'd met him. They'd been a flame of hope, which she'd nurtured, with dreams of a life of adventure, learning, discovery, and *joy.* All things that as she'd told Sebastian she *could've* had. It had only ever been her preventing herself from accomplishing her dreams.

When she'd left Stag House, yes, she'd needed money, but stubborn, resourceful, intelligent as she was, had she wanted to live, she could've. Instead, she'd denied herself, going into everlasting mourning. Instead of honouring Sebastian's memory by living she'd let herself die away, killing what was left of him along with herself. Despite all the good she'd found, she couldn't deny she had regrets; regrets which pierced her soul more with each day here. And she knew, when this was all over, she would face a choice again: *return to the home I found*, or *leap into the unknown*.

A choice made more complex for the realisation she'd had, outside the shop, but also a thousand times since his return, that hers and Sebastian's love had not been mere *youthful love*, but true, everlasting, profound love. Despite not growing with him, knowing all his life had been, she'd always known his heart. And she still loved him, felt that love alive, and reviving more with every passing day within her breast. She'd felt it even before she realised; shifting and transforming, with every moment spent with him. Alive, as it ever was, simple, yet echoing, and transcendent. Confusing, for she didn't know what the Hell to do with it.

Accepting it didn't change the past, or opaque future. Accepting it didn't magically heal and resolve everything between them; mean they could sail off into the sunset together. Sebastian likely wouldn't want it, or her—no matter what his eyes seemed to say at times. They'd been living in a falsity of their own creation; actors playing a role too well.

Besides, the truth was… She didn't want her love, *him*, to factor in what decisions she eventually made for her future. She wanted to make them for herself, as she always yet never had; though love also meant factoring in others. And *this* love, entwined in every fibre, could affect her decisions, which terrified her.

She wanted to deny it, preserve herself as she had thus far. For all she'd encouraged Ginny to love again, not bury herself and reject happiness, Juliana wasn't ready to mind her own words. Even if she knew refusing this love...

Means rack, and ruin; desolation and true everlasting damnation.

'Juliana?' Blinking, she saw her reflection again, the brush stuck in the middle of her hair. 'If you're not finished, I'll make myself scarce again, however you've been sitting there nigh on half an hour,' Sebastian said.

Finishing that last stroke, she set the brush down.

Everlasting damnation...

'It wasn't childish love,' she said quietly, staring at the brush. 'It was youthful love, yet also everlasting love. I tried to rid myself of it for eighteen years. Even in those specks of time when I managed to convince myself you'd done what they said, were the monster they purported, truly believe for *one second* you were guilty... Even then I loved you. It hasn't grown with a shared life, but it has grown, with every breath. I may pray at the altar of science, and rationality, yet I cannot deny my conviction that our souls were enmeshed before we ever met, and nothing either of us, nor the world could ever do, can change that.'

'What are you saying, Juliana?' he breathed, and incredulity and a desperate need for certainty in his voice.

'I loved you then, with all I was,' she said, turning

to him. He stood ramrod straight, his fists clenched, eyes shining mercury in the gloom; alight with hope and confusion. *How often do those two conspire?* 'I'm saying I've loved you all my life, and love you now, despite wishing it weren't so. I'm saying... I always knew, Sebastian. I always knew it wasn't you,' she choked out, tears streaming down her cheeks.

They were the words she'd never had the courage to speak, having always known they would change her life, change *her*.

Realising now, that this damning confession was to be made to Sebastian alone, in this world or the next; though her belief in the latter remained debatable. He alone was to be judge, jury, and executioner and make of her what he would.

Though I wonder if I believe this to justify my heretofore cowardice.

Either way, the die was cast; the time for illusion, dissimulation and fantasy now well ended. They were coming to journey's end, she could feel it in her bones, and she wouldn't wait to speak *these* truths; risk Sebastian disappearing from her life again without having heard them. He'd given his courage, his strength, to her so she might heal from the past, the least she could do was repay that mighty gift.

Even if it drives him from me now rather than at the end of this road; for parting is not an unknown variable.

All truths must be revealed before it's too late; who I am to become will be decided in this moment.

* * *

When one expected the worst of everyone, having seen the worst humanity had to offer, one was rarely surprised. Yet with a few seemingly simple words, strung together in innocuous sentences, Juliana had shocked him to his very core. He was a sailor standing on the bowsprit, watching as a crushing wave engulfed him into the watery depths; an explorer standing frozen on the mountain's craggy rocks, waiting for an avalanche to sweep him into white oblivion.

'I love you now.'

'I always knew it wasn't you.'

How can such words rearrange my entire being?

Everything he'd believed, built himself out of, was ground to dust, set alight, and tossed to the winds. He stood, frozen, her words reshaping his mind, heart, soul, and body; were he to move, his legs would doubtlessly give way.

Had it been possible, he might've felt joy, relief, or a sense of always having known the truth himself, but all he could feel was shocked.

'All this time…' he muttered, after what might've been minutes, or hours, searching Juliana's face for…

A clue this was a jest, that she was toying with him, or perhaps believed it only because of their current circumstances; yet his heart whispered that he'd seen the truth in her eyes that first night in Scotland.

'Weeks we've been here, and you said nothing. Why?'

'Eighteen years I battled my love for you, and the

knowledge of your innocence,' she shrugged, shaking her head, and angrily wiping tears away. 'Confessing…is not so easy. I know I should bear no guilt, for I couldn't have saved you, yet I do, and always will. My words may not have swayed the court, but you might've gone to the hangman knowing I loved you, believed you. All these years, I could've searched for the truth, but I didn't, because having proof it wasn't you, might've made *me feel worse*. I couldn't let myself see that the truth matters, no matter that the dead are dead, because it's about how we keep their memory alive. I never thought myself a coward, but I see now I've been one for a long time. I thought you hated me, for good reason. Admitting I never believed your guilt would've only added fuel to the fire, and I wouldn't have borne it. These past weeks, things have been… good, and coward that I am, I didn't want to ruin it. I convinced myself my helping you demonstrated I believed you.'

'So I must now bear the weight of this?' he shouted without meaning to.

He cursed himself when Juliana flinched, then realised his anger gave him the ability to move again, so he paced, trying to untangle the knots of emotion and…

Everything else.

'I never hated you,' he finally said, stopping before the fire, massaging his brow. 'I tried to. Told myself you should bear guilt for not believing me; for our love not being enough. I told myself loving you led to my demise; that hating you was the only cure for missing you so *goddamned much*. I channelled all my anger at the world for doing what it did to me, to Alice, to Bertie, to you, into that hatred, and it worked for a time; allowed me to survive. But as soon as I said those words in the carriage… I knew them as the lie they'd always been. I thought these past weeks had shown you… I never stopped loving you, Juliana. Only…'

He sighed, shaking his head before he turned back, to find Juliana looking as though *she'd* just been condemned to the gallows, and it tore, and scraped at him, leaving him more adrift than ever.

'What the Hell are we supposed to do with this?' he asked her desperately. 'I beg you, tell me, for I've no earthly idea.'

'Neither do I,' she whispered. 'But I'm tired of knowing things, and feeling things. All I want to know and feel is you.'

If her previous honesty had torn, scraped, and sent him adrift, there were no words left to describe what *that* honesty did to him.

Or what the sight of her rising, then summarily disposing of her nightclothes in one of the most courageous and vulnerable acts he'd ever witnessed, did to him.

Yes, you do.

It gives you life.

And though there were a great many reasons why he should deny her, deny them both, for how this indulgence might destroy them when time came for the chips to fall, he also knew that should he not seize this chance to love her for however much time he had, he would be undeniably cursed.

Who's the coward now?

'Damn you, Juliana,' he sighed, striding over to her. 'There'll be no chance to kill this love after this.'

'I know.'

As Sebastian strode over to her, as much resignation and passion in his eyes as there was vibrating through her, Juliana wondered if they'd ever had a chance of truly killing their love.

No...no chance at all, she decided as his hands slid across her cheeks to cradle them, with more delicacy and gentleness than the ferocity and determination of his manner suggested him capable of. Only, that contradiction between wildness and gentility had always been one of those special things about him. The goodness with an edge of danger; an edge which had grown in their years apart, making the tenderness even more striking.

That contradiction was present in all he was, and tangible in his kiss. In the way he delved into her mouth with exquisite verve and intention—a bite of animalistic passion—whilst his lips and tongue stoked and played, relearning and tempting; sweet, yet untameable. It was in the strength he held back, but poured into her skin, whilst his thumbs gently stroked beneath her eyes. Being with him thus again instantly settled her heart, and she clutched his shirt at the waist tight, bringing their bodies as close as possible.

It had been thus in the carriage, though she'd dismissed it, viewing the transformation he elicited within as dismissible. Now she saw that though there was unmistakeable compatibility, it was so rare it became exceptional. And she'd not had exceptional since they'd been young; not fully yet themselves. There were remembrances of those kisses and touches, however now the growth of their hearts and souls was felt in their connection. A certainty, a lack of hesitation; previously unpossessed self-knowledge. Suddenly, she wanted *everything*; to feel his skin along hers, to see all of him again, as she'd not yet had the chance.

Tugging at his shirt, she pulled it from his trousers, and he groaned though they barely parted for a second as she divested him of it, as though he couldn't bear not touching her. A sentiment she shared, and a problem she remedied by tangling her arms around his neck before his shirt even touched the ground, exploring his mouth this time, though she paused, realising perhaps she shouldn't hold him there. Leaning back slightly, she forced him to look at her, his gaze as clouded with desire as her own. Silently, she asked him, and he merely grinned, that crooked, dangerous sly smile that made her heart race, and took hold of her waist, lifting her so she could wind her legs around him. She peppered his cheeks, brow, and beard with kisses, nipping gently at his lips as he carried her to the bed, the contrast between his slick skin, and the roughness of his trousers, enticingly teasing her already excited self.

Laying her down at the foot of the bed with slow, exquisite yet torturous gentleness, Sebastian languidly rose, his eyes tormenting and igniting her already vibrant nerve endings as they travelled across her face, cataloguing every detail, his lips following swiftly behind; as though deciding which part to feast on next. Brows, eyelids, the skin between ear and cheek, the dip between jaw and chin, then straight down her throat, his tongue flicking lightly against the most sensitive spots—remembered, and learned anew. Down further, in the hollow of her throat, the top of her breasts, her nipples—at which point her irregular, shallow gasps of breath quickened—teasing, and relearning her body, perfunctorily, but without any aim to finish soon.

Onwards he went, and with every touch, she taught him, guiding with every stretch, buck, and sway. Fingertips grazed the space above her stomach, whilst lips and breath tickled the side of her ribs. Further still, across her stomach, along her hips, and just above her sex, when he finally rose fully, and Juliana's eyes focused on the sight he presented.

He'd changed. It wasn't about comparison, but his body was now as she'd suspected—possessing the lean, sculpted tightness of a fighter, beneath the bronze tinge of many days in the sun. In the firelight, he glowed like Apollo, and the sheer magnificence, power, and love she held for him, stole her breath. As did the lust, and unbridled passion mingling with heart-rending softness in his gaze—his eyes darkening to near black. Adoration was written upon him, and she hoped he could see how she adored him; ever would, and ever had. It might've frightened her had she still possessed the ability; only she didn't. Not tonight.

He must've seen, for he nodded slightly, raking his hair back with a look that suggested he knew well how positively roguish and enticing he was, and she grinned, laughing.

The laughter. I'd forgotten…

Sebastian grinned too, also recalling their gift for that, then did away with those last remaining garments, and neither of them were laughing any more. Lifting a hand, she beckoned him, and he granted her wish, prowling onto the bed and over her, until he was safely nestled between her legs, some of his weight on his forearms as he safely caged her in, and they were chest to chest, belly to belly, skin to skin again. The renewed connection, his weight and feel overwhelmed her; how much she'd missed it, too. She drew as deep a breath as possible, Sebastian's fingertips stroking the sweaty strands of hair beside her ears, holding her gaze, anchoring her, as he too acknowledged the weight of *them*.

Holding fast to his waist with one hand, with the other she traced the lines of his face—new and old—before raising her lips to his, kissing him reverently, savouring his taste, and the scratch of his beard, thicker than ever before. Her feet explored the hairs of his legs, as her sex grew readier to receive him, still nestled against her, undemanding yet enticing. It struck her deeper than ever before, their talent for moments of mere appreciation and mindless exploration amidst infinite passion. Pleasure without an end goal; often more intimate than a race to ecstasy.

They remained thus, breathing, kissing, and feeling, for a long time; the sounds and scents of their connection filling the room. Slowly they shifted, somewhat mindlessly, rolling and coiling until they faced each other on their sides, still, barely a hairsbreadth apart. Pausing their endless kiss, Juliana met those now near-black eyes, so steady, and bright with tenderness and love, and reached between them to position him where she desired him most. One breath, one kiss, one twist of his hips, and he was home again, inside her; and, oh, how her body rejoiced to entwine with him again.

They set the pace together; in the carriage he'd relinquished power and control to her, relinquished himself, which she hadn't realised how grateful she was for until now, too overwhelmed by the transformative qualities of any experience with him. As this one was, albeit infinitely more painful, and stunning in its pernicious slowness. They moved together, rediscovering, and learning anew, how to elicit the most incredible sensations. It was at once a lazy drive, each stroke drawn out so tidily it was maddening and addictive; blended with pure lust and pleasure. Slickness dripped from those most intimate places, and every pore, the heat creating an exquisite haze.

Breathing shallowed into determined pants.

Kisses became messier, and quicker.

Still, their eyes held the connection.

Juliana couldn't be certain of where limbs, hands, or toes were; it was as if they touched everywhere all at once. At least until she sensed him nearing completion, and he sought out her bud with his thumb. Then, she became acutely aware of all of him, and her flaming cheeks, as he drove her higher and higher, forcing her to the peaks of ecstasy before he could reach them.

His strokes lost none of their lazy pace, dragging the depths of her every time, yet there was a drive in his gaze, a challenge for her to be fulfilled.

'Come with me,' she whispered, holding tighter to everything; coiling tighter around him. Her mind had room for that last rational thought, for which she thanked it. 'It's as safe as it can be, though I understand if you can't risk it.'

His response was merely to devour her whole, their gaze still holding; though she couldn't focus on anything but the light in his eyes, and then, the light in her whole body, as he brought her to the highest peak of pleasure. He followed not long after her body finished grasping him tight—inside and out—and the final wracks of rapture still echoed through her.

And so they lay panting, touching, sweaty, and slick, staring at each other.

Entwined and enmeshed, as our hearts and souls have always been.

There will be no killing this love.

Whether that was a blessing or a curse… She'd never settled on an answer; and doubted she ever would.

His eyes and love were ever the only answer I needed.

Chapter Eighteen

As they lay together in a tangle of linen and limbs after having loved each other again, softer, more languorously than before, Sebastian found he couldn't stop *touching* her, looking at her, devouring her with all his senses; his fascination with this being that was Juliana at its zenith.

There was incredulity too, that he was here with her, not in dreams, but in this life of so much loss; though mostly it was that eternal fascination for all that composed her. He'd been fascinated since he was a boy—seen her, admired her, studied her for years— but particularly after that day in church. He'd never known it meant so much to her, and instead believed he alone had felt as if his chest had been struck by some mighty blow on high. There had always been this ethereal, unreal quality about Juliana, as though she were a creature of another world, another time, come to visit. Once they'd come to know each other, as strangers, then friends after her father's death, when she began sharing her freedom and knowledge with him, before finally becoming sweethearts…every day there'd been something new to fascinate him.

All that remained, tinged with his incredulity at being granted the chance, for a flicker of time, to love her again, along with new fascination, awe and wonder, at this new Juliana. The woman, in mind, spirit, *and* body, for there was no denying he was struck dumb by her widened hips, softened belly, riper breasts… The lushness of her womanhood. No, he certainly wasn't immune; just as his cockier self was pleased to note Juliana had seemed rather pleased with all *his* mortal coil had become.

Before there was passion; I wonder what it should be called now…

As young lovers, there had been unbridled exploration and eagerness; fun, and love. In the carriage, there'd been remembered desire and knowledge, but now… There was previously unknown settledness and surety in how they were, and because of their separation, layers upon layers of longing and need…

Spellbinding.

Just as these freckles he was currently mapping on her arm, his head resting neatly on her delectable breasts, were; constellations special to the universe of Juliana. She mapped the marks on his back—scars and birthmarks alike—lightly, yet with repetition and warmth that spoke of his same fascination. The same desire to commit the new knowledge to memory; lest it be lost for ever.

The need to remember every nuance for soon, memories alone will remain of us.

Shivering, he pushed that unhappy thought away; it had no place in this night.

'Tell me more of your life,' Juliana prompted quietly. 'I've longed to ask, but, we shared much, so quickly, then needed time...'

He nodded against her breast, taking a breath, preparing as he too was unaccustomed to this exercise, and felt the strain of fear, and uncertainty of where to begin; all of it so sweet and wondrous, yet intertwined with bitterness and regret...

As life is. You're safe; your name, life, heart, always safe in her hands.

'After... I went to Ireland,' he told her, focusing on her velvet skin, and the jasmine of her scent. 'Took what work I could, on ships, docks, farms...making my way the length and breadth of it. It's as green as they say, and when the rain falls on the cliffs, and the sea rises up...it's as though you're traversing the veil into the faerie land.' Juliana drew a deep breath, and he smiled against her skin, letting her imagine it. 'That's what I remember most, though I hated the beauty then. I hated that it was a place we'd wanted to go; that it was so close, yet so far from England. I lost myself and mightn't have ever made it past that time had I not drunkenly joined a crew bound for the Azores. From there... I roamed the Continent—Portugal, Spain, France, Italy, Switzerland, everywhere we'd marked on our imagined Grand Tour—working where I could, more or less scrupulously. I had all this anger which served me well, when I could keep out of drink, which I couldn't properly until I crossed the Alps. The mountains…broke me and stitched me back together. The whistling of the wind. The thin, cold air, the sheer size of them… They sobered me up, though it took time.'

'I'm glad they put you back together. Gave you strength to carry on.'

Sebastian lay a grateful kiss against her skin before continuing.

'It was in Italy I realised how much money I had when I didn't drink it away, and there too I learned you'd been right. I was good with numbers, and my travels had taught me to read the hearts of men. Making money brought satisfaction but no fulfilment. I was still haunted by my demise, devoured by anger, only I channelled it into my own success, and by the time I reached Buda, about a decade ago, my reinvention as Thomas du Lac Vaugris was complete. I'd carried that name since I'd died, but never become the man we'd imagined. The Danube saw my…repurposing. I resolved to do good with the fortune I had then, and focused on reinvesting and speculating on companies and businesses which had worthwhile purposes. I went to Germany, yet no amount of success brought me peace, and that's when I began hiring investigators. Only I was too close to England, too tempted to return, so I exiled myself to Constantinople. But that was yet another place we'd dreamt of seeing, and it was on the Bosphorus I realised I'd run for seventeen years, yet remained incapable of escaping you, and my past. I began making my way back, resolved to finish what my investigators had failed at, determined to...' *See you again, see my father again, clear my name.* 'Find peace, or die trying,' he said instead, which perhaps meant the same.

'Don't,' Juliana reprimanded, the hand he was currently toying with curling to hold his fiercely. 'I watched you die once, Sebastian. I won't again.'

Leaning down, he kissed her fingers tenderly, then turned over so he could see her face again.

His heart pinched, then smoothed out like honey, the love and conviction in her beyond compare.

'As you command, milady.'

'Precisely,' she nodded, raising a brow, and he laughed, heartily; her following his lead a moment later.

My love, only you could make me laugh now.

'I'm glad you saw him again,' she said softly after a while. 'Your father.' He nodded, his heart hurting again as he recalled that meeting. 'I thought to find him many times. There was so much I wished to say, but everything happened so quickly after your arrest, and then you died, and I was...unwell... By the time I had the means to find him, I had no courage. I thought he'd hate me, and I knew he would remind me too much of you. I'm sorry he didn't know you in the end.'

'I might've told him, only it felt crueller. He'd suffered enough. Lived a quiet life, by all accounts, without need, and that was something. I too thought often, of finding him earlier, returning to England, if only to tell him, again, and again, that I hadn't done it. *True* cowardice stopped me. When I had the means to, I ensured he was without need, and he was, without my helping hand, though some days I wished he hadn't been, for it might've assuaged my guilt at having left him, and you, to suffer my demise whilst I found success.'

Juliana merely nodded, and he was immensely grateful; there was nothing to say, to change his thoughts, which though they made perfect sense, made none at all.

But then in a situation such as his, exceptions could be made for irrationality.

'May I ask how you survived?'

Sebastian stiffened, though knew that question would eventually arise, and he knew he could refuse, however...

I am safe; she deserves all I can give of myself.

'Luck and mercy,' he told her, pushing past the lump in his throat which always returned when recalling those moments.

The before, the after, those were easier—not easy, *easier*—whereas the moment he'd been given a chance to live again was overwhelming; perhaps the only thing to keep some manner of humanity alive in him.

Remembering that there was *good* in the world, and you could either preserve it, perpetuate it, or let yourself shrivel and be consumed by darkness.

'They took me down quicker than they were meant to. Whether because of the cold, or because they thought the job done… I'll never know. All I know, is that a surgeon came to fetch my body,' he said, the words difficult to string together, yet easier if he focused on Juliana's warmth, and scent enveloping him. 'A surgeon my father and I knew—he'd grown up near Burndsey—though to call us friends would be overstating the acquaintance. He'd followed my case closely, didn't believe my guilt, and was a rather devout man of God, as well as a radical who thought justice in this country…flawed. When he inspected me, realised my heart still beat, he saw a miracle. He bought himself a few moments alone, and gave me something to ensure I remained insensible until he got me out. Once he had, he took me to his private rooms, and later told his superiors the body'd been stolen on the way. I don't think he would've told me any of it, had I not been so insistent. I remembered the drop, then I woke in warmth, believing it Heaven, until I saw him, and his jars and books, and tools… I had so many questions, I wanted to cry, begged him to just let me die, send me back… I couldn't believe I'd survived, and that he wasn't a demon torturing me with promises of life, and yet, I knew it was real…'

Inhaling a sharp, but deep breath, Sebastian turned his eyes to the bed's canopy, tears trickling from his eyes.

Juliana wiped them away gently, and he found the strength to finish.

'He bathed me, clothed me, fed me, and when I could stand upright, he gave me coin, and sent me into the night. I had so many questions I couldn't ask, for I had no voice, and barely the mind to comprehend what happened, or why he saved me. I kept thinking: *this, this is the greater mistake, that I'm alive.* Yet I walked into that night, and didn't rectify it.'

'Did you tell him? Who you were, ask him those questions when you found him again?'

'Yes. He laughed,' Sebastian told her, chuckling as he recalled that night, so similar to that which had seen his rebirth, when he'd knocked on the doctor's door in Manchester, where the good doctor had gone to see those swept up in the madness of industry had help. 'He said he'd always hoped I'd visit. We sat together a long time, and told each other of our lives. He thanked me for my assistance over the years—anonymous donations to his various endeavours he realised then had been from me. And when I asked him why he'd done it, with no assurance of my innocence, he merely said: *"You did good with your life. Beyond what you did for me, and those I help, you did good."* That was enough for him; though I don't know it will ever be enough for me.'

'Perhaps someday, once we've found answers, you'll have a chance to sit with him again. Perhaps we both will. Perhaps it will be enough then.'

'Perhaps.'

They both fell into silence for a very long time, their minds and hearts ingesting all that had been shared.

Both realising what they couldn't entirely comprehend: that somehow, they could love each other again
in every way, be together, if only briefly.

*And in that, there's hope, miracle, and Fate—no
matter our disbelief in them.*

Chapter Nineteen

If he hadn't lost his faith, he might pray now, for God to grant him peace, a reprieve from the heaving anger tearing him apart; or at least, for a promise, that when his time was spent, he'd be forgiven clutching to anger to the last.

He wished he could release it. Not march to the gallows with anger and fear in his heart; be the stronger, better man. If not forgive, then accept his unchangeable fate.

Nineteen years he'd lived. Longer than some; less than others.

Was there any order, any plan?

He doubted it.

If there was a plan, a God, a supreme being, he'd be allowed to walk up those steps, to that platform, with if not peace, then love in his heart.

If there was a greater design, the designer wouldn't strip love from him; not whilst taking his life. It wasn't that it wasn't fair, it was that it went against all the good books said.

Love, above all.

But the world, God, all of them, had stolen his love. Maculated it.

That was why he couldn't release his anger.

He saw nothing, felt nothing, heard nothing, but cold, and his own breathing, and the rattle of irons as he was marched out, alone, for winter had been cold, and harsh, desperation and crime were rife, but a devil murderer such as he shouldn't ever taint those other criminals, who might have a chance at Salvation.

He didn't—he'd been promised he would writhe in hell-fire.

He wanted to scream that he was already in Hell.

He wanted to tell the holy man praying and promising forgiveness he didn't believe him.

He wanted to reassure the executioner, and the guards too.

Tell them not to worry—his punishment was already underway.

He declined the head covering, refusing to go out without feeling the crisp wind on his face; they didn't argue.

He wouldn't turn away from this travesty even if everyone else would, even the mighty Creator of worlds.

The rope scratched and itched, heavier than expected.

Or perhaps he'd tried not to give it much thought. Not praying for a miracle, but not quite knowing to think of such details.

It was his first time being hanged after all.

He almost smiled at that, realising the truth about gallows humour.

And then he saw her.

A wraith in black, towering above the others he couldn't see—even his father.

He could see her eyes, shining like black marble in the blurred, washed-out backdrop of the world.

It had only ever been her, shining brightly, against dullness.

He hated her. Hated them all.

Yet he loved her so much his heart broke anew, and he was terrified as never before because it was the end, he could feel it approaching, the drop. It was coming, and he wasn't ready because he still loved her more than life, and she was being taken from him, because God, Heaven, and Hell, none of it was real, he saw that clearly then, it would be over, and she would never know...

It wasn't him.

Their love wasn't tainted.

It was the only eternal thing, and he couldn't leave her alone.

He tried to tell her, not breaking her gaze in those final few shreds of seconds before he fell, and he couldn't breathe, and the world was blackness, and he couldn't see her eyes, and this was the end.

Only, it wasn't.

Not quite.

* * *

'I've been thinking,' John said, lowering the shot-gun, and turning to Sebastian whilst the dogs and gamekeeper collected the downed fowl. Sebastian blinked, clearing his eyes and mind, reflexively moving his neck, to reassure him the rope he felt still was only a figment of his dire memory.

'I'd like to talk business, if it isn't too *gauche*. I've never had the mind for speculation, and cannot say I've ever met anyone running such schemes I'd trust with a ha'penny. However, you've a frankness about you I appreciate. A quality which means, I'm certain, you'll tell me if you've no interest in such conversations,' he grinned.

Sebastian smiled as he pondered the man's proposition, releasing this was likely the reason for today's shooting expedition.

Not that there had to be a reason—they'd all spent rather a lot of time together since he and Juliana had arrived—only this was perhaps the first time it had been *gentlemen only*.

Who would've thought. Just the three of us, John, myself, and Rourke.

It was certainly jarring, though admittedly knowing John had perhaps had an ulterior motive to the expedition helped allay some of his nerves, if they could be called thus.

A very strange feeling for a strange day.

The fact that Sebastian wasn't particularly keen on shooting—as the *gentle folk* did, where it wasn't about the necessity of putting food on the table—didn't help, though knowing those birds they shot down would end up at table, did. It wasn't that he didn't know how to behave on such a jolly social afternoon either—he'd learned those lessons well—it was primarily that it felt like an afternoon between friends, and *that* was new.

Thinking of Rourke thus especially was.

It had been three weeks since Josiah's departure, and they'd had no word beyond a note advising he'd made it to London. Though Sebastian felt mired in mud, use-less—after the hundredth time going over the papers, Juliana stopped him, telling him they'd done what they could, and must wait before deciding next steps—and felt too that time was slipping through his fingers, be it in regard to this investigation, or his life as a whole, he also felt surprisingly at rest. He was trying not to worry, *trust*, which was difficult, but made easier by the time he had with Juliana. To love her, and know her, as he'd never had before. Freedom to, as well.

Especially that.

It wasn't stolen kisses in their woodland sanctu-ary, or furtive nights at the cottage. It was holding her hand in full view of the world, and kissing her when he liked. Rationally, he knew that was part of the fan-tasy he was losing himself in, which would shatter at the first sign of news from Josiah, but these past three weeks, he'd not had it in him to care about the end. The future. He grasped tightly to the now, and gave himself over to the dream.

Admittedly, Rourke had become part of that. The time they'd all spent, almost like a true family these past weeks—sharing meals, rides, walks, visits to tenants or livestock markets, or simply going on about their own affairs—it had been *good*. He'd got to know Rourke, as he had Juliana, and that was also part of his current torment. Because with every passing day, he began to hope more, *particularly*, as concerned Rourke.

He hoped with more might than he thought he had, that he'd been wrong. Though there were still moments doubt pricked his heart—the cold vacancy in Rourke's eyes ever occasionally present, as were similar moments of possessiveness to those that had made him initially uneasy—he pushed them away more readily. He hoped that Josiah would come back, with some third act turn, or *deus ex machina* explanation for what had happened to Alice and Bertie—that it had been her sweetheart, a jealous relative, *anything*—and that this would all end...

Without further injury to the living.

Be it Rourke or Juliana, for were I to have been right, you would pay a dear price, my love, and I would never see you harmed again.

Yet even as he hoped more, he despaired more. He felt a worsening sense of impending doom, of collapse. A sense none of them would leave this place unscathed. To boot, as good as things had been, there was no denying Stag House, Barrow Heath still emanated poisonous memories and gloom as a putrid factory might fumes. With every passing day, despite the smiles he gave her, Juliana continued to diminish. Rourke too.

Every day, he saw clearer and clearer, perhaps his true purpose.

To free her, Rourke, and myself from the past. From the hold of this place.

He'd always known this quest or whatever he was meant to call it was about more than him; looking at things starkly, he was alive. He'd survived; Alice and Bertie had not. So many lives beyond that had been changed. He'd thirsted for revenge, and yes, perhaps sought it, as he longed to have his name returned to him. But even once he'd cooled down, and acknowledged that it was about justice, first and foremost, he'd not quite *felt* the entirety of his purpose. Which was that those who'd lost their lives—their names and whole selves, for no reason, for none would ever be worth the price paid—deserved the truth. They deserved for their names and whole selves to be found.

And as for those who had suffered the past—that night, and the horrors preceding it, at least in Stag House—deserved to be free of it. They deserved to be released of this place, as neither Juliana nor Rourke were, in their own different ways.

So I find myself hoping the cost of the truth for the dead will not be paid by the living.

'I do hope your mind is as miles away as it appears,' John said, chuckling, and Sebastian returned to the present. *Where you should remain; as you well know.* 'And that expression isn't your response to my proposal.'

'It isn't, and my apologies. Speaking of business merely reminded me of things I must attend to soon,' he said, and John relaxed, nodding with a relieved smile as they continued on. 'As far as your proposal... Be warned I'm only as honest as the next man,' he added wryly, gaining a laugh from John that came out in breathy puffs as another shot sounded nearby.

They glanced down the treeline to their right, where Rourke was keeping to himself; either to allow John some time for this conversation, or merely because it was as it seemed, and Rourke was pensive today.

'I might claim to some worthiness, as I refrain from calling my investments *schemes* where possible,' Sebastian said, and they continued along, occasionally taking aim, and succeeding, or not, in furthering the spoils for future dinner tables. 'Are you looking for advice, or to invest in something together? If the first, I'm happy to oblige, the second... I wager only my own funds, alone.'

'We are well suited then, for it's the first I seek. You mentioned always seeking to invest in ventures you believe in, which is to be commended, and certainly changed my view of speculation.'

'If one doesn't believe in the venture one's investment will support, how can one justify profit? We live in an age of advancement, revolution, and progress. Those ventures we seek to advance, and support, must therefore be in line with how we want to shape the world; at least in my humble opinion.'

'I agree,' John nodded, taking down another grouse. 'Even on a smaller scale, such as my estate, or Rourke's, we must work together, towards the same goals. It isn't merely about working the land, but finding good people to do so. Keeping those in your care healthy, whilst preserving the land. The toffs might presume to lay claim to that, to England herself, but we too live off it, so we must tend to it.'

'My father used to say such things,' he smiled fondly, forgetting himself. 'Though he was a toff's son, so perhaps that's why,' he corrected.

'Trace any of us back far enough, and you'll find toffs for peasants, and peasants for toffs. But I'm happy you share such ideals. It's a small corner of the world we have here, but it is worthy. I seek to make it a place for my children—God willing we are blessed with some—and my tenants' children, and so on. I know your plans are being decided,' John said diplomatically. 'However, it isn't so terrible a place to settle, despite what you might've heard.'

Swallowing hard, Sebastian took aim, felling a duck; a life he would honour when he met the fowl at table again.

'So you heard Juliana and I were asking questions about that old affair,' Sebastian finally said, deciding to face things head-on.

They might've *paused* their interrogations, however no use denying, and perhaps it wasn't a subject to avoid, considering John's current role as local magistrate.

Good magistrates are hard to find, and one never knows when one might be needed.

'Everyone for fifty miles heard.'

The turn in conversation made them both pensive, and they rested their shotguns on their forearms as they meandered along the frosty, crunching ground.

'I understand the impulse, to enquire about such things. I don't know what Juliana shared, but it was an extremely trying time. For her, and Rourke.'

'She told me some. Of the loss of life, and the man she lost.'

Never to return again; for I am not him.

'We never want to think the worst of those we love. It doesn't help when rumour and fact tangle—be it in Barrow Heath, or Paris. As distraught as Rourke was when she left, once he knew she was safe, he saw it was for the best. Everything had calmed in recent years—until your return—though every few before that, there'd be some new tale being spread about those days. Someone would swear they'd seen the murderer, after years of silence, and that he'd had horns too, and next you'd hear how Rourke went to Scotland for nefarious purposes, when really, he went to find Juliana a doctor, unwell as she was. People have no shame.'

Despite wishing not to, Sebastian wondered if John referred to the same person as had told one of his investigators those same rumours of Rourke's Scottish escapade.

It's of no true import, we'll have answers soon, and this isn't the time or place.

'We didn't seek to disturb the dead,' he told John. 'Juliana's abrupt departure from Stag House left her with questions, and many things unresolved. I think she needs to be reassured, in some sense, it was as it was.'

'Understandable. She lost more than most that night, though you'd think it was Rourke, the way he speaks of what was taken from him. It's why he's so happy she's here. That you both are. It was a difficult way to part, and with his wife's death, he's been alone too long.'

'The two of you are gossiping as though on a Sunday walk,' Rourke interrupted, coming up to stand beside John, with a smile of camaraderie, and jesting. 'I hope your business has concluded, for our sport is suffering, and neither of our households will be pleased if we fail to provide sufficient sustenance.'

'We are for the time being,' Sebastian nodded.

Perhaps for ever, for who knows if I shall ever count John as a—

Present moment. No past, no future.

'Excellent,' Rourke smiled, patting John on the back to get them all moving again. 'Let's not disappoint our households. A few more birds should do it, but let's to it before the weather turns on us.'

So on they went, for that afternoon at least, friends united to fill larders.

Were that it could always be thus...far away from here.

Chapter Twenty

When Juliana, Ginny, and Elizabeth had first moved to Scotland, there had been a blissful period when time had slowed, and for perhaps the first time in many years, she'd felt she could truly breathe, and *live*, without thinking about moving on, to the next post, or challenge, or whatever it was. There had been other instances after Ginny had married Spencer, and that slowing of time had been one of the greatest comforts that life had offered.

There had been moments too, when time had stopped altogether, for instance after Sebastian's death. Only Juliana hadn't ever felt time crawling with pernicious, torturous yet delightful intensity as it did now.

No matter how enjoyable these past weeks had been, how lucky she felt to be reunited with both Sebastian and Rourke; no matter how dreamlike it was to be able to love Sebastian openly, how easy and natural it all felt... She couldn't deny these past weeks had felt like an endless trudge through gigantic drifts of snow; an endless climb to some great peak. And while Juliana had never breathed the mountains' thin air, she understood the deliriousness it could bring; how such a climb could make you forget reality.

Make her forget that she, Rourke, and Sebastian could never be a family as they were now. Rourke had stopped making comments about the future—perhaps reassured by their continued presence—but she regretted them, for they were a reminder, of what couldn't be. Every passing day robbed her of clarity, making the dream life she was stuck in ever more appealing. It made the infinite climb appealing, for she knew only pain and death awaited at the summit. She was caught between pleasure and exhaustion, and if something didn't change, she...

Well, she wasn't entirely certain what she would do. Part of her was tempted to just...*leave*. Pack her bag, say a fond farewell, and disappear again, except she was too far down the path to turn from it. Leaving now meant guilt, regret, and self-recrimination as never before; it meant *giving up*, and that wasn't in her abilities.

Failing is preferable to surrender. Accepting defeat takes strength.

Josiah will come through; or won't—either way we'll have direction.

Perhaps the most unsettling aspect of these past weeks had been her growing desire to be done with the pretence. She longed to tell Rourke the truth, to trust him, to have him on her—on *their*—side. To rebuild, rather than speak half-truths. The impulse was made worse by how Rourke embraced Sebastian, befriended him… It was all she'd ever longed for, and though they never spoke of it, she liked to believe Sebastian saw now, that Rourke couldn't be the culprit they sought.

There's a connection we're not seeing, but Josiah will find it. Then, our truth can be revealed, and we can all move forward.

However, in the meantime she knew telling Rourke anything would doubtlessly come at the cost of Sebastian's life, and Bertie and Alice's truth, and she couldn't risk either.

So we'll wait for Josiah, may his return be swift—

One wish whose utterance I regret, she thought grimly, her heart pounding and breath stilting when, sensing his gaze, she lifted her eyes from her book, and found Sebastian at the library's door.

'Josiah has returned,' she said flatly; the look on his face, resolute and apprehensive, along with the note in his hand, speaking volumes.

'I sent a return as soon as I received his note,' Sebastian told her, dissonance in his voice she recognised well. 'Asking him to meet after dinner. I didn't think you wished to wait until morning.' She nodded, knowing he'd set the meeting so soon for her, rather than himself. 'Juliana, I…'

'I know.'

Only she didn't.

She didn't know anything; nor believe any answers would illuminate her.

They will but further tangle my mind and heart.

* * *

Whether Rourke believed their tale about enjoying moonlit rides, or wished to leave a calm pot unstirred, Juliana neither knew nor cared. All that mattered was that they managed to leave Stag House without fuss, and were about to get answers. Even if only: *there are no answers to be found*. They would have *something*, with which to further proceed; hopefully, far away from here.

Perhaps even with Rourke by our side.

Though I still daren't fully hope, she thought, the flicker of the lone candle hypnotising and taunting, as they both stood around it by the fireplace of Sebastian's once home.

Rubbing her hands, she knotted her fingers, then blew into them gently, in a futile attempt to warm herself from a cold that had nothing to do with the brumal conditions. In a flash, Sebastian was there, taking her hands in his, surrounding her with his warmth and steadiness, and she leaned into him, taking everything he had to give; though she wondered how much he had.

For his fate most of all rests on this night. Doesn't it...?

'How can you be so calm?' she asked, her voice muffled by the layers he sported, and which did heat her cheek as she nestled in the crook of his shoulder. 'I feel my heart will give out, fast as it pounds just now.'

'I'm far from calm, Juliana,' he confessed quietly, wrapping his arms around her. 'I'm so terrified of what this night may bring I can barely walk, nor speak, nor breathe. These past weeks…have been glorious gifts, and yet every day I hoped tonight would come; even while I wished it wouldn't. Now I cannot but meet it; and you alone keep me from running scared into darkness again.'

Disturbingly, his own trepidation reassured her, and she clung to him tighter.

They remained there a long while; though all too soon they heard the crunch of Josiah's arrival, and separated, turning to the doorway, as their hands linked.

One glance at Josiah's shadowed face, worn by days of sleeplessness and travel, along with something else—*life-changing, incomprehensible answers*—and Juliana stilled, bracing herself.

'Evening,' Josiah greeted with a nod, attempting pleasant casualness. Failing for his honesty as he made his way towards them. 'I trust you've kept well. The family send their regards, and Elizabeth misses you,' he added with a small smile to Juliana.

'Josiah…' she breathed, pleading, and he nodded.

'I'm sorry. I know you've both been on tenterhooks, awaiting news, and I swear it wasn't my intention to remain silent. However, what I discovered in London…' He grimaced, shaking his head, and Juliana wanted to shake him; shake it all from him, even as she was frozen in place. 'I couldn't reveal what I'd learned there, without being certain of its meaning. And I couldn't lie, and send reassuring platitudes either.'

Sebastian's hold tightened, as Josiah reached into his

coat, extracting a leather pouch, which he reluctantly handed over to Sebastian.

With a kiss to her temple, Sebastian released her to open it, and extract the papers therein, though Josiah didn't wait to illuminate them.

'His lordship got me access to the records, though I mightn't have found a name had it not been for the old chap there. He put me in contact with others from the regiment, who remembered the lad in the portrait,' Josiah said regretfully, as Sebastian paled. Juliana couldn't see what he saw, not that she tried, merely watching his face, and listening to Josiah. 'They remembered him, how he spoke of his wife, Alice. I went to Suffolk to ensure there was no mistake, and I had friends up north dig up further records. There mightn't have been any to find; a man was asking about the same records some years ago, but the parson grew wary. He told him records from before the turn of the century had been lost in a fire, and to be safe, he hid them, for which he was glad, as there was a burglary not long after. The man disappeared, but the parson kept the papers, knowing they had a dear price. I am sorry, Juliana.'

The way he said that...

'What was his name?' she asked, tears gathering; for her heart knew the answer before he breathed the words.

'Christopher Myles,' Sebastian finished so Josiah wouldn't have to, and she shook her head furiously.

'It can't be, it can't mean what either of you are thinking, it makes no sense—'

'There are records, Juliana,' Sebastian said harshly, meeting her eye, the papers raised in his hand. It didn't make sense, any of it, least of all the regret in his gaze, the pleading, the lack of satisfaction... 'Records of a marriage in Scotland, in 1787, between Robert Florian Myles, and a woman called Mary, which had for issue, in 1788, a son named Christopher. A record of the death of Mary Myles, in 1794. There is no question. Christopher was your half-brother, and your father's marriage to your mother was invalid, having been celebrated in 1793.'

'I know what it means,' she hissed, tearing herself away from both of them to pace. It didn't... It *couldn't*... 'Rourke couldn't have known. The day before Alice and Bertie died, we were in Burndsey, all day. He wouldn't have met her. He *didn't know*, and even if he had, he wouldn't...'

'Christopher Myles passed away in the Walcheren campaign,' Josiah stated reluctantly. 'Alice had no family, but by all accounts, she managed well enough until Bertie was about five. Work dried up, there were harsh seasons, and she might've gone to a city, only she was concerned about Bertie's health. They were well-known in the village, as was Christopher's mother, who moved there from Scotland the year your father remarried, and people tried to help, only Alice was set on giving Bertie a proper chance. No one knew the specifics, only that Christopher had always hated speaking of his father, and that Alice left to find distant relatives who might help her when things became untenable. It fits—'

'It doesn't fit! It doesn't make *sense*. I will not believe my brother did this! I cannot!' she shouted, stopping her pacing to stare at them both, half pleading, half challenging.

'You can, because you must,' Sebastian said quietly, a deadly seriousness in his voice that felled her.

There were no more words.

There was no more breath in her body, no more anything. She had to leave, to…

Run.

And so, run she did, out into the cold night, the men's shouts and calls echoing in the welcoming darkness as she ran onwards. Her lungs tearing with icy knives; tears streaming down her face. Warring with herself, as she tried to piece it together—what Josiah had brought, and everything they'd had—trying to find holes, mistakes, yet unable to focus, for her heart pounding, her gut telling her: *Sebastian was right.* She wanted to be ill, to scream, and run until she reached the ends of the earth, but she only reached the hill where Alice and Bertie had died, and that was the end of the earth, wasn't it?

So in the crystalline, sparkling, and bright moonlit night, she screamed until her voice gave way, and then arms surrounded her again, pulling her close, and she screamed some more.

No.
I cannot believe it.

In those long moments during which he held fast, and held her tight, not imprisoning nor limiting, merely stabilising, Sebastian felt every crack of Juliana's heart, every sorrow, every doubt, every stab of anger and desolation, as if his own. For they were now, his; had always been, and would always be.

Such is love.

Many times he'd imagined this moment.

Well, not this one exactly, but the moment the truth was known to him. Not even revealed to the world—that was an entirely other moment—merely to him. When all his own questions were answered, and he could, if not live in peace, then have some reason for his and others' suffering. He would know there *was* reason; that it wasn't merely senseless chaos.

That moment would be triumphant. Cathartic, and magnificent; as mighty and powerful as those trumpets he'd once believed would sound at the end of days. It would be beautiful, and he would be…*happy.*

What a fool I was.

In his heart, he'd always known the answer lay with Rourke. He'd wanted to doubt, for Juliana, and himself; for this man that might've been *his* brother. Yet he'd seen, known, and hoped, only…

There wasn't merely opportunity in design.

The rest of the supposed evidence that had been twisted to suit the narrative could've just been Rourke taking advantage of the situation to be rid of him. But the weapons, even the location of the murder, and now Scotland…

None of it matters.

You always knew what the cost would be, and still you imagined the moment might be wondrous.

He'd always known that whether or not he was in love with Juliana, he loved her. Finding Rourke to be the culprit, would always destroy her; in a way believing Sebastian himself guilty never could. He'd always known part of the sacrifice for the truth would be Juliana's heart, and had he allowed himself to fully realise that before returning, he knew now he would've let it lie. He would've died with the nocent stain on his own soul, for her.

Good then that I didn't, for the truth was never mine; but Alice and Bertie's.

Its sacrifice was never mine to make or not.

And so now they would both be filled with sorrow and pain—for Sebastian felt it too, not just hers, but his own. Still, part of him wanted to be wrong, to believe as she did there was *something else*, so that the man he'd come to know, become friends with…

Won't share my fate of old.

Though obviously exhausted, he felt Juliana straighten, regaining some of her strength, for another battle, and he slackened his hold so she could turn in his arms, but he didn't dare release her; not trusting her quite yet to hold steady alone.

'He couldn't know, Sebastian,' she repeated, as she

might for the next century, gazing up at him, a plea in her eyes for him to give her another truth. *I wish too, my love.* 'Even if he did there has to be another explanation,' she stated before he could remind her of all the chances Rourke would've had to discover what they had. 'I know you want to believe it, you've been convinced from the beginning, but you've seen it—he's a good man. He's never been violent, despite what Father did to us. He always protected me, there is no evil in him.'

'I don't want to believe it, Juliana,' he told her seriously. In the moonlight, on that frozen hilltop where two lives had been taken; and so much else after… was room only for truth. The sun's reflected rays cut through any remaining pretence; and it was under the moon's light their fate would be decided, as it had been eighteen years ago. 'I never *wanted* to believe it for the pain it would bring you. I see your heart breaking; I feel it, in my own chest. You're right, I've seen the man he is, and I prayed and wished as I haven't in years, that I was wrong. For it to end another way. For a miracle. But there is no other answer. Rourke *has* always protected you. Before, I believed merely from me, but now I see it was from so much more. Destitution, ruin, the loss of your home. Bertie was the rightful heir to all of it, and Rourke couldn't take that chance, not with you on the line, can't you see?'

'There was too much calculation,' she said fiercely, jerking out of his embrace. She stood a few steps away, needing distance; a glinting angel of dark doom. 'He would've had to know, *everything*, and plan, and at the very most I can see him hurting someone in anger, to protect me, but not as happened that night. His heart… it *is* good. Full of love—'

'For you, Juliana. If he believed Alice wanted to take *anything* from you…if he thought her child's existence threatened yours, merely by being born legitimately, whilst you were both found to be children of bigamy… He would do whatever it took.'

'He would've found another way! Killing a child…' The glint of incomprehension in her eyes, reflected tenfold by the moonlight, told him she wouldn't be convinced; not tonight, and not like this. He understood; the reason behind the crime bringing him comfort in its logic, whilst bringing her only more disbelief. 'He would've found another way. He wouldn't murder a child. I cannot believe that, and after these past weeks, surely neither can you.'

'Juliana…'

'I will not believe it unless I hear him say the words.'

'Fine,' he agreed, and she froze, expecting another way forward, even as she knew nothing could be done without Rourke's own admittance of guilt. 'A confession made without duress, in view of appropriate witnesses, would be the only thing to exonerate me. So let us make a plan to have the truth of that time from him, whatever it is, in full view of trusted witnesses.'

'Very well,' Juliana agreed, exceedingly reluctantly, yet aware there was no other choice. He saw it, the moment she admitted the battle was lost; still refusing to concede the war. *Would that I could hope still too.* 'We should have the magistrate present, however the question must be asked… Can we trust John to be objective, despite his connection to Rourke? I would, but then I fear my instincts aren't to be heeded just now.'

'He can be trusted to do the right thing, whatever that may be. We should have Josiah there, as well. His and your connection with the marquess might be required.'

Juliana grimaced; and he understood again her reluctance to involve them, to allow them to know the grim details of her past, yet it also smarted, for it reminded him all too brutally, that he was part of this life she would only ever strive to forget.

As she should; even if it means our time must come to an end again.

'We should get back to Josiah,' she nodded, the long sigh which followed misting her from view for the briefest second. She glanced around, hugging herself tightly, and though he yearned to comfort her, he resisted. 'A night so similar to this one,' she breathed, her eyes affixing on the distant shadow of Stag House. 'I might've seen them. It was clear then too. Even if I couldn't hear them, I might've seen… Just as I used to see you working here from my window. I wish now I could forsake them as everyone else has. But we alone remain to care for them, so we will see it done.'

If there was something to say to any of that, he knew not what it was.

So he strode over, took her hand, and together they

returned to the cottage; Sebastian vowing all the while, that they would see it done. And when it was, he would ensure Juliana could find happiness again; whatever sacrifice it may require, for that sacrifice was his to make.

One that I will make unhesitatingly.

Chapter Twenty-One

It took them three days to organise. Three long, un-ending days which were unlike anything Juliana had lived before. Demanding strength, resoluteness, and patience she was certain had all been used up and sto-len in the preceding days, months, and years. They de-manded the reserves she knew she must conserve; for it wasn't the end. The worst was inevitably yet to come.

The first morning after Josiah's return, she'd cried off everything, citing a terrible headache, which wasn't entirely untruthful. Her mind was too full to properly function, going around in circles, trying to find differ-ent answers, different solutions, all whilst she prepared to face Rourke. To look him in the eye, and pretend nothing was amiss, until the time had come; to not summarily demand answers. She spent the day look-ing through the papers Josiah had collected, wracking her brain again with the events of those days, eighteen years ago, trying to make any other sense of it. Un-fortunately, unless Rourke offered some miraculous explanation, she was beyond loath to admit, nothing else made sense.

Sebastian kept him at bay that day, though he reported back that obviously her brother was concerned, but he'd managed to stave him off checking on her. Sebastian too kept his distance, and had she not insisted, he might've gone to speak to John without her.

'Every step we take until the end of this, we take together,' she told him.

And he listened.

They went together on the second day, *sans* Josiah. Told John everything—except of Sebastian's true identity. They might think they could trust John, but they couldn't risk Sebastian's life again. There was shouting. Debates. Cajoling, and reluctant acceptance. All which bolstered Juliana, for she felt less alone in her staunch refusal to believe Rourke guilty. In the end, John agreed to their plan, for one of the same reasons she'd agreed to return—to prove Rourke innocent *and* uncover the truth.

The third day was the worst, for there was nowhere to go. Atrocious weather confined them at Stag House, and although she had moments of quiet solitude, when she didn't have to face Rourke, when she did… She thought she might give up the game, for she would just *study* him—from across the library, or across the table—and wonder: *could it be?*

Could you have done it, brother?

She would search for any hint that beneath the man she saw, there was one of hellish deviousness and violence. She would wrack her mind for any memory which might gift proof of precursors to his supposed acts that night Alice and Bertie died.

There was nothing.

That third day was as many following Sebastian's arrest had been. Filled with the same thoughts, doubts, fear, and conviction. She would return ceaselessly to the question: *if not him then who?* Wonder again, if she was so blind that she couldn't see such horrors, such evil, in anyone's heart.

Once, I sought to see evil. But as I was convinced then, so I am now; the books were right. At times it's too perniciously disguised to be recognised.

Though Sebastian was with her through this, it felt as if oceans separated them. They were, if not enemies, then in opposition, and all she really wanted, *needed*, was a friend solely on her side. Not on the side of truth and justice at all costs; merely present for her. She longed for Ginny, for a hug, for her friend's advice; though she knew as before, that were Ginny here she likely wouldn't say anything. Juliana would remain silent, push her away, for the same reasons she'd not told any of them anything before.

This task is mine alone. And so I shall face it, alone.

Chapter Twenty-Two

The plan in the end was simple, though it felt anfractuous, and for it, Juliana would indeed be alone. She would confront Rourke in the library with all they'd learned, knowing that were there to be a damning confession to be pried from his lips, she alone could extract it. And damning it would be to her and Rourke both; even as it spelt Sebastian's salvation.

Therefore I daren't hope he shall be saved—not by this truth.

Whatever truths came from Rourke regarding that terrible December night—she admitted there was *something* he had to share—they would be heard by Josiah, and John, posted with Sebastian in the tight confines of a disused servants' passage. A passage which had once been Juliana and Rourke's hiding place—until Father had discovered it. In any case, whatever Rourke had to say, would be heard.

It felt shameful. Deceitful, and underhanded, and Juliana despised it, even as she understood it was the only way. Rourke would say nothing with them all present, yet they needed to hear his defence. Witnesses were necessary; though invisible they must be.

Sebastian wasn't entirely thrilled with the plan either; he'd expressed concern over how Rourke might behave once confronted and cornered. Juliana had made it clear that it would be her alone, or nothing. She knew her brother would never hurt her; at least, she had as much certainty as anyone in her position would, considering their family history, and the history of men. And though she accepted Sebastian had the right to be there, to confront his once accuser, she'd returned to ensure neither came to harm, and having them in the same room would certainly see one or the other injured.

So here she was, standing vigil at the table by the fireplace, the papers Josiah had collected—and of which copies had been made in case—laid out instead of the chessboard, as she waited for Rourke to join her. Praying, as she never had, that this could all end...

Without the horrors I fear it will.

'You summoned, Juliana?' Rourke said, amusement and confounding in his voice. Looking away from the rain-battered window, she found him at the door, arms crossed, wearing a smile matching his tone. 'How very formal.'

Let this end better than I fear...

'We need to talk,' she nodded as he strode over to her.

'So serious, Juliana... What's all this?' he asked,

spotting the papers on the table; the very seriousness he commented on, diminishing his own amusement.

'I think you know.'

'I haven't the fathom of clue.'

'The truth of who Alice and Bertie were,' she said steadily. There was a flicker of something... The tic of his jaw... All minute; all which only she could've spied. *He knows something; he knew of this. Still it means nothing.* 'These papers are proof they were our kin; papers I know you sought to find in Scotland years ago. Tell me you didn't kill them, Rourke. Tell me it wasn't you, and I'll believe it. I see you know some of this, but I need the truth. This has gone on too long.'

'How did you get this?'

'I searched for it, and had a great deal of help.'

'From Thomas.'

'Among others.'

'This is why you came back?' he asked, hurt beyond what she would ever hope him to be; especially because of her.

Lying will only make it worse.

'Yes,' she admitted. 'And no.'

'You came back, not for me, not to be together again, but to dig up the dead,' he said, shaking his head, as though he couldn't recognise her, which clawed at her heart. 'All for a man who's been dead eighteen years, Juliana? Was I not enough? Was your new life not enough? I knew you hated me for showing you the truth of that beast, but to go so far as this, to punish me—'

'Enough lies, Rourke,' Sebastian said, gently, which made it worse, appearing at the door. Juliana glared at him, half murderous, half pleading; grateful that at least the others remained where they should be. *Please leave, my love, before this gets out of hand...* 'She's suffered enough. Let her go. Let them all have peace.'

'This doesn't concern you, Thomas,' Rourke spat, and she knew she was losing him with every passing second.

'Like Hell—'

'Sebastian, please!'

Years, she'd spent, learning to control her emotions, to hide everything for the sake of her survival, and that of those she loved, and in one instant of carelessness, she'd failed every lesson; let desperation, fear, and frustration win.

Closing her eyes, she took a breath, knowing she'd just condemned them to a future of horrors such as she'd feared. When she finally had the strength to re-open them, she watched as Rourke turned to study Sebastian, unbelieving even then. Time, along with her heart, and everyone's breath, stopped.

Then, heartbreak slowly replaced disbelief in her brother's eyes, more gutting than anger.

'Impossible,' Rourke whispered finally.

'Yet, here I stand, awaiting the true reckoning.'

'You...you did this, you poisoned my sister against me, as you did then. I thought you were my friend.'

'Rourke—'

'He was going to take you from me, Juliana!' Rourke

screamed, rounding back on her, tears in his eyes, and she shook her head desperately, her heart breaking as she finally saw.

Rourke killed them.

Sweet, beautiful, kind, gentle Rourke...

Tears gathered in her own eyes, as she begged him silently to take it back. To clarify, to deny he'd meant it thus, but the truth was clear as day, in his own eyes.

I was a fool blinded by love; however this story was written.

'I knew of your plans,' Rourke continued, breaking her heart more, and more, as she'd never thought it could be again. 'Heard you whispering behind hedge-rows, and in that place you'd go by the river. I let you indulge in what I believed a youthful tryst, because he made you happy, and I thought eventually you'd grow up. Only then, you made plans to leave me, and I...'

'I couldn't stay.'

'And what of me, Juliana! What of me? Did you even think to ask me to come with you? No! You were going to leave me here all alone! I'd already been so alone before you came along; you were all I ever had! We only had each other, until *he* ruined everything! And you,' he shouted, rounding on Sebastian. 'I welcomed you, like a brother, I loved you, and all this time you were waiting to betray me as before!'

Before she could even begin to fathom what was happening, Rourke was across the room, launching himself at Sebastian.

Everything inside her felt as if it was being torn out,

and set alight, right there, on the library floor, as they grappled and rolled, punching, biting, kicking, and clawing at each other like animals.

And as with many animals, she knew this fight wouldn't end until one of them was dead.

'Please, stop! Stop it!' she screamed, moving closer, but knowing too close and one of them would end up hurting her.

Neither would forgive themselves, and it would only end the same way.

They fought, men possessed, with ferociousness she'd never seen before nor wished to again. Still, she saw Sebastian held back, seeking only to defend against Rourke's more deadly intent, her brother's savagery surprising her; it was the same she'd never believed him capable of.

And that imbalance was the deciding factor.

Rourke gained the upper hand, pummelling Sebastian into the floor with unbreakable viciousness, just as John and Josiah appeared at the door. Juliana knew they wouldn't prevail in separating the two, so she gestured them to stop, and posted herself as close to the bloody mass as she could.

Someone give me strength to finish this, for still, it isn't over.

'Rourke,' she called gently, as she had so often when they were children, though tears streamed down her face now as they never had. 'Please, you'll hurt yourself.' Rourke froze atop Sebastian, at whom she daren't truly look for fear of seeing she was too late. 'He isn't worth it, my love.'

The words were brittle and sharp, but she knew it was the only way.

'I did it for you, Juliana,' Rourke cried, looking up at her, his mind both present, and faraway. She nodded, that too splitting her inside out, and lowered herself to her haunches, arms open to welcome him. He took the offering, and came to her, his bloody, broken fists encircling her as she cradled him tightly. 'I did it all for you,' he sobbed. 'The truth would've ruined us, we would've lost everything. I couldn't let that happen. Who knows what would've become of you? You saved me from endless torment, and so I had to save you.'

'I know, my love,' she murmured, cold numbing her with infinite grace.

Perhaps there is a God in this moment.

She dared to glance at John and Josiah.

The former was watching her, stunned and disbelieving, whilst the latter, thankfully, was quietly attending to Sebastian.

Finish it.

'Now, tell me of it, tell me of it all. Then we will know peace. It will be all right.'

'Do you promise?'

'I promise.'

And so he told her, everything, as she rocked him, and John bore witness, and Josiah dragged Sebastian away.

He told her of Alice arriving at Stag House the day

before her death, and leaving a note bearing her name, asking to meet him. Of him riding to meet her in Barrow Heath early the following morning, and finding her on the road, and *what a boon it was*.

He told Juliana of the proof she bore—records as they now had, and a family ring he'd instantly recognised as Father's—and how he'd feigned elation, whilst secretly knowing this signalled doom.

He seemed surprised when Juliana asked about the locket—he'd known nothing of it.

After a moment, he continued, and confessed to luring her to a meeting that night, purporting he needed time to *prepare his sister for such news*, but knowing instead he needed time to make a plan. A plan to not only rid them of that threat; but also that Sebastian posed.

And finally he confessed what he'd done to them on that hilltop, that frigid December night, and had the cold not already taken such a gripping hold, Juliana might've retched all over him.

Instead, she held him, and rocked him, and they wept.

Chapter Twenty-Three

~~~~~~

Eight days later

'I wish you'd wake, Sebastian. Oh, how I wish you would wake,' Juliana sighed, turning away from the grim figure in bed, beside whom she'd stood vigil these past days, but who patently refused to return to her. Or to give any indication he would. 'It's unfair to us both that after everything, you're not awake to see… what is coming to pass.'

The *denouement*, the *end, all we've achieved*—words which danced at the edge of her mind, but felt wrong.

Then again, nothing felt *right*; not even the truth's revelation, no matter how she'd told herself it was for Alice, and Bertie. She couldn't see any good; any justice nor triumph. All she could see was yet again, fear, anguish, and regret. Violence, pain, and horror.

The first traces of early spring, emerging with tenacious ferocity through the dwindling frost and storms, taunted her. Not only by being so diametrically opposed to what the world *should* look like to mirror the desolation; but also by reminding her of her promise to Elizabeth. Of all that awaited...

Far away from here.

Though I fear if I find my way back there... I will be late.

Still, despite spring's taunts, Juliana forced herself to gaze out upon the awakening world; to feel comforted by the promises *it* made, and all the hopeful symbolism of renewal it could represent, if she had the heart to accept it.

Though I long abandoned faith, still I believe in sin, and repentance, so why not rebirth?

Besides, it was either look out onto the world, or stare at the walls, or the ceiling, or Sebastian's broken form, and she'd done enough of all that of late. In a way, ensconcing herself here, tending to him, had helped keep her mind off the rest. Off Rourke, what came next, the danger to Sebastian's life; that Rourke had nearly taken him from her again.

If she stood vigil, washed his wounds, changed the poultices, poured broth down his throat, read to him, stayed with him, then she could almost forget *why* she had to. She could almost forget seeing him once John had taken Rourke away that day, still sobbing, screaming her name. Almost forget Sebastian, laid up on a lavender armchair, Josiah tending to him best he could, whilst waiting for the doctor he'd sent a servant for. She could almost forget wondering how different he might look if he survived. Forget the doctor saying that if she hadn't stopped Rourke when she had, there would've been no point; that Sebastian's life hung in the balance, and only time would tell if he would awaken, and if he did, if he would be himself. She could almost forget being forced to remain in this house—Sebastian's condition not allowing departure from it—this house that was evermore cursed, and soul-stealing, and wretched.

She could almost forget everything.

The exhaustion and weariness deeply settled into her bones helped too; especially when the world outside intruded, despite her willing it not to.

Josiah would check on her and Sebastian. He had the decency not to ask anything beyond: *do you need anything?*

John came to inform her of what was happening with Rourke; what would happen. For now, he'd kept Sebastian's true identity secret; Rourke's confession guaranteeing no safety for a convicted criminal who'd escaped the noose. It was a case of rare complexity—the law having to decide the proper order of things—so no risks could be taken. Word had been put about to ensure public support for Sebastian—Juliana daren't even think how quickly the story reached London, popular as it was, nor how she should write Ginny, for though Juliana's involvement and name had been kept out of the papers, connections would not be difficult to make. Still, even with such support, safety wasn't guaranteed until Sebastian's exoneration was signed, sealed, and official. Which considering John and Josiah's tireless work, and championing, would be a matter of days; the law deciding it preferred to exonerate before it executed.

Though we shall have a trial to ensure all is proper...

Juliana too had done what she could, gratitude in her heart for more not being demanded of her. She would've done it, but for now, thanks to the others, she could tend to Sebastian, and prepare for her brother's trial; which she had no idea how to do.

She doubted anyone did.

John, when he wasn't keeping her abreast of everything, would offer words of sympathy, and regret, try to make her feel less terrible, and she hated him for it, chafing against his solicitude as she had against Sebastian's. Celia had come a few times, mirroring her husband's solicitude, but Juliana chafed against hers too.

The servants that remained—only a couple hadn't left for greener pastures at news of their master's demise—were mostly sweet and respectful of her quiet isolation.

The doctor was the worst, going on about local gossip, to the point where she'd finally thanked him yesterday, advising him not to return. There was no point. They knew what they were doing. Now it was merely a waiting game.

A game I no longer wish to play.

'It isn't only because your name, your life are at stake again that I wish you were awake, you know,' she said, resuming her one-sided conversation with her shattered heart; looking as battered and broken as the one inside her chest. 'I wish you were awake for myself. To stand with me. To comfort me as I prepare to lose another I realise now… I lost long ago. I'm going to see him today,' she added, glancing back at the bed, almost hoping that would be the thing to wake him. 'They're moving him for the assizes tomorrow, and after that… They expect everything to happen quickly. As with you, they intend to make a statement. Justice will be swift and merciless.

'Unless he has a sudden change of heart, Rourke won't fight it. John said…he was broken after that day. I told him we were broken a long time ago. I never liked that word. Now I find it apt. I find myself unable to function as the rest of the world seems to, and Rourke never could, I see that now too. Parts of us might've been repaired, healed, made to serve a purpose, but the breaks on our soul remained, as surely as they might've in our bones.

'I've been asked whether I will speak for him, and I still don't know. What to say…whether I wish to. If it would even make a difference for they are set on seeing him hang. I'm living the same nightmare as with you, only now I'm not a child. I'm not helpless. Yet still I haven't learned how to reconcile the love I hold for a murderer. Whether I can speak for him, try to save some part of him as I failed so many years ago with you. I wonder if he deserves my forgiveness. Salvation. But as with you…' She shrugged, tears misting the landscape before her. 'I cannot stop loving him no matter how I try.

'I cannot seem to stop crying these days,' she added,

swiping away the loathsome things. 'I cannot but wonder, and be sad, and scared, and angry, and I hate it. Someday, perhaps, I'll feel something else again, be relieved, *pleased*, even, that we found the truth, that we've given names and lives to the dead, and will get your name and life back, but right now... I cannot.

'It's the rationality that destroys me. I imagine it brings you comfort, or would, or did, or will. To know there was a reason everything was taken from you. It only makes it worse for me, to know he planned it so meticulously. That he took their lives so coldly. For me.

'I thought with all the evil I'd witnessed, read about, heard about, that even if I couldn't see it, I knew the world's true darkness. But I've been proven wrong. Still, I cannot believe Rourke *evil*; as I couldn't you. I wonder what that says about me.

'You're not allowed to die,' she said, her own force and steadiness surprising her, as she turned back to gaze at Sebastian, whose chest rose and fell, while his eyes remained tightly shut; though the swelling had diminished. 'I've said it many times these past days, but I'll say it again. You're not allowed to die, because we didn't do all this, I haven't, and won't sacrifice all I have, for you to not. You're not allowed to die because I couldn't bear the weight of that again. You're not allowed because I need you, and love you, and even if we aren't to have the ending we dreamt of, I won't stand for you leaving me like this.

'I should go. Josiah will stay with you while I'm gone.

'Please don't make me face what comes next alone,' she whispered before she left.

I beg you.

Juliana may not like the term *broken*, still it was the first which came to mind when she saw her brother again, in the dark confines of his cell. It was as clean and dry as one could be however, and that was something. Something for which she owed John more gratitude, as she wagered he'd ensured her brother was treated to a modicum of, if not comfort, then lack of squalor.

Whether or not Rourke deserved such consideration was another question she would long wrestle with, as she did the rest, including her decision of whether or not to speak on his behalf.

It was an increasingly complex question, as the question of sanity posed itself again when she saw him. Though he looked outwardly *fine*—groomed, clean, dressed as well as possible—there was a gaunt, fragile sadness about him, and that look in his eyes she'd seen the day he confessed, which suggested he wasn't entirely present in the same time, and world, had returned, a hundredfold. She suspected it wasn't a recent state, but that his view of the world, of right and wrong, love and duty, and so on, had been twisted and skewed, shaped into something alien a long time ago; though he'd learned to hide it. It didn't excuse his actions, though perhaps, despite the reason behind them, it meant...

What? That he should be spared?

When Sebastian wasn't and others haven't been for less?

You may not believe in an eye for an eye, death for death, however it isn't for you to decide what justice is.

'I wasn't sure you'd come, Juliana,' Rourke said once they were safely locked in together. 'John said you'd visit, but I wasn't sure.'

'Neither was I,' she admitted with a faint smile.

She pondered going to sit beside him, for he looked so vulnerable, like the boy she'd known and loved, only she couldn't quite bring herself to bring him comfort.

'I should never have left you here alone,' she said quietly after a long moment.

It wouldn't have changed what he'd done, and likely wouldn't have changed their now future, however, she had to say it, for in her heart, it was true.

'I wished you hadn't. But I never hated you for it. Much of me was glad you'd got away, saw all I couldn't. I'll be glad for all you will see yet.' Juliana nodded, her heart wrenching as though on the rack; every word twisting pieces of her farther apart. 'John told me he's alive but not awake.'

'We can only wait now.' She wasn't entirely certain whether that was disappointment or shame flickering in his gaze, but he hung his head before she could decide. 'I wasn't lying when I said he gave me the strength to come back to you. I think maybe he loved you a little in the end too.'

'He was a good brother.'

'Why didn't you tell me?' she asked, desperately, and still Rourke refused to meet her gaze. 'There were so many other ways…we could've found one together. We would've. How could you?' she choked out.

'I couldn't risk it. It was my burden to bear.'

'Do you regret it?' she asked, and perhaps *that* was what she needed to know most.

What the world needed most to know; what Alice and Bertie did.

Rourke's eyes met hers, and she saw the temptation of a lie, before resolve, and a full sense of the moment's finality won.

'No,' he told her simply. 'I regret the cost, but not to them.' Clenching her jaw tightly shut, Juliana fought the soul-wrenching realisation, and feelings flooding her. 'There's only one ending for me, Juliana. No words could spare me, so I will spare you speaking them.'

'Thank you,' she breathed, tears streaming as he gave her the last of his protection.

'Will you be there for me, as you were for him?' he asked, her brother again, that boy she'd loved with all her heart, who had loved her, best he knew how, and she nodded. 'What chance did we have, really?'

'I don't know. I suppose we never will.'

'Do you still love me?'

'For ever and ever.'

'But you wish you could stop.' Juliana nodded. *No more lies.* 'So did I.'

Silence enveloped them, barely any sounds reaching them; only the flickering of the lone candle.

What chance did we have...

'I'm not scared, you know,' he whispered, turning to look at it.

'I know,' she said, finding the strength to go over to him, and kissing his head gently. 'You were always very brave.'

He looked up at her, and she smiled down at him; her once protector, who she'd try not to ever remember such as he was today.

Instead, she would keep the memory of the sweet playmate, friend, and guardian he'd been, and perhaps in those future memories, he would have a chance.

'Goodbye, Juliana.'

'Goodbye, Rourke.'

May there be a next life you find some peace in.

May there be a god who can make sense of and forgive what has been done.

Chapter Twenty-Four

If it was indeed justice, and righteousness that saw Rourke Edmund Myles hung on a bright spring morning in March 1833, to the tune of the excited, braying audience, Sebastian couldn't say. Despite all he'd dreamt of *justice finally being done*, the true guilty being punished and so on, it felt nothing like he'd imagined; nothing like justice.

Not merely because he loved Juliana, and felt her heart break over and over; first with Rourke's confession, then every day until his death. Not merely because he felt a piece of her die along with her brother as Sebastian held her hand, and they watched Rourke breathe his final breaths. Not even because despite his initial desire for vengeance, he didn't truly believe that a life taken should be paid for with another.

It was because he saw Rourke for what he was, and always had been: a scared little boy who just wanted to keep the one person he loved, who loved him, safe. He was a boy who'd been tortured and twisted into something terrible, by a cruel father. It didn't excuse his actions, nor the lives he'd taken—there were many others who'd suffered such ills, and never done what he had—still, taking his life, didn't feel like *justice*.

At least to Sebastian.

To the law, to those who'd known Alice and Bertie, travelled up from Suffolk for the trial, to the locals and strangers who followed the case like some serial, it was justice apparently. Very, very swift justice too, which also pleased them.

On the latter point, Sebastian agreed, only because the fortnight or so it took them to try and convict Rourke was long enough to continue the torture begun long ago on many; first and foremost to him being of course, Juliana. Even his own exoneration, a *fait accompli* days after he'd awoken, had been of little joy, relief, or satisfaction, considering all yet to pass. His being far from fully recovered—from his injuries, all that had happened, and the eight days spent in a void of darkness, empty save for snippets of Juliana's voice—didn't help. The most he could remember were pleas to not leave her to face this alone; pleas that had undoubtedly dragged him back into the conscious world. Sebastian had dragged her back here, made her go through this; the least he could do was stand by her side as she faced her brother's loss. As she grappled with all she must to reconcile with Rourke's guilt. As she sat quietly during the trial, wrestling with a lifetime of guilt, remorse, and questions.

Though Rourke had released her from speaking for him, John and Sebastian had. He'd said what he could to shade the otherwise seemingly black and white question put to the court; not that anyone believed it would make a difference, which it hadn't.

It made a difference to my soul, and hopefully to Juliana's.

He wasn't sure what else to do, but be there for her as she faded away from herself. Be her tether, her anchor, as she'd been his. Keep her from fading entirely, hardening, losing herself, and so he did that. Stood by her, held her hand, made sure she ate, made sure he healed so he could be with her, and since she would no longer speak, he spoke to her, reaching out through the darkness, as she had for him.

And now here they were, broken and bruised, yet alive, and he liked to think, healing best either of them could as the world resumed turning, blooms burst, and birds chirped.

Time had resumed its course. Life had resumed its course.

Stag House and all Myles family possessions had reverted back to the Crown. Juliana was glad to see the inheritance she'd never touched go too; calling it blood money.

Sebastian had paid for, gladly, Alice and Bertie's headstone to bear their name, and birthdays. It was one of only two reasons they'd come back here, to Barrow Heath. To lay certain things to rest, before…

Whatever comes next; a future I cannot divine but for its bittersweetness, brimming with many more goodbyes.

'I've seen two hangings in my life,' Juliana said quietly, the most words she'd strung together since he'd awoken, as she stepped back from placing the bunch of lavender on Rourke's grave.

He'd been laid to rest with no marker but a stone in a quiet, tucked-away corner of the estate, where no one would hopefully disturb what peace he could perhaps find.

Josiah had taken care of securing the body, bringing it back, burying it, and so much more, and Sebastian was eternally grateful, as he was to John, who'd suffered Rourke's revelations, yet upheld his duty, and friendship to both Juliana and Sebastian.

There is good in this world, no matter how much any of us would like to forget it.

'Even were those I saw hang not people I loved, it is twice more than any man should witness. I'll never understand those who attend them as though they were spectacles.'

Sighing, Sebastian nodded, trying to find any words which might bring Juliana some version of comfort or peace.

I doubt there are any. It is only time left to hopefully heal these wounds; in us all.

'I'm sorry it ended this way, Juliana. Truly, I am.'

'I know. I'm grateful for your strength, and steadiness, without which I wouldn't have made it this far. But I…'

'Need to go home,' he finished, realising then this was part of what the day held for them.

A goodbye.

Juliana met his gaze, surprise in her which soon morphed to mournful acceptance.

There was a reason we never discussed what came next.

'Yes,' she breathed. 'I love you, Sebastian, with more of my heart and soul than I feel are still alive right now. I wish we could have what we dreamt of once. Start fresh, live happily, renewed and joyful that we succeeded in our quest, grateful for our second chance. Only I can't. Not after everything. I don't know who I am any more,' she shrugged, and he nodded, taking one of her hands in his, and swiping his thumb along her cheek with his other. 'I can barely draw breath without thinking on it. I need solidity, certainty, and you…need to live the life of freedom you never could.'

'I know, Juliana,' he smiled gently. His heart was torn, yet surer, more settled, than it had long been. 'I will love you with every second of life I have left. You've always been with me, and always will be. But I know,' he said again, and she nuzzled his hand, before pulling herself into his arms, tucking into the crook of his shoulder. 'The love I offer isn't the kind you need, to heal, and find yourself again. I wish it was. But I don't know who I am either. I'm a free man, bearing my own name again, yet I cannot even begin to realise it. You built a life, found family, and they're who you need. Pure love, and solidity, will keep you living, and in time, make you smile again. I thought one day, when

I had my name again, I would come back to England, and so I have, but staying having seen and lived all I have… I can't. It would be an unmoored life I'd offer, and lest we forget, one glance at each other, and the past both of us tried so hard to escape comes flooding back. I'm the reason your brother is dead, and you may love me, and forgive me that, but it doesn't change the edge it puts on our love.'

'I never dreamt for life to be as it was in the story-books,' Juliana said, slightly muffled against his chest. 'Today I do. I wish it could be fixed, with the wave of a wand, beauty, love, and joy triumphing over years of hurt and death.'

'It would not be so truthful as life, and you'd hate it.'

'I would.'

'You should leave in the morning,' he said, after what might've been an hour, or a lifetime of them standing there, breathing together. 'Take my carriage. Josiah will see you back to London; you'll forgive me if I don't. I think I'll see what ships leave from Bristol in the coming days.'

Juliana nodded against his chest, before slowly untangling herself.

She slid her hand into his, and with one last look at the bunch of lavender, she turned away from her brother's grave, and on they went, in silence, back to the inn to prepare for their now imminent departures.

May all you souls here rest in peace.

May the truth set you all free; and may it set us free one day.

* * *

'Are you certain you won't take Simpheon?' Josiah asked, and Sebastian glanced over to find the man leaning against a stall, the occupant not bothered in the least, simply snorting and enjoying the occasional nose rub. Despite the obscene earliness, the antelucan light still pervading just outside the stable doors, Josiah looked as tidy and bright as possible.

But then he was likely used to early mornings, considering his profession; or at the least the position he held as a marquess's valet. Whether or not that was Josiah's true profession, or a stop on the road, he didn't know. He didn't know much of the man, beyond that he'd been trustworthy, loyal, and instrumental in getting Sebastian his life back.

So you know him well enough.

'I trust money to achieve much,' Sebastian said wryly, turning back to finish preparing the horse he'd purchased from Young Bernard for his journey to Bristol. 'I trust it to get me where I need to be,' he added, patting the beast, who, in another life, he might've kept for longer than a few days. 'I trust it to buy me privacy, solitude, and the run of places which aren't mine, such as this stable; though perhaps I'm afforded that today as the entirety of Barrow Heath prefers to keep a wide berth, lest I wreak more havoc upon its famed tranquillity. I do *not* however trust money so much as to risk a marquess losing his prized horse, all because the person I paid to return it thought better of it once I was out of sight of England's shores.'

'You'll not be swayed then, from your course.'

'It's a good course.'

'Why did you come back?' Josiah asked, and there was disconcerting taunting curiosity in his voice. Sebastian turned, crossing his arms, and raised a brow, silently saying: *isn't that obvious?* 'No, I mean, why after eighteen years? Feels…rather odd. Ten, fifteen, twenty…any of the more significant markers, I'd understand. But eighteen is *untidy.*'

'Apologies that my need for redemption wasn't timed tidily.'

'I'm only curious. Generally, people, as mysterious or unique as they think themselves to be, are quite similar. They follow patterns, conscious, and unconscious.'

'And you abhor not understanding pattern outliers,' Sebastian finished, relaxing slightly, as a piece of who Josiah was became plain.

'I like to ensure outliers are truly that, not merely following other patterns.'

'So you're implying I didn't return on some significant anniversary because I was following another pattern…?'

'You were being rash.' Sebastian frowned, and was about to throw up his hands, and go back to what he was doing—*too early and late for whatever this is*—when Josiah continued. 'You thought about coming back, getting revenge or justice, or salvation, for years. Dreamt of it, prepared for it. Then suddenly, you come back, with a rather tenuous plan, because it was time?' Josiah shrugged. 'It doesn't fit.'

'What does?' Sebastian asked, more pleadingly than challengingly, because...

Why do I need to hear what this man believes so desperately?

'People make life-altering, rash decisions, when they either find courage, or it becomes impossible for them *not* to act. I think you came back after eighteen years, because you woke up one morning, unable to fathom living another day without Juliana.'

Sighing, Sebastian nodded.

It was the truth, and not one which had been invisible. Or rather it *had been*, for a time, but now... Now the reason he felt no great thunderbolts, or the ground moving beneath his feet, sending him tumbling into an abyss of questioning and doubt, was that he did know. Had for a while now, that *she* was why he'd come back; *that* had been his revelation as he'd watched the sun set on the Bosphorus.

And he'd known, *knew*, that it changed nothing.

'The man who longed for such impossible things is gone,' he told Josiah, though he knew he owed him no explanation. Yet because of the friendship he'd shown, he was owed truth. 'The man I am now knows our love will live on. That Juliana is free of the past, and this place, however much her heart will remain broken, and that is enough. The man I am knows Juliana deserves better than what I could ever give, and that love means putting the other first.'

'I think you're scared, and running away before the hardest trials.'

'How dare you, I stood by her—'

Josiah raised a hand, otherwise remaining relaxed and unmoving, and the undeniable threat stopped Sebastian from taking more than a step.

'It's in the months and years following a loved one's loss that it is perhaps felt most keenly,' Josiah said quietly. 'Not only does the reality of the loss slowly seep into your heart, by that time, all the friends and neighbours who saw you through the early days have resumed their lives. Juliana hasn't only lost her brother, she's lost herself, and every bearing which has kept her going. She's about to return to people whom she cares for deeply, and has always protected, yet whom she must now lay everything she's faced and kept from them, at their feet. She's more alone, and terrified than ever, and you're leaving her to face it alone, because you...want to go exploring again?'

'She has you, and the people she's going home to. I'm doing what I believe best, and for the sake of all you've done for us both, I won't strike you for saying I'm leaving her because I wish to *go exploring*. Think what you will, Josiah, it matters little. We shall not agree, and you won't sway my course. So let us shake hands, and I will thank you, for giving me my life back, for we both know it wouldn't have been done without you.'

After a long moment of hesitation, Josiah nodded, and they did precisely that.

'Take care of her,' Sebastian added.

'We will.'

With a nod, Sebastian turned to his new mount, finished getting the beast ready, and followed Josiah outside.

Juliana was waiting by the readied carriage, looking smaller, more fragile, and yet more at peace then he'd ever seen her. She was a ghost, in the wisps of mist floating on the edges of their world, as the sun's rays threatened to illuminate it; only today she was a ghost ready to move on into the next world, a new life, and Sebastian was surer than ever they'd made the right decision, no matter how much it cost him.

My heart, my soul, my entire being ripping itself from flesh to remain for ever with you, my love.

She offered him a small smile as he came to stand before her, then offered a hand out to his horse, who peeked over his shoulder to investigate a potential new friend.

'So this is it then,' she breathed.

He tried not to watch her too hard, study her too closely, for every detail, from the shadows beneath her eyes, to the wisps of hair at her temples, were torture, as he knew he'd never see any of it again.

Yet, because of that, he forced himself to remember every breath, every crinkle of her clothing, every glimpse of her scent.

'I don't quite know how we're meant to say good-bye,' Juliana said, giving his horse one last stroke, then standing to face him, hesitancy and regret laced upon her shoulders. 'There's so much to be said, so many knots left tangled, and yet...'

'We've said what's important, Juliana. Expressed much of what was left unsaid last night.' He got another small smile for that; which made him share one in return. 'It's fitting, I think, that we part here.' She nodded. 'I'm telling you now so you won't argue with Josiah, but once you're settled back in London, he's agreed to help my driver find another position, and I've instructed him to sell the carriage. Whatever money he gets will be yours. It won't be much, but enough to serve in case you've ever need of it. I know you won't want to ask your friends for anything, and without your inheritance, it will help you feel safe.'

'Thank you. I'd refuse but I know there'll be no arguing with either you, or Josiah.'

'Quite. You should go,' he added after a moment, before he could lose himself in her eyes any longer. 'Never a good idea to waste a clear day's travel.'

'I'll miss you, Sebastian. Write me, someday, to tell me of your adventures.'

He nodded, doubting he ever would.

Perhaps when my life is over. Before, I'm not certain it would be wise for either of us.

Juliana was correct though, this saying goodbye business was confusing, and horrid. There were a thousand words, repetitions, promises, and pleas on the tip of his tongue, none of which felt right; yet none of which he could do without, even though she already knew every single one. Thankfully, she shared his struggle, and knew what was best, so she leaned forward, and kissed him, so they could say that way instead.

It was the sweetest, most chaste, and gut-wrenching kiss they'd ever shared, lasting a century, or barely a second; either way, not even close to enough time to memorise it, and feel everything it provoked.

'You were never a coward, Juliana. You can become whoever you wish to.'

'I love you, Sebastian,' she whispered, before whisking herself away, and into the carriage.

'I love you,' he said, though she couldn't hear.

Tears gathered, but were polite enough not to fall until he'd nodded to Josiah, then to his driver, and they were off.

Then they fell, as he watched them disappear down the road. He let them, before nodding, reassuring himself that he'd made the right choice, and then he mounted his horse, and did as they had, and left Barrow Heath, for ever.

Towards unknown horizons.

Chapter Twenty-Five

London,
One month later

Knowing you couldn't go on as you were, and finding
the will to tread a new path, to make changes, were two
very separate things. Juliana had always been aware
of that strikingly painful dichotomy, yet never had occasion to experience it. Until now.

She knew very well she couldn't continue as she
had this past month, yet remained at a loss of how to
change, move forward, and live again. None of those
sounded appealing, however the alternatives terrified
her beyond words. All the more for she'd lived them
before; after she'd first left Stag House. She'd survived stagnation, purposelessness, and living death.
She didn't wish to again; if only so as not to disregard
the sacrifices which meant she still drew breath, and
walked the earth. Only it was incredibly difficult to...

Find my way. Find myself, and feel as I once did
with those I now call family.

They'd all been wonderful, ever since she'd returned. Demanding nothing, only offering warm embraces, kind words, and gentle entreaties to confide whenever she was ready. Not about the details of events—she'd done that starkly the morning after she'd arrived, though she knew they were aware of most facts, given how word had spread of the affair—but about how she was feeling. Juliana wanted to, except she couldn't quite find the words to express any of what was inside her.

So instead, she simply settled back into a poor facsimile of her previous life; waking, eating, teaching, eating, sleeping, over, and over again. She woke, she ate, she taught Elizabeth, and helped care for baby Justine, despite everyone's objections. Sofia, who'd done a perfectly wonderful job in Juliana's absence, said she would happily continue for as long as needed, but gracefully stepped aside when Juliana assured her it was *no trouble*. It was perhaps the most she spoke to anyone after confiding in Ginny and Spencer *all* her sordid history, when she wasn't teaching Elizabeth.

Elizabeth was perhaps who Juliana felt most comfortable with; being around her was soothing, even if she was as quiet and watchful as the others. Elizabeth was more herself, more apt to pretend they should just resume life where they'd left off. To boot, no matter how wise the young girl was, from having to face truths and situations beyond what any child should, Juliana was never tempted to seek her counsel, or under the impression Elizabeth secretly judged her. And not because she had no idea of what had occurred; Juliana was under no illusion, Elizabeth surely knew most, if not all. Still, Elizabeth neither judged her, nor did anything but treat her normally; not like some fragile piece of spun glass which might explode into a million pieces if it wasn't properly handled. For though she might feel like that, she didn't wish to be treated thusly.

The remaining speck of Juliana's rational self knew the others simply *cared*. Ginny, Spencer, Josiah, the Dowager, the Guaro women—even family friends such as the Waltons, or the Reids—they were only trying to ensure she was as well as could be, and knew they were there for her. And though each of them had lived through trials which made them very apt to give counsel, guidance, friendship, or merely a shoulder to cry upon, Juliana couldn't help but feel chasms existed between them now. Even Ginny... Juliana felt herself drifting further away with every passing hour, because of her own silence, and immobility. Additionally, her speck of rationality appreciated that they only judged lightly, and didn't *judge* her; who she was, her choices, or past.

Her emotional self however, which had lately taken the helm, felt so shameful whenever any of them so much as glanced in her direction, especially Ginny. She felt she'd wronged them with her silence, abrupt departure, and now with her return, tracking mud onto their doorstep whilst remaining unable to move on, heal, as they had. *Wrong*, obviously; still, she couldn't shake it, and so she withdrew further.

You'll lose them, and what remnants you have of the person you built if you continue thus.

Yes, she would. She would suffer a lifetime trapped in her own mind, if she didn't find a way back to those who could help her from the quicksand threatening to pull her into its suffocating embrace.

How—

'Spencer and I have been talking,' Ginny said, and Juliana's eyes slowly focused on the carriages, horses, and passers-by bustling through the London streets below, before she turned away from the drawing room window, to find her friend tentatively heading for her.

It was Sunday, she recalled, hence spending hours staring out of windows, and why the house was eerily quiet—most of them off on walks, or at church if they so believed.

Except Ginny was here, looking like she was delivering the news that the seventh plague's arrival was imminent.

This cannot be good.

Juliana's heart jolted, wondering if this was the moment Ginny chose to end their friendship, and sent her away for being so changed, and—

Calm yourself.

If she does at least it will be something new.

'We were thinking it would be good to get back to Yew Park House sooner this year,' Ginny said with what might've passed for a bright, genuine, smile had Juliana not known her. 'Spencer and Reid will remain, but the rest of us would be so much more comfortable in Scotland. None of us enjoy the Season, so what point is there really, Signora Guaro is the only one who likes it, even Sofia—'

'You come for the Season because your position demands it,' Juliana reminded her gently, touched, yet angry, as she knew *she* was the only reason they were considering returning north so soon. 'Especially with all that's happened these past years, not to mention last year's vote and turmoil, you're obliged to ensure you are known, and seen, and make connections... I appreciate it, Ginny, truly I do. But running away to Scotland again won't solve what ails me, as it healed us once.'

Reluctantly, Ginny nodded, sighing, and slumping into one of the nearby chairs with a lack of grace that belied her position and upbringing.

It almost made Juliana laugh.

'I don't know what to do, Juliana,' she said quietly. 'None of us do. We've tried to give you time, and will give you more, but only if we believe this contemplation is to your benefit. I don't believe it is. I believe you're hurting, and you won't heal so long as you don't speak of it.'

'We healed well enough when we left Hadley Hall, and never spoke of what happened there.'

It wasn't true, and though Juliana knew Ginny was right, she wasn't ready.

'No, we didn't.'

'No, we didn't,' Juliana sighed, turning back to the window. *Just...talk.* 'I watched my brother hang,

Ginny,' she finally breathed. 'Held him in my arms while he told me how he murdered two souls for *me*. I spent half a lifetime mourning a man who wasn't dead, then bid him farewell again because I've no idea who I am. I spent years travelling this isle, teaching children, learning about the world, but I had no right to teach anyone anything because it turns out I know nothing at all. I found a new life with you, and Elizabeth, and I had purpose. I lied to you for years, ran away from who I was, even hid the fact I had money which might've given us a future, all because I couldn't speak of any of it. When Sebastian returned, I promised myself, and you, and Elizabeth, that I'd come back, but I haven't because I don't know how to. It's eating me alive, and I don't know how to fix it, or not wonder how I could be so wrong about my brother, or why I still love him, or if he deserved to die, or if I should've asked Spencer to try and save him, because what he did…he wasn't right, because of what was done to him. Everyone we know has seen darkness, healed, moved on, and where once that inspired me to go back *there*, now I resent everyone for it. Because I can't move. I envy you all your happiness, having found ways to keep your love, because I cannot, and I miss him, and I cannot have him back. I cannot ask him to sacrifice the freedom he's only just regained, ask him to spend a life with someone who reminds him of his worst days, and I cannot ask him to take a chance on a love I've no idea will survive, and he's already long gone regardless…'

Only the sounds of the streets and her own laboured breathing were heard in the long silence that followed, until there was a rustling of clothes, then a tightness around her, as Ginny held her, plastering herself against Juliana's back.

Much as she wished to be free of the embrace, Juliana knew she needed it and so, she melted into it, holding tight to Ginny's hands across her belly.

'If you believe us all happy, and healed, then you haven't been paying attention,' Ginny said, her voice muffled. 'I mean, we are, but it's the work of a lifetime. I'm glad you finally shared what's on your mind, though I'm sorry you've been carrying it alone for so long. What you've lived through…it's only natural to be lost. All of us in this house, and those not here, you know we understand. You never lied to me, Jules. I always knew there was something in your past you weren't ready to confront or share. With how I was then, I'm not sure I would've been able to help you carry it, and that you even worry about hiding the fact you had money is ridiculous. There were reasons for not wanting to use it, and I'm sure that if we'd been in dire need, you'd have helped. But we had a good life, and I would never hold that against you. As for the rest…'

Releasing her slowly, Ginny then took her hand, turned her around, and led her to the chairs, where they sat facing each other.

Juliana wished she could run, only she knew if she did, she'd regret it.

Friends, counsel, love, is what I needed, and now I mustn't reject it.

Only with love, support, and help, can any of us move forward.

'I am sorry, for your loss,' Ginny said, holding her hand tightly. 'What happened to your brother, what was done to you both, what he became... I don't know if you'll ever be certain his death was justice, or that you did right by allowing others to make that decision, rather than using the power at your disposal to try and save him. The great thinkers of every age have debated such matters for millennia, and come to no clear answer. Clever as you are, Jules, you can't be expected to come to one in a matter of weeks, if ever.' Juliana nodded, some of that burden lessening; the burden of: *what if.* 'Spencer and I speak often, of our pasts, who we are now, why we do things, what we feel, why. We have to. Our wounds were deep, and long scarred-over. It hurts to reopen them, but it's our only chance to heal properly. It isn't easy, but it is necessary. Elizabeth, and the Dowager, we force them to indulge too, and were Mary here, well, she wouldn't be exempt, much as she detests such talks. You didn't speak for eighteen years of what you lived, and witnessed. Then you returned there, with a man you'd loved and thought dead... I cannot even begin to fathom what that was like. I wish I could say: *it is done now, Jules.* Only I won't, for it isn't, and never will be. As for this Sebastian...'

Ginny sighed, patting Juliana's hand before leaning back, and turning to gaze out of the window for guidance, whilst Juliana waited for whatever balm these next words might be.

For those up till now had been...

Soothing, calming, strengthening, heart-healing.

'You encouraged me once,' Ginny said, lost in the memories she spoke of. 'To let Spencer in, to love him, to seize what time we had together. To not hide, and deny myself because it was easier. As I recall, there was something about man not being the key to a woman's happiness, but that one man could bring *me* some happiness. I wish I could tell you to heed your own words. Only I cannot,' she smiled softly, turning back to meet Juliana's gaze. 'There are as many good reasons to let love go, as there are to keep it. I don't know which outweighs the other for you. So I'll only say this: you don't have to know yourself to love, and be loved. You only have to know yourself well enough to know what's right for you, and that's something you feel, first and foremost, in my experience. You can learn who you are along the way, and change, grow, yes, sometimes apart, but that's life. If you believe you'll find happiness with us, become who you wish to be, then know, if you don't already, you'll always have a home with us. If you believe that you would be happier with Sebastian, then go, find him, with our help, and blessing, and know, you'll both always have a home with us. We're all here, with you, for as long as it takes to figure it out. Even Reid, who perhaps can relate most of all to what you've lived, though I've heard he's better writing letters.'

'Thank you, Ginny,' Juliana smiled, brighter than she'd thought herself ever able to again, for her friend was right, about everything.

Not having answers wasn't the greatest sin, nor even the greatest obstacle. Not being ready to move on, not knowing who she was, not being healed yet... It was all *all right*. And though she wasn't better, she did feel better; felt the cracks in her heart and soul smarting, a little less. Her strength, if not returning, then not impossible to regain.

They sat together for a long time, until the others arrived back home, bringing joy and noise. At luncheon, Juliana shared conversations, and smiles, with a few. In the afternoon, she played, and laughed with Elizabeth, Sofia, and Justine in the garden. At dinner, she shared more conversations, and smiles, and thought on everything else, a little less.

And that night, as she fell into restful and restorative slumber, she thanked her lucky stars for all life had given her. She allowed herself to wonder, if when she died, she'd be satisfied to know that kiss with Sebastian in the inn's yard at Barrow Heath, would be their last.

The answer in her heart, was a coaxing, tempting: *no.*

It was a goodbye; not farewell.

Chapter Twenty-Six

I should've written a letter, Sebastian thought despondently, grimacing as he glanced up at the townhouse across the street; pink, purple, and orange as its white stone mirrored the dawn's colours. *And I should've most certainly arrived at a sociable hour*, he added with a heavy sigh, the reality of dawn, the quiet streets, only just then hitting him.

Rubbing the back of his neck sheepishly, he looked around, feeling judged by the few passers-by—mostly servants to the houses in this grand part of town, or various delivering tradesmen—even though anyone who even thought to notice him would be more likely to mark him as a potential threat, than an ill-prepared, idiotic suitor unaware of correct courting moeurs.

Which he was.

An ill-prepared, idiotic suitor, unaware of correct courting moeurs.

If coming to beg the woman you loved to give you a second or third chance—*who's counting*—was *courting*. He couldn't say, having never *courted* anyone.

Certainly, he was somewhat aware of how it was done, having a general awareness of various cultural customs, including those that specifically regulated London Society. Which meant some part of him knew very well that he shouldn't just *pop* up at a marquess's door, hoping to have a word with one of his employees—no matter what Juliana said about them being family—just as he really shouldn't just pop up at anyone's door, particularly not at such an unfashionable hour as...

Five thirty in the bloody morning, he groaned internally, as a nearby church rang out the time, mocking him, and enforcing the point about societal rules and courtesy. He might've shouted back across the square at those bells: *I couldn't wait another instant!*, however, that would certainly raise some eyebrows. Except it was all there was really, to explain his uncouth behaviour; he couldn't wait another instant before trying to...

Win Juliana back.

Convince her we have a chance.

Beg her to believe in us.

He respected, understood, heard everything she'd said in Barrow Heath; only he'd also heard Josiah, and what his own heart said.

Oh, he'd tried to ignore the latter two; actually managed it for a solid fortnight. He'd visited the Widow Norton, told her Alice, Bertie, and Christopher's story, then meandered his way through the English countryside, learning to appreciate it before he said *fare thee well.* Until finally, he'd stood on a bustling, turbulent, and thrilling quayside in Bristol, pondering which ship, which horizon to choose, and known the answer was: *none.* At least not until he spoke to Juliana again, with honesty, and a little distance and time from what had happened in Barrow Heath. When he met her with a clear head, and steady heart.

At a reasonable hour, with some notice...
Idiot.

If Josiah could see him now, he'd surely have thoughts on this rash decision—though in Sebastian's defence, it wasn't entirely *unplanned.* In the fortnight since he'd stood by that quayside in Bristol, he'd actually been very busy making plans for the rest of his life; which included ensuring a smooth transition, notably of his assets, from Thomas du Lac Vaugris, back to the newly exonerated, Sebastian Lloyd.

It had been a strange time, which he'd spent mostly holed up in various inns from Bristol to London, as he sent letters, instructions, and dealt with far too much paperwork. Thankfully, the paperwork would diminish—or so his solicitor here in London, who'd he'd finally met yesterday after years of business together, and who'd been helping ensure the transition was smooth, had assured him.

He'd thought of finding Juliana as soon as he'd arrived in the city, but he'd thought better of it, positing one more night to get his mind, and words in order would be a good idea—*might've thought of a better plan than just turning up at her door too, but no—*

and he'd also wanted to settle. To stop, and discover the city. To truly feel, being back in England, as he hadn't but on the road to Bristol—when he'd still believed he'd be leaving imminently. Now it wasn't that he thought he'd settle permanently in London, or anywhere on this island, only, if his plans came to fruition—*plans, ha!*—he'd perhaps be spending more time than originally thought here. So it was best to get to know it. He'd even wandered around Freddie Walton's enterprise, curious about the man he'd not long ago pretended to be a friend to, and—

A curtain moved, catching Sebastian's eye, before he spotted brown curls bouncing on the other side of a first-floor window. Feeling evermore exposed and judged by the little devil whose eyes, even from afar, burned through him, he decidedly wanted to flee, yet found himself unable to, pinned by that very same gaze.

After a rather long moment, unable to do with the awkwardness any longer, he gave what might've passed as a smile, and waved.

The girl thought about it—which made Sebastian actually laugh, right there on the street—before waving back, the quirking of her head telling him, he was not to even *think* about fleeing.

That young lady has supernatural powers; I would swear to it.

He wouldn't have been able to say how long it was in the end that he stood there, time stilling, even the bells chiming the hour disappearing as he prepared for what came next.

Juliana. A speech. Attempting to...

The door to the townhouse finally opened, and there Juliana was, looking rosy and slightly dazed—understandable considering she'd likely been abruptly woken—hastily dressed in one of her usual dark gowns, though to Sebastian, she looked as bright as the clear morn now nearly fully upon them.

As she came out towards him, he glanced back to find who he guessed to be the butler, and a very insistent Elizabeth in her nightclothes, preventing said butler from closing the door.

So we're to have an audience...

Might as well, and perhaps it will aid me to not make a muck of things.

Turning his attention back to Juliana, he took a deep breath, and stood straight, determined to prove himself at least *somewhat* worthy, even despite his eschewance of societal niceties. As she took the last few steps across the street, he searched for any sign that he was unwelcome—but to his great relief, and hope, he found only a glorious mix of utter bewilderment, and glittering excitement.

Perhaps I've a chance.

'Sebastian,' she breathed, as she at last stood before him, studying him with the same intensity, as though she couldn't believe it was truly him. *But then given I seem to always appear like some unwanted ghost out-*

side her employers' homes, understandable. 'What are you doing here…? I thought…'

'So did I. Only, I couldn't. That is to say…' Sighing, he raked his fingers through his already mussed hair, realising he'd forgotten a bloody hat. *Your idiocies are compounding by the minute.* 'Josiah has a theory. He said I returned when I did, because I couldn't face another day without you. It was true. It *is* true, and I… knew that, when he said it, but I believed what you said too. I understood, respected that, still do, and will, but I also… Well, that isn't all there is to it.'

Taking a breath, desperately trying to find the words he'd been practising for weeks, he dared to try and gauge what Juliana was thinking.

All he could tell was that she was listening, giving him a chance, so…

Seize it!

'It won't be easy,' he began, because she needed to know, he recognised that much. 'I wish I could promise the world, a happy ending like in the stories, but I can only promise you my hope. Hope, that we can make it, have a beautiful, glorious life, despite all we've lived, and all that stands against us. Hope, that we can discover together what kind of love we can have. What kind of life we can have. It was always you, Juliana,' he shrugged, keenly aware of the tears pricking his eyes, but unable to do anything about them, because if he moved but an inch, lost sight of her, and the hope growing in her own eyes, the light growing with every passing second, he might lose everything. 'Always will be. Once, before my faith was torn from me, I might've been satisfied with a chance in the next life. Then again... I wouldn't be willing to risk it. We have this life. I'm not ready to wait for whatever might come next to love you. I made that mistake once, and I won't again. I won't ask you to leave the home you've found, tear you from this family, or ask you to choose, but neither can I promise to live here, for ever. Perhaps, there is freedom, and exploration, to be had, as well as this life you've built. All I ask, is that you give us a chance to explore what opportunities we can make for ourselves. And if you want none of it, I'll leave, and that'll be the end of it.'

'No wonder they couldn't find you,' Juliana breathed, and he frowned, trying to make sense of her words. 'Josiah, Spencer, even Freddie Walton, they were trying to help me find you, only none of them could find any trace of you in Bristol,' she laughed wetly, shaking her head, and he grinned, realising what she was saying. 'Ginny talked some sense into me. Made me realise the only answer I needed was to know I wasn't ready for us to be over. It's still such a mess,' she cried, shrugging, and he dared get even closer, running his knuckles along her cheek. She settled into his touch, and at once he felt... *Settled. Home. Alive. Hopeful.* 'So many things between us, so much to heal from... but you're right. Ginny was right. We can find a way together, and so yes, Sebastian, please stay. Please, keep the promises we made to each other lifetimes ago. Let us build something, together. I have hope, and we have time, and love, and I have it on good authority, that with all that, we stand a good chance.'

He might've said something else; but everything had been said.

Besides, his heart was too full of wonder, love, and life, to use words, so instead he simply closed what little was left of the distance between them, and kissed her, with all he was, and had, and ever would have, and ever would be.

Renewing the vows made long ago; sealing new promises made this early morning.

Time lost meaning again, as he lost himself in her, then found himself again; the Sebastian he'd never been, but always dreamt to be.

Finally they separated just enough to be able to breathe, foreheads against each other's, and they smiled, losing themselves in each other's eyes.

'Are you going to invite him in now or not, Jules?' Elizabeth shouted from across the road, and they laughed.

'Ladies do not shout across streets, Elizabeth!' Juliana shouted back without even turning.

'They do today!' shouted another voice, and that had both Juliana and Sebastian turning back to the door.

Our audience has grown...

The marquess and marchioness—the latter of whom had made the last remark—both hastily, but expertly dressed, if not entirely *ready*, now framed Elizabeth; Josiah, and more heads bouncing up between those three, craning to get a better look at the admittedly shocking spectacle Sebastian and Juliana made.

'As if this family hasn't borne enough scandal!' yelled the marquess jovially. 'Now I've a wife and a daughter shouting on the streets at dawn, and a governess mauling a man for all to see! Absolutely shocking behaviour,' he grinned.

Everyone laughed, and Juliana turned to glance back up at Sebastian.

He met her gaze, grinning wider, and more carelessly than he'd ever imagined he might again.

'They'll not be held back any longer, I'm afraid,' she said. 'There will be many interrogations, so brace yourself.'

'I look forward to it.'

For he did.

He looked forward to all of it.

Meeting them, her family.

Making plans.

Building a life with her.

Loving her.

Living, all of it, with her.

So, clasping her hand tightly, they walked on, towards their future.

Epilogue

'Did I ever thank you, Josiah?' Juliana asked, slowly approaching the man, who seemed determined to stand in the corner of the admittedly very full and raucous room. He, like her, didn't enjoy being the object of any attention, and standing up for Sebastian, being a guest at this celebration of her wedding, as opposed to merely a servant in this house, was rather a lot of attention for one day.

'No thanks were ever due,' he said simply, and she chuckled softly, shaking her head, and passing him the glass of punch she'd brought him.

He took it, after some hesitation, then glanced around the room as she leaned against the wall beside him, and did the same.

They were all here, her friends, those she'd come to call family, laughing, eating, playing games, dancing, and singing, as they celebrated her wedding.

My wedding...

Despite the dress she sported—simple, but far more extravagant than she'd wear otherwise, an insistence of Ginny's and Elizabeth's—despite the mountains of food and drink, the flowers, the decorations, and most of all, the morning's memories, of vows, and churches, and hope bright in Sebastian's grey gaze, more luminous than ever, she still couldn't quite believe she'd had a wedding.

That she was married, to the man who possessed all of her, as she did him. The man she'd thought long lost; the man who'd changed her life a thousand times over, merely by existing. She'd abandoned dreams of such a day, such a future, long ago, and so, to hold them in her grasp again, was dizzying.

The whirlwind of the past weeks didn't help. There had been so much talking, between her and Sebastian, as they tried every day to heal a little more, and learn who they were now. Between her and her friends; between Sebastian and her friends. In an amusing turn of events, Sebastian had actually become quite close to Freddie Walton, and was considering investing in his company, and his wife's charitable enterprise.

There had been talk of plans, short and long-term. Of houses to be visited in Italy and Prague before summer arrived too harshly; of Christmases to be spent at Yew Park House. There had been talk of this wedding, papers to be signed, banns to be read, suits to be bought. There had been goodbyes to be made— to Ginny, to Elizabeth, to the others—as Juliana prepared to begin her life with Sebastian. A life of gentle travelling, and exploration; of frequent returns home to her family, who she hoped someday would become his too. A life of healing, discovery, hope, and love. Of wildness, and steadiness.

A life during which neither of us will forget those who were lost; they will never leave us.

So yes, standing here today, Juliana felt about as out of place as Josiah looked, except he didn't have Sebastian's steady gaze across the room to keep him strong as she did.

'I owe you thanks for helping me to this life I never thought I'd have, Josiah,' she said, as casually—so as not to spook him—yet as meaningfully as she could. 'I owe you thanks for being a friend during my darkest hours, and finding the keys to free Sebastian. I owe you thanks for protecting me, shepherding me, and even talking sense into him, before either of us could see the mistake we were making. I owe you thanks for many years of kindness, and friendship, before that.'

'As I said, no thanks due.' Juliana turned to him, raising her brow, and he smiled gently. 'We are friends, Mrs Lloyd.' He waited as that one landed, straight on her heart as he could surely see it did. 'Your gratitude is appreciated, but not owed. The life you have today, you fought for it. You are building it for yourself.'

'All the same, Josiah. Thank you. Not merely because you helped us, but because we are friends, know that should you ever need anything…'

'I know,' he nodded.

With a strange smile that almost spoke of precognition, he downed his drink, then strode away to presumably find another corner to settle in.

A few moments later, Sebastian was beside her, his arm sliding along her waist, as they both soaked in the view of the excited, joyous crowd.

Friends. Family. Love. Home port.

Juliana felt fit to burst with it all—the love, the joy, a resounding peace and happiness which wasn't unmarred by the pains of life and loss, but made evermore poignant for them; though she'd felt that often these past weeks, and it seemed to heal her better, give her more answers, than a thousand doctors or philosophers might've.

'The devil child extracted more unwilling promises from me,' Sebastian muttered grumpily in her ear, taking advantage to also place some kisses beside it.

'Elizabeth is no devil.'

'She has the wily ways of a witch of yore that girl. I think those goats of hers raised her, not you and her mother.'

'Don't let her hear you speak of Galahad and Gawain like that,' she warned, laughing. 'Come now, what precisely has Elizabeth made you promise that has you in such a state?'

'Well apparently, since I've stolen her tutor, *I* am to replace her. No matter that Sofia is taking over in your stead, oh, no, *I* am to impart all my knowledge unto her, in letters, and any time we return, so that she may one day rule the world. I swear, it isn't enough for that girl to have her father and Walton wrapped around her finger, she'll have me too.'

'And you'll be immensely happy for it,' Juliana grinned.

They'd discussed children of their own, but agreed that what they'd already both known in their hearts stood: they were past the lives, past the selves who might've had them.

Instead, they would content themselves with being unofficial aunt and uncle to whatever children their friends had; brought into the world, or brought into their homes.

Sebastian pretended to grumble, then finally shrugged.

'Best to keep on her good side, I think,' he said, a twinkle in his eye.

'A good lesson learned there…'

'Are you certain you're ready to leave them?' he asked after a moment. 'We can delay, start our travels in the autumn, even next year…'

'I'll miss them, Sebastian, always, when we're apart,' she told him, turning into his embrace, and grabbing hold of his lapels; for comfort, and fear she might fall backwards, tumbling into an abyss of elation. 'But I'm ready.'

His smile crinkled the corners of his eyes, in a way she knew so well, and she kissed him, in a fashion so familiar, yet so foreign it made her head spin even more.

Every day, knowledge was imbued, and every day, discovery thrilled her.

Every day, I live the life I dreamt to; every day I become myself.

The ghosts of all I've ever been and ever shall be coalescing into the present.

In the end, Juliana admitted that perhaps, she believed in some versions of ghosts after all.

* * * * *

If you enjoyed this story,
make sure to read
Lotte R. James's
other great historical romances

A Liaison with Her Leading Lady
A Lady on the Edge of Ruin
The Viscount's Daring Miss

And why not check out her
Gentlemen of Mystery miniseries?

The Housekeeper of Thornhallow Hall
The Marquess of Yew Park House
The Gentleman of Holly Street

MILLS & BOON ®

Coming next month

THE TAMING OF THE COUNTESS
Michelle Willingham

'What did Papa want to talk with you about?'

James hesitated a moment before answering, 'He wants me to marry you.'

She blinked a moment, as if she hadn't heard him correctly. 'He what?'

'He believes I should marry you and offer the protection of my title.' He took the remainder of the brandy and finished it in one swallow. 'It would be quite difficult to arrest a countess.'

Evangeline's disbelief transformed into dismay. 'That's a terrible idea. You and I are not suited at all.' But there was a faint undertone in her voice, as if she were trying to convince herself.

'I agree.' Though he hated the idea of hurting her feelings, he couldn't let her build him up into the man she wanted him to be. 'We both know I'll never be the right man for you.'

Her eyes grew luminous with unshed tears, and she nodded. 'You made that clear enough when you sailed half a world away.'

'You could have any man you desire, Evangeline,' he murmured. 'Just choose one of them instead.' He wanted her to find her own happiness with someone who could give her the life she deserved.

The very thought made his hands curl into fists. And that was the problem. Every time he tried to do the right thing and let Evie go, he kept imagining her in someone else's arms. And the idea only provoked jealousy he had no right to feel.

Continue reading

THE TAMING OF THE COUNTESS
Michelle Willingham

Available next month
millsandboon.co.uk

COMING SOON!

We really hope you enjoyed reading this book.
If you're looking for more romance
be sure to head to the shops when
new books are available on

Thursday 24th April

To see which titles are coming soon, please visit
millsandboon.co.uk/nextmonth

MILLS & BOON

FOUR BRAND NEW BOOKS FROM
MILLS & BOON MODERN

The same great stories you love, a stylish new look!

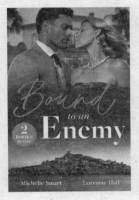

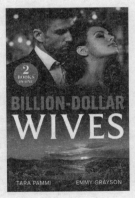

OUT NOW

Eight Modern stories published every month, find them all at:

millsandboon.co.uk

LET'S TALK

Romance

For exclusive extracts, competitions and special offers, find us online:

- MillsandBoon
- @MillsandBoon
- @MillsandBoonUK
- @MillsandBoonUK

Get in touch on 01413 063 232

For all the latest titles coming soon, visit
millsandboon.co.uk/nextmonth